Melting the Blues

MELTING
THE BLUES

a novel

Tracy Chiles McGhee

To Mama Pam
Love you.
Thanks for support
always
Tracy Chiles McGhee
3-6-16

Gold Fern Press

Melting the Blues by Tracy Chiles McGhee.

©2016 All rights reserved.

Printed in the United States of America.

This is a work of fiction. All the characters, organizations, and events portrayed in this novel are either products of the author's imagination or are used factiously.

Books may be purchased in quantity and/or special sales for promotional, educational, or business use. Please contact the publisher, Gold Fern Press at goldfernpress@gmail.com or your local bookseller.

Interior Design: Jana Rade
Cover Design: Rob Allen

ISBN 978-0-9971354-1-1 (hardcover)
ISBN 978-0-9971354-4-2 (paperback)
ISBN 978-0-9971354-0-4 (ebook)

First edition: March 2016

for my daughter, Sasha Ariel,
my most treasured gift

"But still, like air, I'll rise." ~ Dr. Maya Angelou

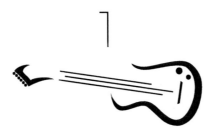

1

The sun was searching for its slippers and Delta bluesman Augustus Lee Rivers was traveling south along a short stretch of tarred road. Having just passed the old mill in his rusty red pickup truck, he was about two miles and a quarter away from the Tail Feather. It was Saturday evening, the whistle had long blown and after a wretched week of withering work and white folks' ways, a good number of colored folks in Chinaberry could be found at the juke joint to shake their blues off. Augustus did his part with the help of his good and faithful guitar he affectionately called Windy City to keep his dream of reaching fame in Chicago close to his heart. He was late to his ongoing gig but taking his own sweet time like the slow rising dusk ahead of him. He figured that since he was wearing his wide-brimmed lucky gray hat to go along with his sharp new money green tie, he had a license to make a grand entrance, not to mention his belief that the patrons were really there to take in the soul-stirring conversation between him and his raw sugar pine guitar with its knots that kept count of the years of deep longing and the moments of fleeting satisfaction.

By the time Augustus arrived to his destination, the sun had retired for the night and the moon had already got lit up with a few shots of whiskey. He stepped out into the fresh scent of clover floating in the air that faded as he neared the wide open door of the liquored and sweat-soaked shanty. As usual, it was packed tight. Upon entrance, all eyes—wide, batting, lusty, bloodshot, beady, plotting, envious, and blind—were on him. He was accustomed to this and moved with aloofness right past the onlookers like he owned the joint and everybody in it. His eyes landed on the welcoming eyes of a lady across the room dressed in sequined gold. She shot him a big, glossy smile through billows of smoke and he flashed a gracious one back before heading to the modest bar.

The band had started without him. The bandleader, local blues legend, Blind Eye Joe, was rocking his head side to side, making his harmonica sing and the crowd sway like delicate branches in a summer breeze. The two other band members let Augustus know they didn't appreciate his tardiness by the flash of red in their contorted faces. Truth be told, it didn't matter what time he arrived. His showing up always made them go deeper into their soul and play their instruments harder. He seemed to have the effect of both adding to their blues and bringing out the best in their music.

Big Lenox, the owner, walked over to Augustus, shook his hand, and gave him a look of understanding that said as long as you showed up, you're alright with me. He ran the Tail Feather with his lady love, Rita Mae, who he sweet-talked all the way from a Harlem brownstone to his southeastern Arkansas shack. The couple ran a tight, well-respected establishment. Everyone agreed to take the occasional scuffle outside and that included Big Lenox and Rita Mae themselves. Every now and then, too many spirits or too much pride would get in the way of good sense and one man would take playing the dozens too far or look at a man's woman too long or knock over the wrong man's drink, or break any number of laws. But mostly, the Tail Feather was a jumping good time of drinking, dancing, gambling, raised skirts, and frisky hands.

When folks needed to slow down to ease their minds, they could count on Blind Eye Joe and his band to bring the low down dirty, dirty blues. Poison and remedy alike lived in any woman blues, early morning blues, careless love blues, jailhouse blues, no money blues, bleeding heart blues, and wayward man blues, to name a few. Blind Eye Joe played harmonica, keyboards, and drums and had done so with the best, up north or down south. But he was the truth when it came to playing the guitar. Augustus had learned mostly everything he knew from him. He earned Blind Eye Joe's respect as a musician and after surviving the Korean War, respect wasn't something Blind Eye Joe doled out freely nor did he take any foolishness. After some time, he invited Augustus to fill Skip Town's place in the band when Skip Town was true to his name.

The rest of the band wasn't too thrilled about Augustus joining up with them. It wasn't that he couldn't play the guitar with great skill or wail the blues with intensity; he mastered both with uncanniness. In fact, by their calculation, he was only second to Blind Eye Joe and third to blues legend Robert Johnson, who Blind Eye Joe had learned a thing or two from in Mississippi years ago. It was just that the band and pretty much all the colored folks in Chinaberry, for that matter, saw Augustus as an odd man out in a restless 1957, where change was beginning to saturate the air like a soft mist intent on reaching a heavy downpour.

Augustus sat down at the bar and ordered a jar of white lightning from Mo the bartender, to try and catch up with the full moon. He planned to join the band the next set and switch places with Blind Eye Joe, as was the routine. He watched a steady stream of plain to pretty ladies negotiating to get drinks on the house. He also looked around and surveyed the room and everyone seemed small from where he was sitting. He assessed again and again that no musician in that room, including Blind Eye Joe, could cut heads on the corner more than him, that no man could take him in a boxing match, and that he could have any woman he wanted in there, whether they were spoken for or not. He took great delight in his private summation.

The set came to a close two songs later and the elder and slight-bodied Blind Eye Joe, dressed in black from head to toe except for his white tie with an unfortunate grease stain, did not hesitate to walk straight over to Augustus with the look and determination of somebody with a chip on his shoulder and an ax to grind. Augustus headed him off with a light, friendly greeting while munching on some peanuts and making a neat pile of the shells on top of a brown paper bag.

"Evening old-timer. I see you aim to give me a run for my money tonight."

"Always but look here. I got something to talk to you about," Blind Eye Joe said as Mo slid him his expected drink.

"What's on your mind, old-timer?"

"Peter Duncan ain't paid Joe Baby for the work he did."

"No disrespect but what's that gots to do with me?"

"You know goddamn well what it gots to do with you. You the one that made the whole arrangement. Called it a big opportunity for my boy. That's what you said. A big opportunity."

Augustus took a hard swig of his liquor and looked right past Blind Eye Joe like there was something more important to see going on across the room than the man with the eye patch standing less than an arm's reach before him.

Augustus had arranged for Blind Eye Joe's youngest son, Joe Baby, to build some wooden shelves for Peter Duncan to put in the diner owned by the Duncan family. The Duncans were the wealthiest family in Chinaberry and they were among Augustus' biggest fans. They called him Hummin' Gusty because he had a special way of humming the blues when he performed. Over time, Augustus fancied that he was like a member of their clan, a sentiment that grew out of his friendship with David Duncan, Peter's younger brother.

After Joe Baby finished the job to Peter's specifications, Peter short-changed him, leaving him without all the money he needed to pay the note on his tractor, and it was repossessed. Blind Eye Joe was furious with Peter, but he knew better than to go against the understood rules to confront him if he wasn't prepared for the consequences.

"A big opportunity, my foot. My boy needs all the money he was promised, not a penny less. He gots things to take care of and another youngin on the way as you well know."

"That's all well and fine and yes, I might've told you Mista Pete was looking for some shelves to be built and that Joe Baby might ought to look into it but beyonds that, I ain't gots nothing to do with that. You or Joe Baby needs to take that up with Mista Pete and leave me square out of it."

"Far as I'm concerned, you all in it. And since you make like you family with them white folks, I expect you to see to it that my boy is paid what's due him."

"Again. No disrespect but you must be clean out your mind if you think I'm gon do any of that nonsense you talking, old-timer."

"Oh you gon do it alright. Either that or give up your take from tonight. Do that and we can call this right here even, but my boy gon get his money one way or the other. Fair is fair no matter how you slice it."

"Now, I know you plum crazy if you think you gon get one red cent out of me. That war must've did a number on you for shore."

"What you just say out your mouth, son?"

"I ain't your son."

By now, a crowd had paused everything and built up around the men. The walls of the Tail Feather leaned inward to hear above the stirring. It didn't take long to gather that everybody had made their assessment of the situation and sided with Blind Eye Joe, including the two other band members, everybody that worked at the joint, the regulars, a few out-of-towners, and a couple of latecomers who didn't even know what the dispute was about. The shaky walls suddenly found the need to brace themselves.

Needless to say, after much going back and forth, the two men didn't see eye to eye and the exchange got so heated that it became the kind of scuffle that needed to be taken outside. Big Lenox made sure of that as Rita Mae tried to protect her new custom-designed lavender silk dress and calm the crowd, who was always eager for a good fight.

So under a drunken-hearted, cold-bloodied moon, the two men stomped outside and the crowd followed behind them, kicking up red clay dust with peep-toe heels and freshly polished shoes, pushing and shoving to get an up close view of the spectacle. As the argument grew louder and more heated, Augustus kept shouting that whatever happened between Mista Pete and Joe Baby was their business and to leave him out of it, but then he went on to claim that Joe Baby's work was shabby poor in the first place and he took too long to finish the job in the second place, *and* Joe Baby did good to get paid at all according to what Mista Pete told him. Any number of folks, both colored and white, would agree that Joe Baby was a dependable hard worker (*just a tad slow charged to being meticulous*) as well as a skilled carpenter taught by Chop-the-Wood himself, the best carpenter from Chinaberry to Helena, Arkansas, for sure.

When Blind Eye Joe heard that, his one visible eye started twitching and with the force of thunder, he yelled "You good-for-nothing, lying mutha…"

Augustus stood speechless while the crowd of bloodthirsty, instigators cheered Blind Eye Joe on until, next thing they knew, the old man drew back and took a powerful punch at Augustus, something many in the crowd had only dreamed of doing in this lifetime. Never in a million lifetimes did they think the great honor would go to Blind Eye Joe, he who wore a patch over what some swore was a socket with no remnants of an eyeball at all, a man who stood five inches shorter than Augustus on his left wiry leg and seven inches shorter on his right, a lightweight weighing no more than a buck fifty who just about toppled over every time he coughed and most of all, he who was Augustus' teacher, the sole one who had a soft spot in his heart for his most advanced student, mainly because he gathered that Augustus' blues ran deep, real deep, and might just run deeper than his own.

A stunned crowd looked at a stunned Augustus who looked at a stunned Blind Eye Joe, who quickly regained his footing after stumbling backwards. He rubbed his knuckles. He was clearly in more pain than the spot on Augustus' face, where he had struck him with all his might and the crowd's solidarity. Augustus raised his fist as a reflex but then slowly pulled it back and down all the way to his side, loosening the long fingers of his large hand that had grown strong from hard labor. Knowing full well that any blow he delivered would be fatal, Augustus took a deep breath and calmly parted the sea of spectators as he went back inside the Tail Feather, grabbed Windy City, and walked out and away. He promised himself that he would never step foot in that juke joint again.

Augustus was sitting in his truck at a turnoff in the woods not far from his house. This is where he had spent the last hour. The moon sobered up enough to lead him there. He wasn't ready to go home but he didn't have anywhere else to go. The night was still young and this was supposed to be his time to unwind. Instead what happened with Blind Eye Joe left him wound up tight in a dim blue ball. He was feeling down and low and maybe even a bit lowdown. He had drifted to sleep but now he was awake again, swollen with mosquito bites and drenched in sweat.

He made Windy City moan about a missed train Chicago-bound, a caring mama turned rattlesnake mean, a white woman forever out of reach, and an old drunk daddy dying in vain. Every weeping chord told the story of his lonesome loneliness and empty emptiness. He didn't know why he felt so lost and lacking when he had a sweet, good-looking, high yella woman waiting for him at home, why he was too damn wrong for his own damn good, and why he couldn't shake his desire to run away from Chinaberry no matter how much he tried. He believed he was meant for bigger and better than the skin and town he was born in and now he wouldn't be able to work all these yearnings out on his guitar up at the Tail Feather anymore.

He attempted to put these thoughts out of his mind with a quick, vigorous shaking of his head. Then he grabbed the steering wheel really tight and looked out the window into the star-filled indigo night by a slither of moonlight coming through the trees. He wiped the tears off Windy City and started the engine to head on home to that wife to see if she could take away some of his misery, to see if she could help heal that jones in his bones just for a little while with some of that sweet, good-looking, high yella woman loving.

Sure enough his wife, Pearl, was waiting for him when he entered their bedroom. No matter what time he arrived, he never found her sleeping. She told him on many occasions that she just could not rest until he made it back home safe and sound. Right away, she asked him why he was there so early, was he alright, where that bruise on his face came from, did something happen down at the Tail Feather, and was he hungry. Augustus offered no words of explanation, just slid into bed and kissed her hard to quiet all her questions and before long, he entered the embrace of her loving spirit to quiet all his demons and found some release in the throes of lovemaking.

His Pearl was a good wife. Both in their late-30s, they were approaching sixteen years of matrimony. Augustus courted nearly every respectable light-skinned woman in Chinaberry and its outskirts before deciding on her. Not only did she have hair that flowed and swayed with her hips as she walked, she was kind-hearted and smart too. He reckoned it wouldn't be too hard to care for her in exchange for the comforts she would surely bring. Pearl bore him three children, two years apart, with soft, curly, jet black hair to his liking. The children were given the names of Isaiah Lee or "Eye" as they called him, Charles Lee or "Boy" as they called him, and Ruby Lee or "Patty Cake" as they called her.

Before long, the old house hushed its squeaks, the entire Rivers family arrived on the shores of dreamland, and the moon, all tuckered out, rested its head comfortably on the horizon.

2

It was any given day and Pearl had chores to do and the heat had not spared her just because she was a sanctified woman. She removed the last of the clothes off the line dried by the generous sun and folded and placed them neatly in the laundry basket. She bent her head down and brought the bottom of her hand sewn apple green apron up to wipe her forehead of sweat.

Next, she entered her old but spry home to prepare supper- fried chicken, collard greens, potatoes, and corn bread. Everything on the menu required a secret ingredient to make sure it would be mouthwatering, make you wanna "slap-your-mama" delicious. Pearl sang and checked the skillet, flipped the chicken, wiped her brow and yawned, stirred the greens, put her hands on her hips, tested for doneness, hummed, shifted her weight, checked the pan, inhaled the aroma of love surrounding her, smiled with satisfaction, and placed the lids back on the pots.

Everything at a simmer or cooling, Pearl slipped off her apron and made herself a full mason jar of sweet tea from the icebox, gulped it down as a reward for her work that began at five o'clock that morning with milking beloved Sadie the cow. Milk was needed to drink, to cook with, and to make butter through churning and cheese through pressing, aging, and waxing. The children also had risen early for chores before setting off to school. Having no inside running water, they took the walk down the long trail to the spring, three children with a big bucket in each hand, to get water from the steady stream in the woods and bring it back to Pearl for daily use. She boiled this water in big pots on the wood burning stove to use for drinking, cooking, cleaning the home, and bathing. She would also boil the water in the old rusty round-bellied cast iron wash pot under an open fire in the backyard to soak the family's clothes with lye soap. Augustus had done his part by chopping and gathering wood before heading to the fields. The Rivers family had to work together to survive. Everybody had a role. Everybody had a string of verbs to perform.

Pearl looked around her well-loved home and all was in order. She decided to go back outside to rest a spell on the porch. As soon as she opened the screen door, she was met with an unexpected breeze. She suddenly felt incredibly light, like her wings had been freed up from carrying the weight of life and she was flying high above the heavens. That brief moment of freedom passed almost as quickly as it came but she stood at the door with her eyes closed tight and took a good long breath to hold onto the feeling a little while longer.

Then she walked over and plopped down on the wobbliest chair on the porch, the one that had her name invisibly engraved in its top rail. The chair, a fraternal twin of a set, "breathed" a sigh of relief once again because it didn't collapse at the careless flounce of its favorite occupant. Made of wood and dressed in chipped slate blue paint, the chair had a seat made of prickly, frayed, wheat-colored straws which poked every which way like a porcupine in need of a serious haircut. Pearl's waist, proportionately slim, curved outward into an ample bottom that was long immune to the prickliness of the straw and proudly spilled over the sides of the chair. The gray-brown, thick planked porch was the sturdy greeting to the Rivers' humble five-room shack that sat regally atop cinder blocks. It, meaning the porch, was a frequent meeting place for the family and their guests. It was also the perfect place to take some time for one's self as Pearl often did at least once per day, especially as she waited for Augustus to arrive home from a long day of farming. Wearing a light cotton dress, Simplicity Pattern #4849, sewn in a high-spirited pink, yellow, and green floral print, she rocked her body to a feel-good song she sang in her head, all the while fanning and swatting flies. Her ripped flyswatter had been wounded in several battles but could still do the job with the right amount of gumption and precision.

The determined sun tried to force itself through the expansive crown of the towering oak tree firmly planted in the front yard but was met with some resistance in the sturdy branches and thick leaves. This deeply rooted tree provided a measure of shade that made sitting on the porch bearable. A rainbow of daisies, four o'clocks, daylilies, and sunflowers hugging the front of the porch divided by four steps and framed by piles of rocks, released a fragrant bomb that tickled the slight point of Pearl's nose.

Pearl's hair was pulled back tight away from her face in one long French braid that was wound upon itself round and round and then pinned up so as not to touch her neck and make her hotter than need be. Small beads of sweat traveled from her fine-haired hairline and rested on her full cheeks that she had stuffed with chewing tobacco she had found in her embroidered dress pocket. From the other pocket, she removed a handkerchief and wiped her face with one big clockwise swoop, cleansing away both sweat and tobacco spittle that had escaped from the corners of her rather tiny-lipped mouth. Pearl always kept a pretty lace-trimmed, white hankie tucked somewhere to wipe away the blood, sweat, tears, snot, and spittle of life, and to occasionally add some flair to a "Sunday-Go-to-Meeting" suit pocket. Of course, the hankie had to be triangle-folded and placed just so for a lady such as herself.

Only ten minutes of solitude passed when out of the blue, Patty Cake, a big burst of green and yellow, came running onto the porch, startling Pearl and nearly knocking over the ever-present spit cup she used to discard that which needed to be discarded in the process of chewing tobacco and dipping snuff. Augustus hated Pearl's tobacco habit. He asked her all the time, "Why on earth would a lady have such a taste?" To him, it just wasn't seemly.

"Patty Cake, stop that running, chile, before you fall and break your neck!" Patty Cake ran into the house to be first to get a sip of water.

Next came Charles in his too-short, hand-me-down overalls chasing Patty Cake, who *did* knock over the spit cup as he ran into the house.

"Boy, haven't I told you time and time again not to be running in and out that screen door and to watch for my spit cup! Now go on in there and get the mop and clean up this mess and hurry up before your daddy come up that road!"

Charles went to get the mop as Pearl continued her lecturing. He started out fast but slowed down once out of the sight of her.

Eye stayed home from school that day. Every now and again Pearl let him. He was much further along in his studies than everybody in the whole school. The two teachers had to find special lessons for him.

"Boy, you need to be in there reading and getting your lesson like your brother. What's taking so long! Stop mule walking like you got all day."

If Pearl could hear what Charles was saying under his breath as he used the dipper to get a sip of water and another and another, Lonnie Wilson, the town undertaker, would be digging a grave for him that very moment.

Patty Cake didn't like to hear yelling unless it was her own. She fell out on the floor inside of the front door and started kicking her feet in the air and crying loud enough for Pearl to hear but out of her reach.

"Now Patty Cake, what you in there crying about? Bring your dusty behind out here. Hush up and stop that crying before I give you something to cry about. I was out here getting some peace and quiet till here y'all come."

Patty Cake stood before Pearl with her head down and tried her best to take her bawling to a whimper as quickly as she could, all the while gasping for air up through her snotty nose and wiping tears with the back of her hand.

"Straighten up your face, girl," Pearl said shaking her head. She closed her eyes and said a short prayer. She then softened her spirit and consoled Patty Cake by pulling her close and putting her arms around her. "Come here now chile...Hush...Hush." She reached into her dress pocket and pulled out a butterscotch candy she was saving for Eye once he finished all the pages of that big book he was reading. Handing the candy to Patty Cake, she whispered, "You better not tell your brothers that mama gave you this treat, ya hear?"

Patty Cake said "Yes ma'am" in a tiny voice and her tears dried up instantly. Glee now covered her from her wide smile all the way down to her bare feet as she sat down calmly on the porch floor and waited for Charlie to join her. She sucked the candy for a while and then sneaked it back into the crinkly golden plastic paper to save some for her Charlie later when her mama wouldn't be looking.

Charles cleaned up the mess before taking his place on the porch, sitting with his legs hanging off the edge with Patty Cake and Eye, who had emerged from reading his book just in time to get the satisfaction of watching Charles mop the porch. He was disappointed that Charles didn't get a whipping this time. His mama must be *real* tired, he reckoned.

Eye whispered into Charlie's ear out of Pearl's earshot, "You bug-eyed dummy. So clumsy. Got two left feet. Ha! Ha! Big dummy, you and Patty Cake both! Ha!"

Charles ignored him on the outside but called him a mama's boy in his mind and moved to the steps to sit closer to Patty Cake.

"Let's play patacake, Charlie," said Patty Cake.

"OK but just one time," Charles insisted.

Pearl's dinner was beckoning. The crispy fried chicken and the rest of the fixings were bursting with flavor and more than ready. All that was needed was the arrival of Augustus for the family to partake in the delectable glory. All four had found a calm and were sitting in silence staring off down the road, hoping to get a glimpse of Augustus coming around the bend first. Time passed, passed some more, and then tapped itself on the shoulder to hurry up.

"Here he come!" Patty Cake jumped up and shouted.

Sure enough, it was Augustus sauntering up the graveled road, in a sweaty, ragged short-sleeved plaid shirt and dirty denim overalls. He spotted his family sitting on the porch from a distance looking like four different kinds of bad news to him. He was moving forward with his feet but walking backwards in his mind.

"Heeey daddy!" Patty Cake's voice rang out.

The rest spoke one by one until Pearl's voice was the last to trail off.

"Evening," Augustus responded out of obligation with the tip of an imaginary hat.

"Supper's on. Just waiting on you," Pearl finally got her chance to say.

Augustus' eyes lit up. The aroma of all that good food danced in the air, making a path to his nose for him to follow straight into the kitchen. One thing Augustus did look forward to about coming home was Pearl's good cooking, which always had the right mixture of seasonings cooked for the right amount of time. He couldn't recall anything that she didn't put her foot in. As a matter of fact, Reverend Willis, the Rev, once said she must have soaked both feet in the mustard greens she brought him while his wife Helen, First Lady, was down sick for weeks. Of course he didn't say it in earshot of his wife or Augustus, but he pulled Pearl close and whispered in her ear that his wife's cooking lacked flavor and most things she cooked were either too dry or too soupy. He told her to feel free to sneak him a plate whenever she could even after the Missus got better and she could also add some fried chicken and pecan pie and whatsoever a plate could hold.

The Rev wasn't the only one who came calling to see what Pearl had cooking in the pot. On the one hand, Augustus took pride in hearing everybody speak highly about Pearl's cooking. On the other hand, he believed that they were just taking advantage of his wife's kindness and he would be as mad as he was wrong when he went to get a slice of pound cake and Pearl would scream at him not to touch it because it was for so-and-so. So-and-sos were always calling on her to cook this and that for church dinners, the sick and shut-in list, bereaved families, weddings, funerals, folks moving up north, folks visiting down south, good news, bad news, or just because somebody woke up with a sweet tooth that day. Pearl didn't pay his complaining any mind. Her cooking gave her joy and a whole lot of pride. She considered it a gift from the Lord and using it was one of the ways she thanked Him for His many blessings. As for her sewing, it would do for a living and it suited her boss, Miss Perry, just fine. Nope, her fingers did their best when they were snapping and shelling and chopping and slicing and kneading and stirring, and spreading love.

"Augustus Lee Rivers! I know you ain't stepping foot in my kitchen with those filthy hands!"

"Aw, woman, I was just looking in the pot to see what you done fixed good."

"You already know what's in them pots. Now go on and clean your hands good and I'll fix you a plate."

"Yes ma'am, anything you say," Augustus said in an agreeable way that made it clear that he wasn't going to let anything separate him from chowing down.

He couldn't help but to admit that he had the best wife that a colored man could hope for. It wasn't her fault that he had yearnings in a different direction. He did appreciate her, even though he never showed it in a way that would make a woman smile on a bad day. He had been his most attentive during his courting days. He initially was attracted to her because he could clearly see the blue veins flowing through her body that carried enough white blood for him to latch onto and fall in love with. But it wasn't just Pearl's skin color and kindness that made her a suitable mate to Augustus. She also owned land and he knew land ownership could save him from being a run-of-the-mill cotton-picker. He had a notion in his head that he was born to be a cut above the rest, the rest being coloreds. He had a drum major instinct and wanted big things.

Augustus came from a family of sharecroppers and that was not the kind of life he wanted for himself. Growing up, his parents and he and his sister (*may they all rest in peace*) lived in a two-room cabin on the edge of a cotton field along with other colored families. From sun up to sundown, from "can to can't," every able-bodied member of the family plowed and chopped cotton, mostly in June and July, and picked cotton in the fall. Around early September, the head of the household hauled the collective pounds to the white bossman who owned the living quarters, the land, and the commissary. He would tally up the family's meager earnings— half for him, half for them, or more likely than not, how he saw fit, regardless of what the numbers said. The family would get paid at the end of the season or many times break even for a place to live. It was a hard life but for many, it had an expected rhythm, one you could count on for survival until you could do better but for many, better never came.

In fact, Augustus' father, William Lee Rivers, was known as the best cotton-picker on the plantation. Unfortunately, over time, he grew feeble from weak knees, a liquor-soaked liver, and a bad heart. Sadly, he dropped dead right on the cotton field at only fifty-two years. The bossman dug him an early grave for his troubles. Augustus, even as a small boy, took note of how everyone became tense when the bossman came around. Their music changed. Their rhythm shifted. He noticed that all the bossman did was walk around and give orders and the coloreds did all the work. He noticed how big men became small around the white man. He figured there must be reasons for all this. One thing became clear. He wanted to be a bossman. So when Augustus' mother Ursula, was kicked off the plantation after her husband died, Augustus swore to himself that he would not pick cotton his whole life like his daddy did. It was a deep-down promise. And since Pearl inherited several acres of land from her father, that gave him the break he needed.

He was his own bossman. He farmed his own land for a living. Of course, this meant he had to be a better than average businessman and a jack of all trades. Besides farming and singing the blues, he was also a junk dealer. Because of his hard-earned position with white folks in Chinaberry, he was able to get a lot of the discarded items they considered junk, which he in turn fixed up to be treasures. He was very good at this. Had to be to take care of his family. Pearl, of course, made up the rest and sometimes the most.

Pearl was drawn to Augustus for her own special reasons too. In some ways, he was exactly like her daddy, a white man, and in other ways, he was absolutely nothing like him. The very fact that her daddy was white but left his world of social status behind in Connecticut to be with a colored woman in the deep south made him his own man. A successful banker, Benjamin Rothschild was tall and blond with streaks of early gray, light in his step although he carried the weight of nobility on his broad shoulders. He had bigness, wildness, and entitlement in his eyes that said, whatever I want, I shall have. He came to Chinaberry to visit an old chum from his college days on the occasion of the old chum's father's funeral. Their exchange of fond memories over gray clouds and bourbon eventually led to a conversation about a piece of land that belonged to the old chum's father that the old chum was looking to sell. His father had received the land to collect on a debt. After some thought, Rothschild decided to purchase the land, mainly to help out his old chum who seemed burdened with sorting out his father's affairs.

The two men were relaxing with full bellies in the quiet of the parlor in the inner sanctum of their respective thoughts. There was a soft knock at the door accompanied by a high-pitched *Howdy do* that trailed through the air, made its way to the heart of the parlor where it found Rothschild slowly stretching into a yawn, just in time for it to safely land in his wide open mouth that intuitively snatched at the howdy do. Rothschild quickly covered his face from the height of his nose to the cup of his chin with his large hands to forever capture the sweet sound and delicious taste of the howdy and the do dancing on his tongue. Next thing he knew, his old chum was introducing him to Grace Isabella Johnson, doll-faced with flawless skin who stood a tiny five feet inches tall, smiling and holding a freshly baked peach cobbler brought over in condolences for the grieving family, whom her family had been connected to in one way or the other over the years as small towns go.

Rothschild decided to extend his stay in Chinaberry. He had been enchanted by the spell cast by the stunningly beautiful Grace, whom they called Teeny. Well, a few called her Cinnamon for her skin tone but that didn't stick. But only Rothschild called her Dulcinea, because to him, she was sweet as could be. He was not the first to be captivated by her but he was the first white man who dared to wear his heart so openly and obviously on his sleeve despite the consequences. Grace was taken by his charm and fearlessness but resisted his advances and refused his gifts because she was accustomed to living in fear with certain matters. But there wasn't much privacy in Chinaberry and not much room for the boldness of Rothschild. This kind of race mixing was unlawful and intolerable.

Old chum distanced himself from Rothschild. The white townsfolk of Chinaberry didn't quite know what to make of this extreme notion of nigger loving by such an elevated man, so to make sense of it they ripped him of his white skin and treated him like any other colored, which to them was far worse than being hauled off to jail or killed for that matter.

Grace rejected his offer to take her back to Connecticut with him. Her parents were old and feeble and she wouldn't dream of abandoning them. Finally, to be with her as he desired, Rothschild was forced to reveal that he held one-eighth of Negro blood in his veins. The colored and white folks all breathed a sigh of relief and celebrated that one drip drop of blood and they were allowed to marry. The groom had a quaint little home built for the two of them on his newly purchased land. They created a little heaven there for themselves and Rothschild hardly ever left the house. He grew weary of being a white Negro so he spent most of his days reading and writing and waiting for the return of his Dulcinea, who managed to maintain a small foothold in the old world that existed before they constructed their own. It was as if they were put on earth just to love each other in a home that was made to their exact specifications and dimensions. For this love, Rothschild gave up his loftiness before men. All that was required of Grace was to become a little less Grace and a lot more Dulcinea.

Even when their only child Pearl arrived nine months after their "I do's," and tried to enter their world, she was met with the coldness of the borders of their love so she was always on their outskirts. She learned to read signs of love from them to get by—an extra spoonful of buttered rice, a door held open, a brushing of hair, a tied bow, a faint song heard through the cracks, a pretty dress, a stack of books, a word of caution, a tucked quilt, and occasional smiles. Such gestures came few and far between, but they did come like bursts of light. Pearl became good at sensing love even if it wasn't expressed through heartfelt words or the greatest of care. Years later, she knew even before Augustus did, that they would have a special love, much like her parents, that others wouldn't understand but come to envy because of the honesty and acceptance it contained. It would be a love for which she would never apologize.

After supper, Augustus went out on the porch and Pearl followed right behind him. She wanted to ride the good mood she knew her food put him in, if only for a blessed moment.

"Augustus, me and some ladies from church gon get together for a quilting bee to make a nice quilt for pastor's anniversary and I aim to have our house as the meeting place."

"Oh no you ain't! You know I don't want them cackling church biddies up in my house. You just go right back and tell 'em you done changed your mind. You can even tell them it's on account of me. I don't care none how you put it. But they ain't gon be up in here as shore as my name is Augustus."

"Humph, it ain't like I don't know your name. Now look here *Augustus*, you know it ain't my way to go against you but I wasn't asking for permission. I was just alerting you to the fact."

"Well, I'm just alerting you right back that I'm the bossman around here and I set the rules."

"Now, you must need glasses because you ain't seeing straight. You might just be the bossman but this here is *my* house and my land first and yours second. I feel as though I have a say about who I want to be in here, especially when we conducting the Lord's business while you ain't seen no part of a church since our wedding day!"

"I should've known you was gon put the Lawd up in it some kinda way. I see you done made up your mind anyhow. You go on and do what you set out to do from the start. I won't be here when they come. I can bet you that. As a matter of fact, you keep right on ahead disputing me and I won't be around here- period!"

Pearl tried to contain her smile that wanted to pop out. She kissed Augustus quickly on the cheek as he pushed her away and then she went on about her business and left him to his.

Augustus grabbed his guitar, let out a huge sigh, and commenced to humming the blues.

It wasn't too long after that when his peace was interrupted again, this time by his youngest son. Charles had been listening from his bed but was drawn toward the music Augustus was making outside that was making its way inside. Those sounds stirred something deep within him that he didn't understand but whatever it was, it made him want to get right up under the source, to feel the vibrations as close as his daddy would allow. Augustus really didn't mind having an audience. He kept on strumming his guitar and humming until he came to a stopping point.

Charles asked him, "What is it that you humming about, daddy?"

"I hum the blues, son."

"What's the blues?"

"The blues is what concerns you real deep."

"What you mean? Concerns you?"

"What bothers you. What you ain't gots that keeps you from what you want. Could be a piece of change, some liquor, a good-looking woman, or some new threads. Depends on the person, I reckon. You see, whatsoever's on your mind is between you and your guitar. Your guitar listens whiles you playing and it talks back at you. Most times, it's trying to tell you what you *do* gots and depending on your mood, y'all argue, fuss, and fights but sometimes y'all sees eye to eye and that's a whole another tune altogether. No matter which way, y'all thick as thieves. But you see, all this is beyond your comprehending right now but keep on living. Like your mama sing, you will understand it better by and by. Ha! Yeah, keep on living." Augustus raised Windy City by the neck and shook it in the air, feeling real proud about how he just put his words together like a smart talking preacher man or a big-city lawyer.

"Daddy, what you ain't gots? What you and your guitar talks about?"

"Now boy, didn't I just tell you that's between me and my guitar. You gots to listen to the music and try and figure it out if it's for you to figure."

"Well, can you teach me how to play?"

"Before it's all over, I reckon I can but right now you ain't got no blues. Just mind me and your mama and get your lesson. That's all you got to worry about."

Charles thought to himself that he sure enough did know about the blues. His brother was always the blues. Sometimes, his mama was the blues. Everybody picking on his little sister, calling her slow and him having to fight all the time was the blues. Not being smart like Eye was the blues. Wanting some sweet potato pie and mama saving Eye the last piece was the blues. Wanting to go far, far away from Chinaberry was the blues. Having music inside him that he wanted to let out but didn't know how was the blues. He promised himself that he would play music one day just like his daddy. By then, he figured he would have plenty of blues stored up.

Augustus returned to his guitar and played and hummed on. Charles closed his eyes and took it all in. And the sun, after feeling unwanted all day long, finally switched places with the moon and sang its own blues.

3

The day was about the same as the others but the sun was too lazy to even put one foot out of bed. In its place, the storm clouds had risen but they didn't have any reason to shine. Once again, the weekend had rolled around and Augustus didn't want to go home. A month or so passed of not going to the Tail Feather. Instead, he found another spot to play the blues on the regular and that was Duncan's Diner.

He was driving along as usual in his old reliable pickup truck on his way to the diner to release some blues. This path suited him far better than going straight home, where the never ending annoyances of the wife and children were sure to be waiting to greet him at the door.

Close ahead was the old, rickety, gray-planked bridge one must cross over to get downtown. It looked like the slightest step of some poor soul could collapse the bridge into the murky green creek that meandered below. But going over it was just a risk everybody took with faith when they needed to get to the other side, as did most in Chinaberry at some point in time.

Another truck, this one brand new and soft powder blue, was coming down the road from the opposite direction. Behind this other wheel was none other than Mo the bartender, who was driving like he was floating on a cloud, confidently and purposely without a care in the world. No doubt, he was on his merry way to the Tail Feather. He stretched over to look into the rearview mirror and while he rubbed down his shiny black, conked hair edges, he pondered just how he came to be so damn fine. In the midst of contemplation, he noticed Augustus in the distance at the other side of the bridge. He proceeded to drive.

Only one truck could pass the bridge at a time. Witnesses in nature, including the trees, the river, and the birds, had seen that Mo had arrived to the edge of the bridge first and therefore had the right of way. Perhaps Augustus was more determined to get to Duncan's Diner than Mo was to get to The Tail Feather, because he sped up and entered the bridge with such speed and determination that it forced Mo to put his truck in reverse and yield the wrong of way to Augustus. As Augustus passed, Mo threw his arm out the window and gave Augustus the middle finger, all the while cursing and honking his horn violently. Augustus never even looked his way. Instead he looked over at his guitar, smiled, and patted it like it was his partner in crime and they had just gotten away with a caper.

In hardly no time at all, Augustus arrived at the diner. Since declaring that he would never play at the Tail Feather again, he only played music on his porch, in his truck, or for whites only in a back room of the diner. There was a big white sign trimmed in red with navy blue lettering that spelled out in all capital letters Duncan's Diner that was the first hello to its customers. Either Miss Lizzie, Peter's wife, or Miss Patsy the cook and waitress was the second hello. That is, if you were white and entered from the front door. Augustus looked through the large glass window and saw that all four red vinyl booths and all six stools were filled. Miss Lizzie spotted Augustus through the window and waved and smiled at him and he returned the same. Then he made his way to the back porch, where colored customers were served.

With his guitar in tow, he entered through the back door because he had special permission to do so from the Duncan brothers. He then hooked to a room to the left. This small, dusty room was more of a cluttered storage room but contained two round tables, a few mismatched chairs, and a large quilted Confederate flag outstretched and nailed on the wall. It was a makeshift club for its one and only opening act and headliner, Hummin' Gusty Rivers. "Management" had a special corner carved out just for him with a stool and a mason jar to collect pennies. He wasn't performing for money or tips though. He was performing because it made him feel high to receive such special consideration. The honor lifted his blues all the way to heaven.

His audience was waiting on him for the show to begin. Without further ado, Hummin' Gusty took his place on the stool and pulled his guitar out of its old, beat up case. He started strumming and soon he was wailing a song about a woman named Josephine who took his mojo and his money that he couldn't get back unless he went to Chicago oh to Chicago, but he didn't have the money and the mojo to get to Chicago, oh to Chicago... He sang until it morphed into his signature hum, the reason David Duncan had ordained him with the name Hummin' Gusty in the first place. He strummed and hummed, his dark brown eyes rolling back in his head until they closed all the way and then it was as if he was singing the blues in a packed club in Chicago and then he laid his eyes on Callie—Callie Mae Lewis, always Callie, the woman he lost in every song, the forbidden fruit, his forever blues. Behind his eyelids, she was sitting at a table directly across from him smiling, sipping on a drink, and looking back at him in a way that said just wait until we get home, baby.

He sung three more songs before striking the final chord. Then he slowly raised his head and opened his eyes to see the reality before him: a four-man audience looking dead at him like they had been hanging onto every note. Present were brothers Peter and David Duncan, both the spitting image of their deceased father, Walt Duncan. They looked to be identical twins, but were actually eight years apart, Peter being the oldest. Both had stringy, dirty blond hair they combed backward from a severe widow's peak, several rows of forehead wrinkles pronounced in extreme emotion, droopy gray eyes, perpetually red noses, large thick-lobed ears and half-smiles that bore enough charm to forgive the look of caricature they were born with. At six feet three, David was the taller by two inches. But overall, to describe one was to describe the other but for height and spirit. If David's spirit was a cup, it would be half full, whereas Peter's would be half empty on most days. Then there was bald-headed, porky, and jovial Bubba Smith, the "Mr. Tag along, go along" one, and to round out the posse, wouldn't you know it, Callie's husband, George Lewis, smart, athletic, with a reputation for being a decent but dry fellow.

Well, they all clapped and hooted and hollered at their star bluesman. David slapped Hummin' Gusty on the back and started the tipping off with a shiny nickel. Bubba exclaimed, "I don't care what ya say, that nigger shore can handle that guee-tar." He dropped a penny in the jar and headed back to the main part of the diner to order a fried fish sandwich before the kitchen closed for the evening. Augustus just smiled.

As he was packing up his guitar, Peter came over to him.

"Gusty, you always bring the house down. You shore you ain't got a hit record out? You shore is talented."

"Thank ya, sah. I reckon it just come natural. Plus, been playing a good long while now."

"A bluesman like you should be up north in Chicago or Harlem, one or the other. Don't tell me that thought ain't never crossed your mind?"

"I suppose it has. Takes more than crossing though," Augustus said.

"What if I told ya I got a way for you to take a trip up yonder to test yourself out?"

"I would say my ears are right open, Mista Pete. You're smart. If anybody know how, you do."

"Well then, you'd do good to listen. Here's the deal. Imma get straight to the point. Look here Gusty, I can give you more money than you ever seen, enough to not have to worry about farming no more, enough so you can settle your debts. You can head out to Chicago to live tomorrow if you want to, not just to play in the club but to get your own band together and make some recordings. Heck, with what's left over, you can get you a nice shiny car, and have all the good-looking women you can fit in it. Now what you think about that, Gusty?"

"Well, that sounds mighty good but why is you fooling with me, Mista Pete."

"I ain't fooling with you none. As God as my witness, what I'm telling you is the God honest truth. Course, Imma need something from you."

"What on earth do I gots that you want?"

"Land, Gusty. I want your land, all the acres you sitting on."

"My land. I don't rightly know if I can sell you that, Mista Pete."

"Shore you can. Selling is a heap better than me taking it," Peter laughed.

Augustus let out nervous laughter.

"Now I'm fooling with you. Listen here, what if I told you that you can keep the land. I don't want it until you pass on and that ain't no time soon by the looks of you."

"You mean to tell me; you will pay me for the land but I can stay on the land until I pass on."

"I didn't stutter. That's the deal. You ain't got to answer right now. Think on it long as you need but don't breathe a word of it to nobody, including that wife of yours. Now let me carry that guitar for ya. Big star like you shouldn't do his own toting."

"Go 'head Mista Pete, messing around with you, I'm gon get a big head for shore."

"And just maybe, some big pockets," Peter remarked with that half-smile and Augustus returned with a full one.

Peter's pa would be so proud of him at this moment. If there ever was a son who loved his pa, it was Peter Duncan. Walt Duncan was a big man in Chinaberry. He was a businessman who got his early bigness from being the son of the town's mayor. From the moment he was born, he had the force of law wrapped around him like a quilt and he passed a sense of entitlement down to his first son, Peter. It was the highest duty and honor for a father to teach his son good and proper Christian, family, and southern values. Walt took his job very seriously and Peter was a model son, always eager to learn and please.

If you saw Walt, you saw Peter at every stage of his life getting a lesson—in his truck learning to drive, in the woods learning to hunt, at the creek learning to fish, in the yard learning to play baseball, and everywhere they went, learning to handle coloreds. From a young boy on up, he was taught, when it came to coloreds, there was a code to be followed at all times and at all costs and he better take heed lest he dishonor God, his family, his nation, his race, and himself. And so the code was passed down by a caring and loving father and Peter tried his very best to abide by it as warned.

Augustus saw an empty porch up ahead and wondered what he had done to deserve such. He smiled. If he was extra lucky, the house would also be empty and a nice warm plate of one of his favorite meals, any of them, would be there waiting for him with all the fixings. Just the thought of it made his mouth water and him move quicker. He even skipped up the steps. But what he saw when he opened the door made him almost jump out of his skin. It was a house full of folks!

Before Augustus could even put his eyeballs back in their sockets, three men in dark suits stood up and approached him with the kind of greetings that demonstrated they had been raised well or trained well. The tallest one hugged him and the other two gave him a firm, vigorous handshake like the pleasure was indeed all theirs because it was clear that none of it belonged to Augustus. He just stood there in his overalls, speechless with a blank face. Pearl quickly joined the circle of menfolk, bringing with her a smile big enough to cover anyone in the world who didn't have one, especially her husband.

"Look who done come all the way from Little Rock to see us. Cousin Rudolph, you know we calls him Esquire now that he's a big-time lawyer, graduated from Howard University two times, yes he did. Wished his mama could've lived to see it. God rest her soul. And now he working for the N. Double A.C.P. and these here his friends, Mr. Trotter and Mr. Scott; they N. Double A.C.P. lawyers too. Ain't that something! Gentleman, this my husband, Mr. Rivers." Pearl's words rolled out like a runaway wheel. She prayed Augustus wouldn't show out too bad, that he would muster up some politeness so she wouldn't be embarrassed.

Augustus managed to mumble a "Good evening" and took a quick exit into the kitchen.

The guests looked at each other with a degree of awkwardness, resumed their seats, and continued to eat Pearl's famous chess pie. It was so quiet you could hear a feather land. The children were in their room on their best behavior, even Patty Cake. They were occupied by the gifts that Cousin Esquire's wife, Cousin Gloria, had sent them with love.

Pearl excused herself and followed behind Augustus. By the time she got in the kitchen, he had washed his hands and was standing at the stove about to grab his plate.

"What they doing here in my house? I know you ain't tell them they can stay here."

She sighed, "They don't have no need to stay here. He staying at his mama house. His baby brother still keeping the place up. Plenty space for them over there."

"What he bring them highfalutin Negroes here for? They look to be up to no good. You know folks don't take too kindly to strangers around here." Augustus raised his voice on purpose, at the same time noticing that there was barely enough food for him to get seconds.

"Shush now. Besides Esquire ain't just visiting me. They're here on official business and I ain't gon allow you to put highfalutin on them just because they got education. I'd be right proud for Eye to follow after any of them."

"And what kinda business is that? The kind that get colored folks in a whole heap of trouble? Stirring up matters that ain't none of they business? I hope the white folks don't catch hold to this."

"Humph. Let you tell it. They will. What goes on up at No Ways Tired Baptist Church ain't none of the white folks' business. That goes for the Duncans too. All these young men wanna do is to speak to the congregation about some new laws that's done passed for the betterment of the race. Reverend Willis know all about it and told them to come on and he would round folks up. Ain't no more to it than that."

"Well, you ain't going. That's all that concerns me," Augustus said while eating his way down a cob of sweet and salty corn drizzled with butter.

"Now why would you fix your mouth to say such foolishness? This my family and my church. You know I gots to be there. Besides, I for one, want to know what's going on in this world. Lawd knows, we need some brighter days. If these young men done come all this way, then the least we can do is to make them feel welcome and listen to whatsoever they gots to say."

"Woman, I swear you wouldn't listen to me to save your life. They make you out to be so prim and proper but I know better."

"Reckon I know better too. You ain't twice as bad as folks say. You are three times worse."

"Humph, you got a *real* smart mouth on ya, don't ya? All I know is, you go against your husband every chance you get. I can't do nothing with you."

Pearl softened her voice and added some flowers and music to it. "Is that right? You mean to say, you can't do *nothing* with me", she crooned as she sauntered over to her husband.

"What about this?"

She squeezed her way in between the table and the chair where Augustus was sitting and he accommodated her as she sat on his lap. She placed her arms around him tight, loosened her lips and led her husband's tongue into a slow dance until he took the lead. She felt his bulge harden against her hips, hips that had widened after bearing him three children and they widened some more still as she rubbed against him. She felt his bulge dance in excitement. She felt his heat rise and his heart pump. She heard him breathe her name and then she felt his love. She jumped up and planted a quick smooch on his forehead.

"I gots to go tend to my guests till we head out. I saved you a big slice of chess pie and Imma have some more dessert for you when I get back from the meeting," Pearl said with a wink.

Right as she got to the door, Augustus said, "I best carry you up there. I'll wait for you to get done in the truck."

Pearl rushed back over to her husband and hugged him. He shooed her away, shifted in his seat, and picked up a meaty neckbone as he watched her walk out the room and thought to himself, "Damn."

Esquire and the two other suit-wearing civil rights lawyers had driven all the way from the capital city of Little Rock to Chinaberry to discuss a case called *Brown v. The Board of Education*. It was a good thing they came too. Chinaberry was the last to know just about anything that went just beyond what they already knew. There weren't but so many televisions in Chinaberry and not a one was owned by a colored family. Not many even had electricity for that matter. The lawyers greeted the congregation warmly and they were lukewarmly received. They were generally a gracious welcoming people but they had built some walls up toward strangers, and that is what Esquire now looked to be with his air of big cityness and education drawing a line in the dirt between them. He left home years before to go off to school without so much as a visit since his mama's funeral. That didn't sit too well with the lady pillars of the church.

Unaware of the rules of proper conduct he'd broken, Esquire cleared his throat and explained to the congregation how the N. Double A.C.P. had fought hard to make a better way for colored people by changing laws that crippled the race, laws that said segregation was fine in public places as long as everything was separate but equal when in reality it never had been. The congregation nodded in agreement that separate was definitely not equal. Then Esquire shared how another N. Double A.C.P. lawyer by the name of Thurgood Marshall was convinced that the best way to uplift the race was to make sure that there was equality in education by changing the laws that sought to discriminate on the basis of skin color. He went on to say that this brilliant lawyer was a hero and that he was the one that took the case called *Brown v. The Board of Education* all the way to the highest court of the land, the Supreme Court, to argue for equality and had won a major victory for colored people all across the nation. One of the others followed that up by saying that winning this hugely important case meant that the whites had to let the Negroes attend school with them, that their children didn't have to walk so far anymore when there was another school that was closer to most of them, that they would have the opportunity to learn in a much better building than the one they were accustomed to, and they could get their lessons in books that weren't falling apart with torn pages.

A great many of the congregation chose not to come to the meeting. Some remembered the 1919 Elaine Race Massacre that occurred just a couple of counties away, when colored farmers had the audacity to meet in a church to talk about their rights and over a hundred blacks in town ended up dead or jailed, tortured, and sentenced to life by white folks. A few still were haunted by the cries of a fourteen-year-old boy named Emmett Till, who was exercising his right to be a carefree boy on a summer day when he was brutally murdered in Mississippi two years prior for the alleged transgression of flirting with a white woman. And one or two knew the tragic story of how George W. Lee, also in the neighboring state of Mississippi, had been shot in the face and ran off the road because he was fighting for voting rights. They also recollected how over the years, right in Chinaberry their very own loved ones had been stripped of their right to live for breaking the white man's laws. To the ones that didn't come, they reckoned that anything having to do with coloreds getting some rights ended up deadly wrong. No, they would come to the regular church meeting come Sunday morning, but they didn't want any part of this meeting about rights unless it came with an absolute guarantee of the right to live and be left alone.

Among the ones that did come, some thought all of this sounded good but a greater number thought these big-worded, sharp-suited men had lost their damn minds in a book somewhere if they thought for one minute that the white folks in Chinaberry were going to let their children mix with theirs in the same school or anywhere else for that matter. The lawyers repeated that this was their right, but those in attendance really wanted to know how they were supposed to exercise these so-called rights and live to tell it. They figured the best thing they ought to do was to continue to make due like they had been doing. Yes, they could use a better schoolhouse and such and such but they reckoned their children were plenty smart, going further in grades than many of them, and the teachers did just fine providing them with lessons. They couldn't see how all the talk of integration was going to do anything but stir up trouble, and trouble was the last thing they needed with white folks. Trouble meant trouble with their livelihood, trouble meant trouble with their lives.

However, there were three sets of parents that left that June meeting determined to register their children in the whites-only school when the new school year came back around. The N. Double A.C.P. promised that they could count on them to help them every step of the way with legal support and some financial support should they lose their work. But the very next day, not a one showed up to the meeting Esquire set up to get the plan together. The white folks got to every last one of them and talked them out of it with threats, intimidation, and acts tailored to fit each family.

It looked like the "all deliberate speed" the big-worded, sharp-suited men talked about at that meeting was going to take a while longer, especially since the law had passed three years prior in 1954. Pearl packed Esquire and his friends up enough food to last them for their journey home and a week after, thanked them for coming and bringing books and toys for the children, a pretty lavender scarf for her, and a fancy striped bow tie for Augustus that caused a smile to slip out of him when he saw it. She placed the courageous men at the top of her prayer list so they would be protected from all hurt, harm, and danger as they made their way back to Little Rock to continue the struggle for equal rights for coloreds. Then she watched them drive off into the distance, leaving dust, broken church windows, new dreams, and a smidgen of hope behind them.

Admittedly nosey, the sun peeked through the window of the Perry family's corner room, on the second floor of their home. Pearl felt the shine on her forehead while she sat at the antique mahogany sewing desk, slightly hunched. She peered downward and concentrated on her work. She held the silk pink fabric in place with tired, achy hands and stitched the seam with precision, lowering the presser foot. This party dress must be perfect, the one most envied, Miss Perry had drilled in her seemingly a million times.

"Pearl!" Miss Perry raised her voice after Pearl didn't respond the first two times. Gertrude Perry, all fiery-red hair and freckled pale skin, was Pearl's boss. The Perry family owned the town feed store and the only dress shop in town. Pearl had been employed as her *modiste*, fancy word for personal dressmaker Miss Perry insisted on using, for years before Miss Perry decided to open a shop and share Pearl's skills with others and of course get paid handsomely for it. Pearl's mother had been Miss Perry's mother's modiste and the sewing and tailoring and designing skills had been passed down to her. Pearl was a reluctant apprentice but she knew better than to not listen and learn. It was a respectable profession and she was not inclined to be a domestic. Pearl's dressmaking skills were advanced, her designs beautiful and desired by all the ladies who could afford fancy dresses. Miss Perry told her all the time that she didn't know what she'd do without her. On the other hand, she was barely tolerable most days. Pearl did her best to tune her out so she could get her work done in peace, be paid, and go on about her business that extended well beyond the desk and window.

"Pearl!"

Pearl heard her call all three times but ignored her and kept right on sewing on the fancy new Singer sewing machine. Pearl was getting acquainted with the machine Miss Perry had just bought for her the week prior. It was called the Model 206. Miss Perry told her that she would be able to stitch much faster and even zig zag stitch but Pearl missed her old machine she had named Susie Singer. The machine and she had learned to dance together so much that the pain in her fingers could be masked. With this new machine, she felt the ache in the joint of her hands. The second nature feeling she had with Susie Singer would have to be earned over many more hours of sewing with the Model 206, and then only after that, could it earn a special name.

Frustrated at Pearl's lack of response, Miss Perry took off her apron, left the kitchen, and marched upstairs to Pearl's sewing room.

"Now Pearl, what's the matter with you? Don't you hear me calling your name?" Miss Perry spoke in a singsong falsetto voice that irritated Pearl to no end.

"Oh, howdy do, Miss Perry, you been calling me? You know when I gets to sewing, I can't hardly hear nothing."

"Oh Pearl. I declare. You just too much. I wanna know how you coming with my dress. We got to keep you on track or there's gonna be some mighty angry ladies when their dresses not ready for the party. Now, tell me, how you coming? When can I try mine on? You know mine has got to be the very best as the hostess. That's called being the belle of the ball. Ha!" Miss Perry laughed at herself as always as she stood in front of the floor length mirror, fixed her hair, and admired herself.

Pearl didn't answer but kept her pace sewing. Her granny had taught her how to cook. Her mama had taught her how to sew. Cooking was a joy. Sewing was a living. Miss Perry kept right on yapping and Pearl put her sewing on remote and her thoughts trailed off. She imagined that the gown was finished and it was the day of the party and she was there to help squeeze Miss Perry into the dress and button all the many pearl buttons down the back of the dress. Miss Perry would be standing in front of that floor length mirror as she did half of most days and she would just be so tickled pink. Pleased with her vision of loveliness, she would twirl around and around and tell Pearl that she really outdid herself, even hug Pearl as long as no one was looking. Then it would be time for her to welcome her many guests. Everyone would compliment Miss Perry on her beautiful dress, but as the night wore on, the dress would slowly unravel itself without Miss Perry realizing it. Pearl would be at the top of the staircase watching the entire event unfold. Finally, just as Miss Perry would give a welcoming speech to her guests, the dress would suddenly fall to the floor leaving her in her French brassiere and bloomers and everyone would gasp and try to hold back laughter as Miss Perry ran out of the room embarrassed and in tears.

Pearl accidentally let out a giggle at her imagination.

"Pearl. Pearl! You hear me, Pearl? Chile, I think your ears need checking! You hear me calling you?"

"Yes ma'am, I hear you."

"So tell me. When can I try on my dress? When will it be ready?"

"Soon. Very soon. Be patient, Miss Perry. It must be perfect for the belle of the ball."

Miss Perry let out a squeal of a laugh. "Pearl, I declare, you are sweet as molasses. You might just be my best friend in the whole wide world." She fixed her hair once more in the mirror and then twirled around and said, "Now stop your slothfulness. It's just not biblical."

Pearl stared at her without expression and couldn't help but to think non-biblical thoughts.

"Oh my! See what you just did. Made me forget all about my coconut pie. I'll be back to check on you in a bit."

Pearl held her breath until she could no longer hear Miss Perry's steps and then exhaled with a giggle. She had learned that laughter sometimes was a better cure than tears when the light at the end of the tunnel or the kitchen knife with the sharpest blade was too far off. She also took extra joy that Miss Perry had no idea that she could cook. For her, she would bake no pies.

Just as Pearl wound down her work day, Augustus had already left the fields and was headed to the Reynolds' General Store. Alongside the Duncans and the Perrys, the Reynolds family were one of the few who owned places of business in the town and big brick houses to go with them. They had employed Augustus' mama, Ursula, as a domestic for nearly twenty years after she left the plantation when her husband passed.

Today Augustus had gathered some absolutely beautiful, plump, juicy, ripe tomatoes in a straw basket. He was excited. He knew Callie, the only daughter of John and Abigail Reynolds, was working in the family store, which she did from time to time to help out. He knew she would be mighty pleased to get those tomatoes he picked especially for her. They weren't for sale. They were a gift. Callie loved fresh tomatoes to put in her famous tomato soup and Augustus loved to see her eyes light up and smile even though she went out of her way to dodge direct eye contact with him. He did the same so they were quite a sight to watch as their eyes darted back and forth and looked to the right and left of each other.

Callie stood pretty tall and was slender like a pencil. She had blond hair she wore in her signature bob with a bouncy flip. She had a perfectly oval face, large wide-set eyes, rosy cheekbones, a pointy nose and a deep dimpled chin. There was something very stiff and jerky about her move-ments as if her perkiness was controlled by a puppeteer. To Augustus, it all added up to pure loveliness. She was wearing a light blue dress with teeny tiny white polka dots. Augustus knew the blue was a perfect match to her eyes even though she had his back to him.

Truth be told, he probably knew the number of pores she had on her face. She was his first love. It all started when they were youngsters and the "it," whatever it was, had carried into their adulthood.

To this day, Augustus had a reoccurring dream about Callie. In the dream, he'd be lying on his back in a lush green field underneath a bright summer sun. He'd look up high, and in the distance see the face of young Callie, looking like an angel to him, floating, her doe-like blue eyes closed shut, but curly lashes fluttering, her thin-lipped mouth, closed shut but wide smile looming, her dimpled chin pointing upward, exposing the length of her thin, delicate neck, her loose ringlets of hair blowing in the wind. She would sway to and fro above Augustus like a pink balloon as he'd hold the long string tight below. For fear that she'd fly off into the sky, little by little, he'd carefully pull the string toward him, drawing in her bodiless head and neck until it rested comfortably on his chest, his prized possession. He would gently and lovingly palm Callie's head into his eager hands, and just as he'd close his eyes to plant a kiss on the center of her forehead, the head would explode and just like that she'd be gone, a pin-popped, shattered balloon with pink fragments all about him. His tiny-framed, naked body, with eyes wide open in shock, could see Callie's rubber, fabric remains get sucked into the horizon. This nightmare of a dream was fodder for his blues.

Augustus composed himself and took a deep breath before entering the store. Callie was not facing the door. She was standing on the footstool placing a jar on the top shelf.

"Howdy there, Miss Callie," Augustus said, startling her.

She looked back and stumbled backward and fell down off the stool. Augustus rushed over behind the counter.

"Oh Lawd! Miss Callie, is you alright? Let me help you up," Augustus said as he offered his hand to help her.

She reluctantly accepted his hand and allowed him to pull her up to her feet.

"I'm fine, Gusty, fine. You nearly scared me half to death. You mustn't sneak up on me like that. What's got into you?"

"Now Miss Callie, you know I didn't mean to scare you none. Look, let me make it up to you. I brought you some nice tomatoes here. Ain't they purdy? Look here," He picked one out of the basket and extended it to her.

Callie quickly wiped her hands on her apron and then accepted the tomato and smiled as she examined its entire glistening, red surface.

"Yes indeed, Gusty. This is mighty fine and is gonna find its way into my soup this very day, yes indeed. Thank you, Gusty. That was mighty kind to think of me and to bring them way over here out your way."

"It was no trouble a' tall, Miss Callie. No trouble a' tall."

She looked to the right and he looked to the left but somehow their eyes still met. Then he did something like a bow and backward skip with a tip of his hat and said good-bye. She just stood there holding the tomato and smiling. She didn't say good-bye until he was long gone out the door because she had savored the moments in slow motion and had to catch up with herself.

Callie had put Augustus in a good mood and he was not quite ready to go home to break that mood. He decided to pay a quick visit to see his good friend David to stay on a high note.

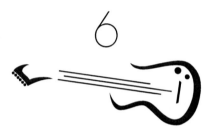

6

David Duncan was sitting on the edge of his porch playing checkers with his young son Richie. It really was too hot to be outside as evidenced by the sweat running down their faces. But David decided being outside felt better than being cooped up inside. His wife Mary Faye brought them some water but they had gulped that down before she touched the screen door handle to go back inside to tend to baby Jane and to finish cooking supper. Now those two empty silver tin cups lay beside them just as parched as they were. A loud growl from Richie's belly made the point that his hunger was inching up on his thirst but he put all that aside because things were starting to shape up nicely for him on the board.

"King me!" Richie yelled, pointing to and tapping the black checker on the far left side of the wooden board.

David said," I'll be. You might have a chance of beating me yet."

Just then David heard Augustus' loud truck make its approach. Soon as he did, he commanded Richie to go inside with his ma.

"Pa, I don't want to. I'm finna win. No fair!"

"We can finish later on. Now scat like I say."

"Pa!"

"Richie," David said in a tone that only Richie would recognize as a sign that he meant business. With that, Richie got up and left holding an etching of the checkerboard in his mind until it was time to return and march toward his planned victory.

David gave Augustus a friendly smile since he was glad to see him. Richie was sent in the house because David didn't permit him to be around Augustus too much, even though he taught him to call him Uncle Gusty. Augustus was his friend but he didn't want to raise his son in a way where he'd be accused of being a nigger lover. He'd grown use to his brothers, cousins, and friends calling him that. He knew the pain of being teased. His friendship with Augustus had gotten deeper over the years but it began as adults. Over time, he cared less and less of what others thought but wanted to let Richie get older and make his own choices when it came to race mixing.

Augustus came to the edge of the porch and David hopped off to the ground to greet him with a tight, close body handshake that stopped short of a hug.

Just then Mary Faye came out with a pitcher of water. She waved a quick hello to Augustus with a slow moving smile, refilled David's tin cup, retrieved Richie's empty cup and disappeared back in the house.

Augustus and David were neck and neck in height, two of the tallest men in Chinaberry. David always joked that that's why they saw eye to eye but really it was music that brought them together; Augustus' music and David's love for it held the unlikely friendship together.

Augustus was born with his mother's song in him. It was a song that held longing and endurance. He was also born with his father's drums in him. The drums carried fire and spirit. Augustus was given his first guitar from a neighbor at the age of twelve. Instantly the song inside him found release through his fingers and lips as rhythm and hum and breath. A chant repeated in his head told him that he was seeking. The pounding of the drum in his soul sounded like someone calling his name in the distance.

Somewhere within these musical expressions David was pulled into a space just outside of Augustus' blues one day when he heard him playing inside his truck. From that moment, he was drawn in, but Gusty's blues must never become his blues. He must never reach the unbearable point of no return. And Augustus was happy to grant him that space because it meant that he could travel to the space at the edge of David's freedom, which is all he could hope for.

Augustus was very much in tune to when his music produced a rise in emotion in David and it influenced the way he played. If he could pull David into that space, he was pleased as both a musician and a man.

"How you doing there, Mista David? What you know good?"

"Ah hey, Gusty. Come on. Let's sit down. Too hot to be standing."

"Yes, yes, shore is hot." Augustus eyed David's tin cup full of water and swallowed his saliva.

Although David was thirsty too, he didn't drink without being able to offer some to Augustus.

"Been expecting you to come around. I see you got Windy City with you. I don't think I ever noticed all those scratches on it. How long you had that one?"

"For quite some time, I reckon. Blind Eye Joe give it to me. Ain't no telling how long he had it before then." Augustus couldn't help but to glance over at the water again.

"Well, one thing's for sure. The way you handle that guitar is a real gift. Wish I could play like that."

"Well, I could teach you a couple tunes on it. Been asking if you want a lesson and you steady saying no."

"That's alright, Gusty. Imma leave that to the professionals like you. If I've said it once, I'll say it again; you should be up north playing."

"I ain't gon lie. I reckon I think about it time to time but then again, I'm happy right here playing for y'all. Yes sah, I shore am."

"Well, if you ever change your mind, just let me know because I could see to it that you make that trip."

"You don't say. You sound about like your brother now."

"Well this we agree on but you know for yourself, we don't agree on too much else."

"Now that's the God honest truth. Y'all about as different as night and day."

"True. True. But speaking of Peter, have you given any more thought to the deal my brother's offering?"

"Yes sah. Was wondering if you was gon bring that up. I shore have. Can't hardly think of nothing else."

"Is that right? Well, at some point you need to make up your mind because the offer ain't gon be on the table forever, you know. There are other considerations. Now I'm a pretty patient fellow but I can't say the same for my brother and he wants to go on and close this deal. Really, it looks to be something good in it for the both of you. That money can put you in a real good position. Opportunities like this don't come every day to your kind. You know that, don't ya, Gusty?"

"You speak the truth. And I'm thankful that Mista Pete would even consider me for the deal."

"Let me ask you this. You ain't letting your woman control your thinking, are you?"

"Oh no, sah. Not in my house."

"Alrighty then. I expect you'll let him know what you decide by sundown tomorrow."

"Yes sah. Shore will."

"Good. Good. Hey, why don't we meet up at the diner later on and you can bring Windy here and show them why they call you Hummin' Gusty. How's that?"

"Now you talking. I can smell Miss Mary Faye got supper on so I ain't gon hold you. Let me make my way home to see what the Missus got waiting for my hungry belly and I'll meet up with ya later on."

Augustus had some real thinking to do. He had a decision to make that just might put his life on a different path. Just being in the position to make such a decision made him feel important, so his good mood was intact as he jumped in his truck.

In the midst of a smile and his thoughts, he saw David running toward the truck. He came around to his window and reached in his pocket, pulled out his billfold and handed Augustus a limp ten-dollar bill. "Sorry to trouble ya, Gusty, but mind taking this to..."

Augustus cut him off as he took the money, "No trouble a 'tall, Mista David."

They parted ways. Now Augustus had one more stop to make before heading home. Turns out, Richie and Baby Jane were not the only children David had, just the only ones he claimed, the only ones that were full white. He had one whose brown-skinned mama received ten dollars a month and a big bag of groceries from him courtesy of his tried and true delivery man, Augustus.

7

"Patacake. Patacake. Baker's man. Bake me a cake as fast as you can. Roll it up. Roll it up and throw it in a pan!" Charles clapped with Patty Cake as she chanted and squealed with delight. After a few times, he reached his limit of playtime. He eased away slowly so as to not make her cry. She did not like things to be abrupt and he was always mindful of that. He woke up Patty Cake's dolly taking a nap on Pearl's straw chair and handed it to her. They exchanged a smile and then he skipped away from the porch and entered the house. He went into his bedroom and pulled back the ratty, baby blue, corduroy spread. He then climbed into the old rusty iron bed covered with layers of peeling white paint. He grabbed his feather pillow and propped his head up by doubling it up for extra support. He hated sharing this tiny, cramped room with both his brother Eye and Patty Cake. Patty Cake had a cot all to herself but he and Eye slept together. His side of the bed was pushed tight up against the wall, which held the only window in the room. In late fall and early spring, that window provided a welcome breeze but in the winter, it was he who caught the brunt of the freezing cold draft long before it reached his brother's side of the world. To make matters worse, Eye's wild, long-legged sleeping left Charles coverless most nights. But what he really hated most about this sleeping arrangement was the fact that whenever Eye was there and he needed to get out of bed, he had to scoot all the way to the foot of the bed to exit. He learned the hard way that climbing over Eye was not an option, unless he wanted to get knocked in the head or off the bed.

Content to be with himself, Charles looked out the dust-clad window, as he often did, and put his dreams off somewhere in the distance, past his mama's flower beds, the strawberry and blackberry patches, the oak, sycamore, and pecan trees, past his father's garden of beans and greens, past the dense woods, and even past where the earth meets the sky. Although his dreams were far away, he didn't see any harm in having some. There had to be more out there beyond Chinaberry, Arkansas, and he hoped to get at least a piece of it for him and his sister one day. The rest could fend for themselves for all he cared.

Just as he placed himself firm in his dreams, a door slam brought him back to reality. Pearl was home. He could follow the path she took even though he couldn't see her. Pearl was heavy-footed and anyone in earshot could hear a combination of her stomps and the creaks on the stressed wooden floors. Basically, Pearl's daily arrival from her work as a seamstress signaled a series of obtrusive sounds. Slam. Stomp. Creak. And last but not least..."Charles! Boy, get in here!"

Charles didn't hesitate. He rushed into the kitchen and headed straight for Patty Cake, hunched over the wash pan. He let Patty Cake do the dishes even though he knew it was his turn.

He forgot all about her while he was wrapped up in his dreams.

"Get over there and wash those dishes," Pearl commanded. "You know Patty Cake can't get them cleaned worth nothing plus I know the water done got cold. Go boil some more and hurry up."

"Can I please dry," Patty Cake begged. Charles gave her the tattered, plaid dishrag so she wouldn't sulk the rest of the evening.

Pearl sat down at the large round table that was smack dab in the middle of the kitchen and closed her eyes. She needed a moment of rest before getting supper on, and before Augustus came in from the fields with whatever attitude he had thrown over his shoulders from events of the day or the story of his life.

Just then Eye ran in, slamming the screen door behind him and startling the house into attention. He brought another set of noises. Slam. Stomp. *Mama!* Smooch! He landed a big sloppy kiss on Pearl's eager cheek and placed in her tired and achy hands a gold envelope. It was his report card.

"I got *all* As," Eye bragged in a singsong manner.

"Well, let me see, baby." Pearl softened her voice as she opened up the envelope and pulled out the card. She squinted her eyes, quickly skimmed it, and then broke out into a huge smile. "Look at that. You shore did. Good for you. That's my baby," she cooed as she drew him close and gave him a big hug. "Now where's yours, Charles? You ain't showed me nothing since I walked up in here. You better not be hiding it either."

"I didn't get mines yet, mama," he lied. It was hidden inside the four-drawer chest of drawers. One of the drawers belonged to him. Eye, who always seemed to have at least one more than him in most things, had two drawers and Patty Cake had one. Charles knew he would have to produce that report card the next day or Pearl would go right up to the schoolhouse and embarrass him in front of everybody. But all he needed was one more day. That morning, he had seen Pearl cutting up some apples to make apple fritters to eat after supper. He didn't want to get a whipping *and* miss out on apple fritters. Nope. That didn't make any sense at all.

The next day, Charles was prepared for his fate. Slam. Stomp. Creek.

"Charles! I know you got that report card. Now bring it in here!"

Charles turned away from the window, shut his eyes, and took in a deep, deep breath. He already held the gold envelope that sealed his fate. His hands had been trembling with nervousness all the way up until he heard Pearl stomp through the door. Now his hands were steady as strength traveled down the surface of his body from his head down to his toes like a warm gelatin that quickly formed into a hardened shell. And then Charles felt like a fully prepared, armored soldier.

"Charles! I know you hear me. Boy, don't make me come in there!"

Charles opened his eyes and almost actually smiled, not about the situation, but because Pearl was predictable in a funny sort of way. He mocked her all the time in his head and under his breath. He erased any semblance of a would-be smile from his face and walked quickly with mustered dignity into the kitchen. Without saying a word, he handed Pearl the envelope. She snatched it, although it was well in her hands before the actual snatch. She opened it and slid out the folded card and opened it with anticipation to confirm what she already expected. Pearl squinted her eyes again and then widened them as they darted from the right and left and to the right again, making their way down the list of subjects. Her neck joined in on the side to side motion. To Charles, her whole body was swinging back and forth like she was dancing to what she was seeing. English F. Math F. Spelling D. Science F. Social Studies D. Physical Education D. Citizenship C.

"Boy, all you got is Ds & Fs except in Citizenship! Boy, go out there and get me a switch! And don't take all day! I'm tired."

Charles turned his back to her to exit out the door. He waited until he got off the porch and turned the corner before he rolled his eyes and started muttering under his breath, calling his mama a mean cow. He was headed to the sycamore tree in the backyard taking his own sweet time. On his way, he trampled one of Pearl's flowers in her flowerbed on purpose. It was a nice pretty purple one with a yellow center that looked like a smashed egg yolk by the time he got through stomping on it. This made him smile real big. Then he made it to the trunk of the tree where he picked up the switch he had already pre-selected that morning before leaving for school. This one was not too thick or thin and had a smooth surface. His experience told him that it was perfect if such a thing was possible. He then returned to the house, handed Pearl the switch at arm's length and proceeded to run from her from one small room to the next to tire her out some more. Then when she was breathing heavy, he let her catch up with him. On the inside, he took his whipping gallantly but on the outside he flinched and screamed and jerked about on the floor and dodged blows and promised to do better and begged Pearl to stop in order to give her enough satisfaction to complete the deed and go get supper on. He was hungry.

Right in the middle of the spectacle, Eye walked in and saw what was going on and burst into laughter. Pearl turned to admonish him and at the same time she stopped the whipping along with her chant of you better-STRIKE-get your-STRIKE-lesson-and-learn-STRIKE–them books-STRIKE-you-hear-me! She was panting. It was as if she welcomed the break that Eye's interruption was giving her. She had been tired when she walked in the door. Now all that chasing and whipping had worn her out completely but she still had to cut up and fry the chicken, make some rice and biscuits and warm up the butter beans before Augustus got home. Yes, both Pearl and Charles were happy to see Eye.

At the same time, Patty Cake slowly walked into the room, rubbing her eyes as she emerged from a nap. Her thick mounds of hair that needed a good untangling was smashed on one side of her head along with the imprint of sleep and a stain of dried milky white saliva on the corner of her mouth.

"Charlie, play patacake with me!"

Charles stood up, brushed himself off, wiped the forced tears off his face and headed back to his room. Patty Cake followed close behind even though he had not answered her. As he played patacake with Patty Cake, Charles could hear Pearl and Eye talking and laughing down the hall. She was telling Eye to get a good night's sleep because she was going to allow him to go fishing with her and her friend Little Bits. That was to be his reward for getting such a good report card. He didn't too much care about the fishing part but he loved being up under his mama and her fishing buddy, who always had a treat for him.

They planned to get up well before the sun the next morning, which was Saturday, and go to a creek that was a good distance away. Of course, Little Bits would drive since Pearl didn't know how. Charles heard the whole thing. It wasn't hard. His ears were open and the house was small. On top of that, he believed that they were being extra loud to make sure he could hear their plans that didn't include him.

He also heard the grease popping and crackling in the cast iron skillet. He heard it all. This talk made his head feel heavy with locked-in tears rising to the inward temple of his forehead. He wanted to cry again, this time for real. What he was feeling was far worse than the whipping. He held back the tears since he was playing with Patty Cake and didn't want to upset her. He looked toward the window and pictured himself trampling on all of Pearl's prized flowers, even the fuchsia ones, which were his own personal favorite. He could easily sacrifice them to spite her.

After some time, Charles heard a third voice. Augustus was home. As usual, he didn't announce himself with big sounds when he entered the house like the others. He never seemed happy to arrive home, even though he was tired from working in the fields all day. Augustus would always hesitate before opening the screen door, let out a big, heavy sigh, and then close it gingerly behind him as if he didn't want to wake up a sleeping baby. To him, coming home to Pearl and the children gave him the feeling of missing the last train to Chicago every day.

Augustus put his troubles and contemplations to the side when he caught a whiff of supper. While he ate, savoring every bite, and sopping up with a biscuit what his fork or hand couldn't scoop up, he exchanged the necessary amount of words with Pearl to give her just enough pleasing to cover his meal. After that, he complimented her as he customarily did and took his full belly out to the porch to soak in the night air and to find a free moment for himself, free of the sun on his back in the field and free of Pearl and the children reminding him of what he didn't have and what he wasn't.

He grabbed his guitar as he headed out the door. He posted himself on the edge of the planked porch to the right of the steps as he always did, and looked up at the stars a good long while as if he was searching for meaning in their positions and relative brightness. Finally, a mosquito that landed on his strumming hand reminded him that he was holding his guitar. He quickly swatted the pest away before it was able to feast on his salty sweat and sweet blood.

Then he commenced to playing his guitar until he was moved to wail a hum loud enough for the moon to turn a quarter. Pearl could hear him from inside while she stood at the kitchen sink near the window. Without there being any words to his hum but a lot of longing, she took it for a passionate love song, figuring it was meant for her like any wife would with a bent toward fantasizing. She let her eyes smile along with her mouth as she finished cleaning up the kitchen.

The music entertained her and made this last chore of the day seem bearable. Truth be told, many of Pearl's fellow church members at the No Ways Tired Baptist Church called this music Augustus played the devil's music. Pearl never engaged in such talk. She opined that the music coming from her husband was as worthy as the gospel she sang in the choir. The devil could cause the blues but it did not dwell in the blues. A song sung from deep down in the soul is either a sign of God or a cry for God. Either way, it's all God's business. Who were folks to judge what music made God clap hands and tap feet; that was her thinking anyway, at the time. Not all shared it but some felt it in between Saturday night when they strutted into the juke joint and Sunday morning when they marched into the sanctuary.

She was done drying the dishes by the time his song ended and the music stopped. She dried her hands on her apron, untied it and placed it on a rusty nail on the floral wallpapered wall by the enclosed back porch used to store wood and this and that.

On her way to her bedroom, she hesitated and almost went outside to join Augustus but thought better of it. Since the music had stopped, she had best leave him to his thoughts. He'd be coming inside soon enough, she reckoned. To keep herself lifted, she began humming her own tune which asked the Lord to remember *her way beyond the blue, do Lord oh do Lord oh do remember me*. Still humming, she walked on to their bedroom.

She wondered how long Augustus would be before he joined her in bed. She wouldn't have minded a little loving to close the day.

Augustus wondered how long it would be before she fell asleep. He wasn't in the mood for any loving that depended on him. He had too much on his mind. He had a decision to make, a big one. He picked up his guitar again and this time played a melancholy tune that came close to being a baby's lullaby. Before long, Pearl's soft snore joined in the melody and Augustus sensed correctly that it was safe to join her in bed. Before going inside, he took one last look up in the sky. The moon rolled its eyes at him.

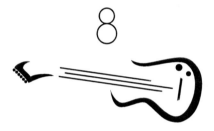

8

Augustus was out of time. Peter wanted an answer. Would he or wouldn't he sell the Rivers land? Augustus had asked himself this question over and over again. Pearl had not been a part of the figuring. To him, this matter did not concern her. It was a decision he had to make alone. It was about his future as a musician and his future as a man. The best way to describe it was to say he was at a crossroad. He saw David earlier in the day at Reynolds' General Store, and the two of them agreed to meet together with Peter later that evening at the diner after it closed. Augustus went around to the back of the building like he normally did and cracked the door open to the makeshift club room where he performed sold-out shows to an audience of four. The room was empty. He didn't think it was his place to go inside without the Duncan brothers being there so he decided to stand there outside to wait on them to arrive.

He leaned against the wall and felt more and more uneasy as the seconds turned into minutes. His stomach growled. He could smell the spicy scent of Miss Patsy's famous fried chicken which over time had settled into every crevice of the diner's walls. He sure wished he had some wings, his favorite piece of the bird. He started humming to pass the time away and to take his mind off both the hunger and the decision he'd have to make soon. A minute or so passed and then out of the blue, he heard David calling his name from the main part of the diner.

Startled, he took his back off the wall and yelled back, "Here I am back here, Mista David."

"Come on in here, Gusty. We been waiting on ya." That was Peter's voice.

Augustus' ears popped and mouth dropped. He was amazed that the Duncan brothers were actually inviting him into the diner where only whites were permitted and served. He placed his hand over his mouth to contain a smile he felt was getting so big it might trail off his face. With just a second of hesitation, he walked with great pride to the entryway into the diner. He stopped short at the one step you needed to climb to enter and peered in. Just in case he mistook what Peter was saying, he waited for additional words of permission to move beyond the threshold.

"What you doing just standing there? Come on in here and take a seat," Peter said, pointing to the empty side of the booth where he and David were facing, he seated on the inside and David comfortably seated on the outside.

Augustus measured his steps while looking around. The red vinyl on the booths shined much brighter and the chrome throughout the room sparkled more than he imagined looking in through the front glass window. He remembered when the Duncans closed the old diner down for a few weeks and opened back up with everything brand spanking new. Both whites and coloreds alike came to see the big changes revealed, but of course only the whites were allowed to go inside for the celebration. Miss Patsy had a party of her own for her favorite customers in the back and passed out enough free food to feed an army. And here Augustus was walking across the spotless checkered black and white floor or better yet, floating across it.

He tipped his hat to the Duncan brothers and slid into the booth, not quite knowing where to place his eyes so he looked downward and focused on a piece of paper that lay on the table.

"You hungry? Patsy left plenty chicken back in the kitchen. I think it's some more tater salad too if my greedy brother here ain't ate the last of it," Peter joked.

"Gusty, don't listen to him. Plenty food left to fit your appetite. That is, if you don't count Patsy's pound cake. Now every crumb of that's gone," David said while rubbing his belly and laughing.

Augustus just smiled and fidgeted with his hands underneath the table, rubbing the length of his thighs while he rocked slightly in the booth. He was trying to find his comfort in this new space. The two brothers smiled back and waited for his answer about the food.

"No sah but thank ya kindly just the same," he answered, hoping they wouldn't hear his stomach growl. He was indeed hungry but didn't want to overextend his welcome so soon.

Peter pushed a half full bottle of Ancient Age one-hundred proof Kentucky straight bourbon whiskey his way. "Well, you look thirsty. Go 'head. Drank up."

"Yes sah. Thank ya sah. Can't say I ever had this kind of whiskey before."

"First time for everything. This is what you'll be drinking every night when you start playing in Chicago."

Augustus took a big swig and let out a big *ah* sound. He was hoping it would put him to ease.

"Well, Gusty, we here to take care of business. All I need for you to do is put your 'X' on this here dotted line," Peter said as picked up the piece of paper Augustus had fixed his eyes on and handed it to him.

Augustus received the long piece of paper in his hands and brought it up close to his eyes and squinted. "Pardon me, Mista Pete but I done messed around and forgot my reading glasses and I can't see to read worth nothing without them. You might should just go on ahead and explain exactly what it says."

"Ain't much to it. You just sign over your twenty acres of land and you'll receive three hundred dollars, plus I'll allow you to stay right there on the land till the day you die." Then Peter took money out of his billfold and counted the bills on the table until the last words he uttered were, "Three. Hundred. Dollars."

Excitement swooped down on Augustus like a hawk. He had never seen that much money in all his life and he liked the looks and the smell of it. The idea of him leaving there with that heap of money in his pocket sent his thoughts into a spin.

Peter grinned at his reaction and David got up on his own cue and went to the booth next to theirs and bent over. He came back and placed a black, hardshell guitar case on the table in front of Augustus.

Augustus' eyes lit up more but he didn't quite know what to make of this unexpected guest now sitting next to the cash that seconds before he had wanted to scoop up and feel the greenness of for himself.

"Go ahead. Open it, Gusty," David urged.

"Yes sah, yes sah," he blurted out.

Taking a deep breath and steadying his shaky hands, Augustus unlatched the brass handles on either side of the case and opened it with great wonder and anticipation. And there resting on a bed of plush, purple velvet was a brand-new Gibson J-185 acoustic guitar, sleek and smart, golden at its center, copper penny brown at its inner edges, and framed by a thin black line around its hourglass curves. Augustus saw the sun rising from the center of that guitar. Its swirling colors were like a new day slowly spreading across every rounded corner of the night sky to reach the sacred moment before dawn. He couldn't take his eyes off it nor could he put his words on it.   He took the whole of his heavy right hand and caressed its polished belly. It felt like well-nourished skin. It was soft like a woman. It was surprisingly warm to his touch. Had it been soaking up heat and saving it just for him? He was thinking that he could carry a guitar like that across his back and never need a coat again even in the thick of winter, even on the coldest day in Chicago. For sure, it could hold summer. Now, he was bound to find out if it could withstand the freezing cold and hold his blues too.

Augustus looked up at David and David nodded in the affirmative at his silent request. Then he slowly lifted the guitar out of the case. He took her into his arms and cradled her and she responded by inviting him to make music with her. Then he strummed her for the very first time. The sound was rich and big and beautiful just like he had imagined. He was already falling in love. David's eyes said play her some more. Peter's face was frozen with his notorious half-smile. Augustus played his new woman until he found the center of her desire and the center of his blues, his soul's release. He heard her moan. Then he commenced to hum a new life carved out of the bones and flesh of that guitar, three hundred dollars and an empty bottle of whiskey.

The next day, Augustus woke up with the chickens, but Pearl and Eye had awakened before both the chickens and the sun to go fishing as planned. Augustus let out a long yawn, rose up, sat up on the side of the bed and stretched, and then yawned again, the second time even wider than before. Then he headed to the outhouse for his morning relief. He wore a long nightshirt with navy blue and white stripes. Pearl had sewn it for him. He returned to the house and followed the faint aroma of breakfast to the kitchen where he found some thick sliced, hickory-smoked bacon with the skin still on waiting for him along with some grits, biscuits and thick sorghum syrup. Still standing, he picked up one of the slices of bacon and began his ritual of eating all of the bacon, lean and fat, down to the skin first. Then he returned to the crispy skin he saved for last and devoured it like it was the best crunchy treat in the world. He thought to himself that he sure was going to miss all this good cooking.

As soon as Augustus finished breakfast, he was already thinking about dinner, which hopefully would be some catfish if Pearl and Little Bits had any luck fishing. He would even settle for some no-name creek fish. Heck, he was in such a wonderful mood, they could come back with the bait and he might dance a jig.

And to top things off, he had the house all to himself or so he thought. He figured that the boys went with Pearl and she dropped off Patty Cake at Miss Mattie Ann's house. Miss Mattie Ann loved to watch kids and she didn't mind watching Patty Cake. Oftentimes, when Patty Cake had her crying spells and had to leave school early, Charles would walk her over to Miss Mattie Ann's house that was just down the road from the schoolhouse. Her only son and daughter-in-law had moved to Washington, D.C. and took all three of her grandbabies, leaving behind a room full of playthings. Sometimes Patty Cake liked to hold playthings when she went into her stillness.

As Augustus walked back to his room, he thought he heard a noise coming from the children's room. He went over and looked in and there balled up on the bed was Charles whimpering. His eyes were bloodshot. The creak of the door startled Charles and he jumped up and tried to wipe his tears as quickly as he could, but it was too late. Augustus had already seen them.

"Boy, what you still doing here and what you crying like a baby about?"

"Mama said I couldn't go. She said Eye got the good report card so he could go. She even took Patty Cake. It ain't fair."

"Well boy, ain't no sense in you crying now. You should've got your lesson. Straighten up your face. You thirteen. You too old for that. Now put your overalls on. We finna go fishing ourselves and I'm gon take you to a special spot over on the Duncans' land. Mista Pete showed it to me. Big beautiful lake full of jumping fish, ready for the taking."

"They gon allow you to go fishing on they land, daddy?"

"Yeah boy, Mista Pete said anytime I wanna go fishing over there, just come on. Don't be asking me no questions. I'm the pappy. You the youngin. Now hurry up. We done already missed the best time to go, if we wanna get any nips at all."

A great wave of happiness overtook Charles. He was thinking, just wait until mama and Eye find out about this. Wait until he comes home with the biggest fish they ever saw! He ran and put his overalls on. Those overalls came well above his ankles. Eye's were so long, he had to roll his up. Once again, Charles got the short end of the stick. Today it didn't matter though; he was going fishing with his daddy!

Augustus drove his truck down the overgrown red dirt road heading to the fishing hole. He was inching along slowly enough to stop short of running over a long, checkered, red, gray, and black garter snake as it slithered across the road, belly full with the likes of a bullfrog. Charles joked that maybe they should stop and grab it to use as bait for the big fish they were about to catch. Augustus laughed. He was glad to be on a secret trip with his son, plus he was in a happy mood about his other secret, the deal he'd made with Peter Duncan.

To have the money in his possession, there was a fullness in his chest like he had never known before. He still could hardly believe it, all that money plus the most beautiful guitar he ever did see for land that he didn't truly have to part with until he died. The way he understood it, that land wouldn't do him any good after he was dead and gone anyway, nor did he intend for his sons to be farmers. On the other hand, he felt that money that he got for the land sure could provide him with just the fresh start he needed so he could get some good living while on earth. Pearl could wait around until she made it to heaven if she wanted to, but he wasn't saintly so he reckoned he couldn't count on flying away some glad morning and entering the pearly gates.

As far as he was concerned, he got the better end of the deal. Maybe Peter just wanted to help him out as a friend, to give him a taste of freedom, he was thinking. Whatever the case may be, he was pretty sure that he was the richest colored man in Chinaberry at that moment and there was no telling just how rich he'd be after he made it big in Chicago. He hadn't yet decided when he was going to leave but he definitely was leaving. He was bound to go. And he decided that he couldn't afford to tell Pearl before he did so. She would just wake up one day and he'd be gone. He figured this way would be better than a long good-bye and seeing a bunch of tears. Plus, if she protested too much, she might even wind up ruining all his plans. No, he couldn't chance that; when he returned a rich man, she wouldn't have anything to say about how he left.

He also decided to put the money aside for safekeeping until he ironed out the details of his plan. Two days earlier, as soon as he left the diner after making the deal, he returned home and walked to the furthest point of the property to the sycamore tree, a place he often went to think on life or to take his mind off life. He took the money out and counted every last one of the bills again and placed them in a rusty tin can and buried it deep near the tree's trunk.

Augustus tried to take his mind off his dreams and keep his eyes focused on the road. He had not been off in these woods since he was a little boy when his daddy's buddy Doc Brown and his wife Miss Ernestine lived back there in a little shack. Every time he and his daddy would pay them a visit, they would find Doc Brown lying on a cot on their sunporch with his gray-haired chest and mountainous belly exposed. For some reason, Augustus would fixate on watching that belly go up and down like it was ocean waves he had never seen. He was both repulsed and mesmerized and wondered why Doc Brown didn't see fit to put on a shirt.

Doc Brown would rise up long enough to shake his daddy's hand out of respect, lay back down and start back talking a mile a minute about this and that and repeating a lifetime of stories with all predictable endings that his audience could recite word for word. Yet and still everybody pretended to be interested and laugh at the right spots in the story. Miss Ernestine would just be sitting in her rocking chair, rocking back and forth, fanning, patting her head when it itched, nodding, and saying, "Yes Brown, I know." or "Yes Brown, I remember." But she had stopped laughing a long time ago or even listening for that matter. He reckoned that's how they spent their days besides minding the chicken coop.

Doc Brown and Miss Ernestine made their living selling fresh, brown eggs. As a youngin, Augustus would be excited to go inside the coop with Doc Brown. He found it fun to make tiptoeing around chicken poop a game. He would watch Doc Brown gather eggs from the nests with great excitement. He liked thinking that maybe Doc Brown would be attacked by chickens but he never was. Anyway, that was a long time ago, before the shack and the coop burned down. After that, Doc Brown had a stroke and was put in the old folk's home until he died and Miss Ernestine went to live with her eldest daughter in Magnolia, Arkansas, and some kind of way, Peter Duncan obtained their land.

They continued their journey to the creek. Augustus didn't recall ever going further than where the Browns lived. That is, until Peter Duncan took him there the day before. After Augustus took him around the property and he surveyed the land, both were in a celebratory spirit. Peter told him to hop in his truck because he wanted to show Augustus something. Then he drove him to a new neck of the woods. Augustus experienced a mix of nervousness and glee during the drive and the walk to the surprise place. When they finally reached the destination, it was like discovering a magical place he didn't even know existed. Peter told Augustus he and his brother David had recently cleared the land of trees to make timber and Peter's younger cousin, Todd Duncan, had moved into a trailer on the land right near the creek.

Augustus was drifting in his thoughts again when Charles tapped him on the shoulder.

"What's that you say, son?"

"I said are we almost there?"

"Oh yes, we real close now. Just a bit more up the road."

"Good, because I'm getting tired of riding."

"Tired of riding? Why, that's the easiest part. Not shore what kinda fisherman you gon make if you already tired."

"That's alright because I don't wanna be no fisherman. I just wanna catch some fish."

"Is that right? Well, what you wanna be?"

"A bluesman like you," Charles blurted out. "I want to learn to play the guitar just like you, daddy. Remember you said you was gon teach me. And I don't care none if you don't teach me using that new fancy guitar you got from Mista Duncan. Maybe you can use the one you been had?"

"Hmmm. I reckon you due a lesson but I put that other one out in the smokehouse so ain't no use in bringing that one up because I don't aim to go backwards. I guess if you real careful I can teach you a little something on the one I gots now but that depends on how big a fish you catch today. You still tired?"

"No sah. I'm raring to go!" Charles said, bursting from the seams.

"I figured you'd 'liven up real quick." Augustus laughed.

He came to the turn of the road that would lead to the creek. A true driving path hadn't been cleared yet to the fishing hole. There was just an overgrown dusty road that you had to follow to get there so the ride slowed down considerably. Peter told him that he could go fishing in the creek in the back of his cousin Todd's trailer any time he wanted. He encouraged Augustus to come back the next morning early if he wanted to catch a big mess of fish. He added that he might just be up there himself the next day and Augustus told him that he might just be up there himself too.

Finally, they reached the spot Augustus marked on a map in his head where they would have to leave the truck and proceed on foot. Augustus parked and Charles got out the truck, hastily slamming the door before Augustus could hardly take the key out of the ignition and put it in the pocket of his overalls. Augustus quickly followed, both eager for adventure and a good time. He directed Charles to grab the box and bucket from the trunk and he grabbed the two poles.

Now Augustus was feeling grand. Not only was he feeling the happiness stemming from his newly acquired riches but the ride to the creek had made things clear in his mind. He was certain of his plans now. He was going to go to Chicago the following day. Wasn't any use in waiting around. He wasn't meant to be playing in a small-town juke joint with a bunch of lowlife Negroes cutting a rug and his audience at the diner was just too small a crowd. Up north, people, especially white folks, from all around would come near and far to see him perform on stage. They would pay big money to admire him and his talent. He would cut an album, too, that would be a big seller. Of course, with fame and fortune, he could have his pick of white women, least ways the ones who would be too happy to be with any talented colored man like himself. He hadn't decided if he would have a whole bunch of them, a new one every night or just take up with one special one even prettier than Miss Callie, and she was about the prettiest one he had seen to date. He reckoned he'd just see what struck his fancy as he got settled into his new life. He also planned on getting some book learning so he could learn to talk proper like educated white folks. He might even associate with some educated, high-class Negroes, no promises, just depending. He pictured the Duncans traveling to Chicago to pay him a visit in his new spot. He would show them tip-top hospitality.

He would make sure Pearl and the children were well-taken care of, but it wouldn't be no place for them in his new life. Maybe he'd send for Charles when he got older to show him what being a musician was really all about. He figured that the God his wife served wouldn't have seen fit to make a way for him to get on a path to his dreams if it wasn't meant for him. As long as they were set up real nice, they would be just fine. Yes, Augustus Lee Rivers, the one they call Hummin' Gusty had big, big plans. As a matter of fact, he was thinking, his luck was so good, he was all set to catch a mighty big fish for Pearl to fry up for supper.

He and Charles started off to the creek. They made their way with deliberate high steps through the thick bush with tall, runaway weeds, shrubbery, and limbs, Augustus taking the lead with confidence, Charles trailing behind trying to keep pace so he wouldn't get left behind. The smell of pines was so heavy; they were toting that too. As they got further from the road, Charles' excitement turned into anxiety and fear. He darted his eyes to the left, to the right, behind, on the ground and straight ahead because he could never quite make out the direction of the crackling, buzz-ing, hissing noises that were moving right along with them down the dark, damp path. He had no idea that they would have to walk so far into the woods into this strange place he had never been. With such trepidation, it no longer felt like a special treat to have the privilege of this journey. His long skinny legs were already getting tired and his load, seemingly getting heavier and heavier, stretched Charles's scratched-up arms to their limit. It was quite a lot to manage but at least the dense trees formed a giant leafy cover that kept the sun at bay, except for determined streams of light that helped to guide the way.

"Daddy, you shore this the right way and them Duncans don't mind us coming back up in here? It shore is far."

"I reckon I know where I'm walking. I was just here and I already told you I was told I could come here whenever I please by Mista Pete himself. I guess that make it alright. Now keep up. We almost there. Just a little piece more. Wait!" Charles jumped.

"Hush. You hear that?"

"What daddy? What is it?"

"You hear them fish flapping about? They must hear us coming to get them," Augustus said, bursting out into laughter.

"Daddy!"

"See now. Look here. We here now."

A wide open meadow parallel to a creek opened before them and the sun was let loose again. Charles smiled and adjusted his eyes to harmonize with the sun. The excitement rushed back. He made it. It was time to fish.

Augustus investigated the landscape before settling on what he determined to be a good spot. Once situated, they cast their rods in the water and patiently waited for some first bites. Augustus hummed. Charles whistled. Augustus hummed some more. Charles whistled some more. After about twenty minutes of humming and whistling and sitting still with their eyes fixated on the water, they hadn't received any bites so Augustus suggested that they try another spot. They walked along the shore looking closely at the water until they lucked upon an area that had a big school of fish for the taking.

Augustus lit up. "Well, I'll be doggone! We not gon need no fishing poles at all to catch these ones here. All we need is a net. Charles, I'm gon chum with them while you run and fetch the net in the truck."

"Daddy, why can't I stay here and do the chumming?"

"Boy, the quicker you get to stepping, the closer we get to supper!"

Charles let out a big sigh. There was no way he wanted to walk that trail alone but he knew not to let on any fear with his daddy, plus he didn't want to seem ungrateful for their special fishing trip. He would just have to be brave. He said a quick prayer and went back to the opening of the trail. He took a deep breath. His plan was to look ahead and walk as fast as he could. His fear that something might jump out the woods and catch him made sure he didn't dillydally. He actually made it back to the truck in no time. He thought to himself, going back seemed to always be easier and quicker than going forward. He grabbed the net and headed back, a little more comfortable this time since he had already survived the path two times at this point.

As he approached the opening to the creek from the wooded area, he heard voices, his daddy's and another he couldn't make out. And then he got close enough to see a strange white man talking to his daddy. He stopped short in his tracks. His eyes widened. Something told him this was a time to be unseen *and* unheard. The white man let out a cackling sound and raised his voice as Charles stood still out of sight and watched on and listened as best as he could.

"But you got this all wrong, now. Mista Pete told me it would be just fine to come down here to go fishing. No sah, I wouldn't be here if he hadn't said so. No sah."

"You're about the dumbest nigger I ever seen!" Todd Duncan, a lanky twenty-something year old chuckled. "I shore wish you had your guee-tar so you could play me a tune before I shoot you dead. You must be a crazy fool, thinking you gon get all that money and Pete just gon sit around and wait for you to die. Just like my cousin say, this like taking candy from a baby. Best to get to praying for your Maker to come save you. Might just change my mind but I gots every right to shoot you. Don't you know trespassing on my land is against the law!" He chuckled some more while pointing a gun at Augustus.

Charles could now see that the man had a gun in his hand pointing it at his daddy. *Oh No! Why! What was going on?* He looked around as if he could summon an answer from the trees but they looked away, as if they had resolved that there was nothing they could do to stop what was happening. Charles felt like his heart had cracked into a thousand pieces and each piece was beating on its own, shooting around his body, and about to explode. He didn't know what to do but then a thousand beating hearts told him to pick up a rock, run up behind the man and throw it at his head so he did. A gunshot rang out and the man fell to the ground. Was his daddy shot? Both collapsed to the ground and neither were moving. Charles stood frozen and his thoughts came racing back. What had he done! He ran over to his daddy. Oh no! He saw blood. His daddy had been shot. Was he dead? He dropped down on the ground and looked at Augustus in the face searching for life. He saw none. He buried his head into his chest and started wailing, "Daddy, daddy! No!" His daddy couldn't be dead. He smothered himself into Augustus' chest searching for his heartbeat. As soon as he did this, Charles felt Augustus' stomach rise. He quickly looked up at Augustus with all hope in his eyes. His daddy was alive! Charles looked over to the other man and he still wasn't moving. He looked back down at his daddy. Augustus was moving his head left to right, trying to place himself, breathe, and find words all at the same time.

Then he muttered, "How you doing Mista Todd? Mighty nice of you to let us fish out here ...fish nipping good today...don't need no bait...just a big net."

Charles kept asking him if he was alright but he kept muttering words that didn't make any sense to him. Charles pinpointed where the blood was coming from. It was coming from his right arm.

"Daddy, get up. Come on daddy, please. Wake up! We gots to go before that man gets up!"

Augustus slowly rose up and almost fell back down when his knees buckled. He kept muttering but he followed Charles' lead. Charles guided him as fast as he could back through the trail to the truck. He now knew exactly where to step and where not to step. There was no fear.

He was focused. Augustus followed also. He felt no pain. His mind was working to erase the memory of what just happened. Charles helped him into the passenger side of the truck, felt around for the keys in his daddy's overall pockets and took them so he could drive. Augustus had taught him how to drive as soon as he could turn the key in the ignition just like he had taught Eye before him.

Charles sped as Augustus lay pressed against the window, bouncing to and fro, still bleeding and now moaning loudly. Charles looked over at his daddy and had a thought that he tried to shake out as quickly as it came but it lasted a good long minute. No matter how big a fish Eye caught, he wouldn't be able to top saving daddy's life! With this in mind, he dodged and dipped and drove on, feeling every bump in the road as a growth spurt. Charles Lee Rivers had gone into the woods a boy and came out of the woods a young man.

10

Pearl and Little Bits had a successful fishing day. The two of them spent the late morning chopping, fin removing, filleting and cleaning a big batch of catfish. Now Pearl was in the kitchen coating the fish with cornmeal and seasonings and dropping them one by one in the grease to fry with the love and pride of a fisherwoman, chef, wife, mother, and friend. She imagined that the Rivers family would be quite pleased when she rung the bell to announce suppertime. She also invited Little Bits and her family over, plus the Rev and First Lady to take part in the fish fry feast. Augustus would not be pleased with those extra mouths, but Pearl figured that he wouldn't mind the company so much after his first bite of fish drenched in hot sauce or maybe even a crispy hush puppy.

Her next thought was, where in the world was Augustus and Charles? And then...

"Mama!" Charles yelled, running into the kitchen. "It's daddy! He shot, mama! He shot!"

"What, boy? What's this you say now? Calm down."

"Mama, It's Daddy! We was in the woods and..."

Pearl looked up and saw Augustus standing in the entryway. Her eyes darted to the blood but before she could even call on the name of Jesus and get to him, he collapsed on the floor with a loud thud.

Pearl let out a terrifying scream. A piece of fish flew out of her hands, landing on the floor. She rushed to Augustus and at the same time Patty Cake and Eye came running into the kitchen from hearing all the commotion. Pearl was kneeling on the floor over Augustus and yelling questions out to anyone who could answer them. Augustus was speechless but Charles rambled off what happened. Eye turned to Charlie and yelled, "This is your fault!" Patty Cake was wailing at the top of her lungs. Charles went to the corner and dropped to the floor with his back against the wall. He hung his head down and pressed his hands over his ears to block out the noise and the sound of gunshots going off in his head. Pearl took off her apron and tied it around Augustus' arm to try to stop the bleeding. Then she demanded that everybody calm down to receive her orders.

"Eye, take the truck and run get Reverend Willis! Be careful, ya hear." He heard. He left.

"Patty Cake, go fetch a pillow off my bed!" Patty Cake walked in the opposite direction toward Charlie. Pearl looked over. "Boy, get up offa that floor and take your sister outta here and hurry back. Patty Cake, don't you come out that room till I say so or I'll tear your behind up, ya hear?" They jumped and did as they were told. Charles took one second too long returning so Pearl yelled even louder, "Boy, get back in here!" Charles reentered the room. "Now run get Leroy and tell him to come quick and bring his truck." He stood frozen, looking at his daddy lifeless on the floor. Pearl was just about tired of yelling so she jumped up and shook Charles by his shoulders, "What you doing just standing there? Go on!"

He left but came back with a pillow and Augustus' guitar and laid it beside him. Then he obeyed his mama's order and took off. Pearl pushed the guitar away and propped the pillow under Augustus' head. Then she got him some water and forced him to sip some. He was breathing better. She stayed with him on the floor, wiping his forehead and hers too with the same handkerchief and singing softly to soothe him until everybody could be rounded up.

"...Hear my humble cry... Do not pass me by! Oh Lawd...Hear my humble cry."

Leroy, Little Bits' brother, was the first to arrive. His instruction was to carry Augustus to the only place they could go to get him some healing, Miss Rosalie's shack off in the backwoods. Pearl prayed that Jesus would touch and steady Miss Rosalie's gifted hands so they could touch and heal Augustus with love, life, and light. The Rev arrived on the scene, followed by Eye in time to help Augustus into Leroy's truck and add a quick prayer. The Rev convinced Pearl to let Leroy take care of Augustus and advised her to grab what she could out of the house. She, Charles, and Patty Cake could ride with him and Eye could drive over alone.

As soon as they got to the Rev's house, Tim Collins, one of the deacons at the church, was there waiting with his youngest son Johnny, a friend of Charles, to lend a helping hand and haul Charles wherever he was to be taken because everyone was clear that he couldn't stay in Chinaberry. Pearl decided with the counsel, condolences, and comfort of the Rev and First Lady that Charles would be sent to stay with Pearl's cousin Esquire and his wife Gloria in Little Rock.

The devastating news of what happened swept through the town. The Rivers family had been put on the top of every God-fearing family's prayer list. Even those that weren't on good terms with the Maker used requests they were saving up for an emergency for the family's protection. This was a town with a long history of colored folks coming up missing so in between prayers, they counted their loved ones, one by one, and their blessings by the biggest numbers they could imagine.

But with the prayers also came talk fast and furious, talk from folks who believed they could speak from authority on the whys and the how comes of the situation.

"I figured something was gon happen like this one day. Don't ask me how. I just did."

"That's what happens when you mess around with them white folks. Can't trust them as far as you can throw them."

"Thought he was too good for us. Humph. Now look what done happened. I bet he turned white as snow when he saw that gun in his face."

"And that poor Pearl. Simple as he is, don't know how she ended up with that fool in the first place."

"If I had me a high yella, pretty gal like that and thick as molasses too, I shore would know what to do with her. Some folks just don't know when they got a good thing. It's a crying shame."

"Always cutting the monkey for them crooked Duncans. I guess he see now they don't give a rat's ass about him."

"What make him think he could go over yonder to that fishing hole in the first place? I guess he lost his mind for shore. He was a fool right when he went that far in them woods. You couldn't pay me nothing to go somewhere a colored man got no business to go."

"Plus them white folks done pumped his chest up, got him thinking he better than everybody because he can play a guitar. Hell, he ain't no

Blind Eye Joe, that's for shore. Now that's what you call a bluesman right there if ya ask me."

"Well, all I gots to say is, you reap what you sow but even still, God don't like ugly and no matter what you think of Augustus, them white folks treated him far worse than him treating anybody on his worse day."

There was a string of, "You right about thats" and "That's the God-honest truths" heard anywhere the conversation was taking place. Then, having got out everything they believed had to be said on the matter, for that day anyway, they all went back to praying and figuring on how they could each help the Rivers family, who lived in a well-kept house at the bottom of a red dirt road on land with flowerbeds and gardens and big-trunked, long branched, leafy trees until something akin to a violent tornado had struck, leaving them torn asunder in a mountain of debris.

Miss Rosalie saved Augustus' arm. It just needed some tender loving care with her special healing gifts and natural ointments. Augustus didn't utter a word the entire time she patched him up. She placed his arm in a sling and told Leroy to tell Pearl to continue to doctor the wound until Augustus was fully mended. That was the best that she could offer. There wasn't anything she could do about the darkness that had settled deep inside his spirit. His eyes were vacant and she could see and feel that there were heavy gray clouds pregnant with grief weighing down on him. What Augustus was experiencing was a matter of the heart and soul. The healing he would require besides the arm was beyond her calling.

She gave Leroy a message to pass on to Pearl, which was to seek the counsel of Old Lady Miss Corinthia. She would know what to do for Augustus. As for her, she offered up a prayer, sent the two of them on their way, and enjoyed herself some good catfish for supper thanks to Pearl.

Eye, Charles, and Patty Cake did as they were told and sat quietly on the Rev and First Lady's living room couch. They did not dare move. There was a sharpness in the air and none of them wanted to get cut. It was again a time to be seen and not heard.

Then with First Lady by her side, Pearl called Charles over to her. Holding a big stuffed flour sack, she grabbed his hand and walked with him outside to the porch. First Lady followed behind them and positioned herself in front of the door from the outside. The Rev stood at the foot of the porch steps. Deacon Tim stood against the passenger side of his truck and his son Johnny sat in the truck on the same side, sucking on sugarcane while watching everything unfold. The house now empty, Eye and Patty Cake found the nerve to get up and were looking out the screen door from inside. As Charles looked around and saw everyone staring at him, it felt like he was the only one unaware of something he needed to be aware of.

Pearl sat the sack down filled with clothes for Charles on the porch swing and stood in front of him. She placed both of her hands on his shoulders and looked down at him directly in his eyes and said, "Charles, you did good to save your daddy. You're a real hero but the white folks ain't gon stand for it. It's best you go stay with Cousin Esquire in Little Rock for a little while so you be safe. Once things settle down, me and your daddy come get you."

"But mama, I don't want to."

"Hush now. Deacon Tim about to carry you right now. Ain't no time for dillydallying."

"I'm not going! Where's my daddy? I want my daddy!" Charles cried.

"You best lower you voice and calm yourself. I ain't gon say no more. It's decided."

Just then, Patty Cake ran out of the house, forcing First Lady to move quickly to grab her and take her right back inside, kicking and screaming. Pearl blocked out all of the commotion and stayed focused.

The Rev jumped on the porch, grabbed the sack and announced sternly to Pearl, "OK now, they best get going." Charles knew better than to utter another word of protest. Pearl led him to the truck. Deacon Tim was already in the driver's seat with the key in the ignition. Johnny had scooted over to make room for his friend. Charles climbed into the truck slowly and looked straight ahead. Pearl shut the door behind him and leaned in through the rolled down window as Deacon Tim revved up the engine.

Then she blurted out with tears, "Now don't get up there and forget everything we done taught you and embarrass us. Make shore you mind your manners now, ya hear. And you know to respect your elders and to always say yes ma'am and yes sir and please and thank you and excuse me. And please, please pick up after yourself and keep yourself clean, especially in and behind your ears and don't forget to sit up straight at the table, bless your food and clean your plate. It don't pay to be wasteful. And don't be fidgeting in church and say ya prayers every night and I do mean every night. And Lawd knows, it won't hurt ya to pick up a book every now and again like your brother. Just act like you got good sense, you hear?"

Charles reluctantly faced Pearl but when he did, his face and heart softened. "Yes ma'am, I promise, mama, but please don't cry."

"Boy, I ain't crying." Pearl quickly wiped the tears that had betrayed her.

Patty Cake burst through the front door again and came running to the truck with Eye close behind chasing her and Charles jumped out the truck and hugged his sister really tight, looked hard at his brother for a couple of seconds, and then hugged Pearl and got back in the truck. First

Lady made her way to Charles and hugged him through the window best she could. Not to be outdone, the Rev came over and placed a dollar bill in his hand and stepped aside.

Pearl leaned in and whispered something in his ear and placed something in his hand too. Deacon Tim nodded at Pearl and she stepped back. Then he waved and drove off with the boys and enough fish sandwiches to see them through to their destination. Pearl, the kids, the Rev & First Lady stood and watched until the full moon moved to the side to make way for the arrival of Leroy and Augustus. The onlookers took a deep breath in unison and released their good-bye momentarily to ready their welcome. All but Patty Cake, of course, who took several breaths.

Todd Duncan was left with just a scratch but the members of the Duncan family and their buddies did not take too kindly to one of their own being embarrassed, especially by a little colored boy. It took about two hours to round up the boys to handle the situation. They decided to wait until sundown to go over to the Rivers' house. From their experience, visits such as these were just better suited for the night when the folks they came calling upon were tucked away in their beds and could be caught off guard for the sport of it. They met at Peter Duncan's house and headed over to the Rivers' home, kicking up dust along the way in a caravan of three pickup trucks of six hate-festering boys acting under the color of their own laws.

When they arrived, Bubba shot a bullet in the air and yelled for Augustus to come out with Charlie, said that the boy just needed to be taught a lesson. They yelled for a good while and when Augustus didn't come out, George banged on the door. When he still didn't come out, Bubba threw a rock in the window. Then George busted the door down. They didn't realize that the Rivers family was not there. Pearl had filled the Rev's trunk up with as many things that they could take in one trip—some clothes, Pearl's quilts and cast iron skillet, Eye's books, the family Bible, some photos, and Augustus' two guitars. It was Charles who remembered to grab Windy City from the smokehouse.

The boys were angry to find an empty house. They had to let Augustus know they had been there so Peter lit a match and just like that, they watched the house burn down.

Charles did not feel like a hero on the long ride to Little Rock. The sound of gunshots rang repeatedly in his head and tears streamed down his face from his bloodshot eyes. Deacon Tim and Johnny pretended not to notice him crying. Leaving home was something Charles had always yearned for, but he wanted the glory of setting off down the red dirt road on his own accord and with Patty Cake by his side. That was not to be.

Once he arrived at the Carters' house, he was in a strange place with strange smiling people. To him, his kinfolk's home was dressed up better than some of the white folks back in Chinaberry. And even though he had a bedroom all to himself and there was a bathroom in the house, that first night, his heart ached for the narrow side of the bed he shared with Eye. There was only one thing he knew for sure that actually made him feel better in a way; his daddy would never be able to claim he didn't have the blues now, not after what he had seen, not after having to leave his family, especially Patty Cake, and not after losing the music his daddy made just outside his window, that "wanting something you ain't gots" kind of music that touched something inside of him like nothing else did.

Two days had passed since Charles' departure and Patty Cake had slid off the side of an upside-down smile into a sea of sadness. Without her Charlie, there were no circles and songs for her to find her natural rhythm.

She sat alone in places no one bothered to look with her head buried in her lap and her hands folded at her ankles. Even Eye was out of sorts with his baby brother gone and his mama otherwise busy tending to Augustus. The bigness he assumed as he paraded around cloaked in his mama's favor was now gone. And without Charles there for him to tower above, to tease and taunt and trip, Eye felt half as tall. He poured himself deeper into his books, nearly pressing his forehead against the ragged, yellowing pages like he was trying to climb in between them and hide behind the words.

And for two whole days, Pearl had not been able to cook up magic in her kitchen, sit in her chair on *her* porch, see all her children flying about like butterflies and hear the bass in her husband's voice and the soulful chords of his guitar. Her life drained out of her. There was only one thing she knew that could get her through this band of heavy rain; she put on her spiritual armor and held on with all her might to God's unchanging hand.

As for the legendary Augustus, with deep brown skin bathed in ancient, dusky rivers and loved by a luminous sun and moon, he wished nothing more than to be an antonym of himself. His "what you ain't gots that keeps you from what you want" engulfed him. His blues were in every shade of blue. They wanted to rush through his lips in the solace of a hum or in the release of a cry or find escape through his fingertips on the strings of his guitar but they were trapped and not knowing what else to do, they began to gnaw at his spirit.

He did not speak, could not speak or was refusing to speak. No one knew for sure what the case was. Had he suffered a nervous breakdown? Could it be a stroke? He didn't give any indication. He just slept curled up most of the time, head on one pillow, and the other pillow squeezed against his chest. At least he appeared to be sleeping. His eyes were closed. Every now and then, he'd get up to use the indoor facilities or sit up and stare off into the distance, like he was looking beyond the walls watching something no one else could see.

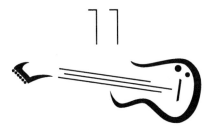

11

"**A**ugustus? I see you sitting up. That's good. Now why don't you talk? I brought you something good to eat. Look here. I gots you some chicken wings, black-eyed peas, rice, a slice of tomato and your favorite-candied yams, nice and sweet with an extra pinch of cinnamon like you like them. And Sista Helen made some fresh buttered rolls and you know that's about the only thing she can make good. And once you done with this, I might even have a big slice of my lemon pound cake for you. It's nice and moist. Now how's that?"

Pearl handed Augustus the food on a wooden tray, which he accepted with an expressionless face. Whatever his condition was, it didn't seem to affect his appetite for Pearl's cooking. Pearl sat in the rocking chair catty-corner to the bed and watched Augustus eat even if it might be im-polite to do so. She just couldn't take her eyes away from him. What was he thinking? Would he ever speak again? One affectionate thing Augustus did was compliment her after he finished a meal. She waited for him to do so now out of habit but he didn't speak. What he did do was tap his empty plate, indicating that he wanted seconds. That would have to be enough of a compliment for now. Pearl smiled and got up to oblige him. But as soon as she hit the corner, she let some tears escape out of Augustus' sight. She had to be strong. That dreadful day had got a hold of her husband's tongue and it was going to take a whole lot of praying to loosen it from its stronghold.

12

Ordinarily, the Rev did most of the visiting in Chinaberry, but since taking in the Rivers family, the Willis house had a steady stream of visitors. They came as good neighbors come in times of need and loss. Most came not because of Augustus but in spite of him. They came and brought food, some with a few coins or dollars they had faith would stack high when bricked together. They came to hold vigils and pray and sing and tell stories or tall tales. They came to sit, some until their plate was empty, some well past their welcome and the moon's nudge. Some came to get in the good graces of Pearl, others to get in the good graces of the Rev and First lady, and others came who knew God was watching and their turn could be next. Still some just came to see up close what was going on to go back and report to others who didn't come since they were not accustomed to coming any other time. Even Big Lenox and Rita Mae came, bringing a collection taken up down at the Tail Feather and yes, Blind Eye Joe contributed. Nobody wants to see somebody up and in become down and out.

But Augustus still wasn't talking. It was time to call on a professional. Finally, against the wishes of the Rev but with the blessings of First Lady and at the invitation of Pearl, Old Lady Miss Corinthia came escorted by a carved mahogany cane, draped in a deep purple shawl, with a drum strapped over her shoulder and a heavy bag of healing tools nestled on the hunch of her back. She came bearing her gift of sight into the soul and was led straight to Augustus' room to see what she could see and do what she could do.

She told Pearl all she needed was to be with him for eight hours and no one was to disturb her. When she walked in, Augustus didn't even notice her because his eyes were fixated on the wall. She knew him because she knew his mother's mother. She also knew him because he was her spiritual child. She called his name. He didn't look her way. She looked around the room. She listened to the room. She looked back at Augustus. She listened to Augustus' heartbeat and breathing. She reached into her bag and took out a jar of oil. Slowly, she bathed the door and window in oil. She returned to her bag and pulled out a cloth and unfolded it, revealing sage which she placed in every corner of the room. She then asked that the Holy Spirit reside in the room and cover Augustus. Then she knelt on the floor beside the bed, closed her eyes, and played the drums as she sang a song that had been handed down to her in the language of her foremothers. This she did for several hours. She beckoned what had been lost from Augustus' soul to restore his wholeness. The spirit filled the room. It would remain in the room until Augustus called it forth by name to return to his body. All he had to do was recognize it and call it by name and not only would he be healed but generations would be healed.

While Old Lady Miss Corinthia chanted and gave thanks to the Great I Am, on the far left wall Augustus began to watch his life play out like a black and white film out of focus with the scenes all out of order and in slow motion. It was if he was putting together a puzzle with fuzzy impressions as the pieces. Which pieces were the four corners? Which formed the inside? Which pieces connected?

He saw baby Augustus swimming, tumbling, and frolicking all about in his mama's ocean womb. In this safe and warm belly home, he could hear her humming and singing as she moved about her day. Her heartbeat soothed him when it wasn't racing. When it raced, he kicked more but to him, it was play. He felt most joyful when he was wrapped in her rhythm. It was as if they were dancing a special dance together. When she moved fast, he heard her heavy breathing as wind. Every now and then, her rhythm was interrupted by jarring movements or the crashing of waves, which he rode gallantly. He felt his mama's temperature and could sense when she was at the mercy of the sun or experiencing a cool evening breeze. But late at night, when she went to bed and all things else were quiet and still, he felt her body tense up. It squeezed against him and made his home feel smaller and darker. Her nerves became electric. He flinched and dodged their jolts. There was no more song. In this hour, she opened up her deepest wounds and sunk into her very worst fears. She didn't feel the wonder or the gift of the miraculous life inside her. She saw darkness when she thought of his future, which she deemed to be a perilous one devoid of hope. Her faith was at its weakest; it was not the faith of her mother and her mother's mother. Her hopeless thoughts kept her restless. Her restlessness made baby Augustus restless. He felt worry and sorrow far too soon. Her body cried so he cried. As she cried, she would pray softly.

101

He wasn't able to recognize the words she spoke but they agitated him and burned his budding ears. He would kick against the hand that followed him as he twisted and turned, a plea for her to quiet into the breathing that was his first sense of security, not this frantic syncopation that made him want to use his still-forming lungs to scream. Their bodies would fight against one another until they both grew tired and drifted to sleep at the same hour, minute, and second.

The rhythm would return the next day as she walked to the cotton field. As she picked cotton, he felt the calm of her escape from the unbearable reality she had no choice but to bear. She shared the hum and song and dance with baby Augustus while she kept pace with the others despite her extra belly load. One day soon, her water would break in the field and Augustus would be birthed there in a sea of stark white underneath a brilliant, sun-drenched sky as she shouted out in agonizing pain.

But what had she prayed that entered into the budding ears of baby Augustus while he dwelled inside her womb? Years later, as a little boy sitting on her lap as she rocked him to sleep and recited the Lord's Prayer, he would recognize the words as being one of her nightly prayers. He would never discover the words of the rest of her prayers because those words were never uttered out loud but perhaps he heard them all the same and carried them with him. Her desperate plea to God was to please grant him a weapon to fight with if he must be born to struggle. Out of this supplication, Augustus entered the world.

Old Lady Miss Corinthia had followed Augustus' eyes to the wall. She had seen what he had seen. The only difference is he could only see one puzzle piece at a time, while she saw the entire puzzle. In the eighth hour, she said a final prayer and left the room. She found Pearl in the living room sitting alone with her head hung low. She called her name and startled her.

"Miss Corinthia, did he talk to you?"

"No child, not with his mouth but in spirit. It is not time for him to speak."

"When, Miss Corinthia? What's wrong with him?"

"There ain't nothing wrong with him. He has already been restored."

"Well, why ain't he talking?"

"There is nothing wrong with silence. Leave him to himself in that room at night. It is not a marital bed at this time. It is a revealing bed in a seeing room. He needs to be silent and he needs to be still so he can see. He has to see it with his own eyes and call it by name."

"What, Miss Corinthia? What he gots to see?"

"He has to see it and call it by name. Have faith, my child," she repeated as she walked out the door. "He has got to see it and call it by name."

∞

The Rev, carrying his Bible, arrived home and caught Pearl in the hall as she was coming out of the room checking on Augustus.

"She gone?"

"Oh yes. She not too long ago left."

"It's about time she left. What in the world was she doing in there all that time? I left out of here sun-up and she was still here when I came back sundown and then I left again. If she was still around, I was gon have to escort her right out of here. I know y'all think that old woman got special gifts but I can't be shore exactly what the gifts are and who give 'em to her. If you ask me, she is just plum crazy."

"Now Rev, you know Miss Corinthia is as harmless as they come. And you know good and well, she helped to nurse First Lady back to herself. You done forgot that?"

"Well, that's what y'all say. I'm surprised y'all got her to come out that shack in the sticks. And I don't know how y'all outnumbered me on bringing her up in here in the first place. So if it's all the same to you, I feel strongly that I need to go in there and check on Augustus myself and end the night in prayer with him. Make shore it's Jesus that gots the final word."

Pearl barely heard what the Rev was saying. She was still reflecting on what Old Lady Miss Corinthia said right before she left. Her words actually lifted a burden from her heart. She no longer felt like anything was wrong with Augustus, just that he was in need of some time to sit with himself. She had faith that everything would be alright and in due time Augustus would see what he was supposed to see and do like Miss Corinthia said and call it by name. This would be her new prayer, simple as that.

"Pearl."

"Oh yes, Reverend Willis, go right ahead, I'll be in there directly. I'm gon finish cleaning up the kitchen. Had to rest a spell. This been about the longest day if I ever saw one. I'm sure Augustus is tired too," she said in a way to let him know he shouldn't stay in there too long.

The Rev entered the room and found Augustus staring at the wall. He sat down in the rocking chair next to the bed.

"How you doing, Augustus? You comfortable?" Of course Augustus did not answer. He never had many words for the Rev even when he was speaking. He didn't too much care for what seemed like extra attention paid to his wife.

The Rev sat down in the chair and placed his Bible on his lap.

"You mind if I read you some scripture, Augustus? I know things don't look too good right now, but I'm here to let you know the Lord's word can comfort you through any situation."

Augustus shifted his body away and turned his back to the Rev, who ignored the body talk and proceeded to open the worn, deep burgundy leather Bible. He had marked the Book of Job in advance. Although he opined that Augustus was certainly not a good Christian, if one at all, Job spoke of great suffering, and with the loss of Augustus' livelihood, house, and good playing arm, he thought it was fitting.

The Rev was certain that if anyone could get Augustus to talk, it would be him. It was no secret that the Rev had not always been a devout man so he figured that if God had brought him from a mighty long way, he had the power to do the same for even Augustus with his ornery, selfish, high and mighty, devil-music playing ways, in his opinion.

The Rev was a man with a past. His royal blue zoot suit and sharp black fedora with the long, gold feather that acted as an antenna for trouble had given way to a black robe and white collar. It was a rainy, Thursday evening about a quarter to seven while he laid drunk, with swollen eyes and a bloody nose, face down in his vomit of baked beans, sin, and folly. The same night, he made it to his granny's bedside just in time at what was to be her final hour. Her prayers had availed. She had received a miracle. He told her he had confessed his sins, asked for forgiveness, and given his life over to Christ on the journey there; he was saved. She surrendered while he held her hand and recited the twenty-third psalm, *"Yea, though I walk through the valley of the shadow of death, I will fear no evil: for thou art with me; thy rod and thy staff they comfort me."*

Later, Vernon T. Willis would be a natural in the pulpit, precisely because all that heard his testimony and witnessed his new walk recognized him as a shining example of God's grace and mercy. And since in his previous life, he had led astray a long list of sanctified women with vulnerable hearts in his home church, he visited churches in distant towns with plans of finding a suitable First Lady who wouldn't have his sordid past so close to her heart and so incessant in his ears.

The spirit led him to his first cousin Linda's wedding in Money, Mississippi, where he officiated. When he announced to the groom, "You may now kiss your bride," a gorgeous lady wearing turquoise blue sitting in the second pew with beautiful almond-shaped eyes and sunkissed, cocoa brown skin flashed him the prettiest smile he ever did see. He knew instantly that he had found his First Lady. At the reception in the church hall, she caught the bouquet and he arranged for himself to catch the garter. Then he set about making his plan to capture the heart of Helen Peterson come to pass. He was adept at sweet talking with empty promises but now he had to sweet talk in Jesus' name. He was up to the challenge. For a season, he journeyed to Money every Saturday to court her properly and he successfully did so to her liking, the liking of her two grandmamas, her mama, her three aunties, her four sisters, two best girlfriends, and a host of others who didn't really have a say but wished her well nevertheless as she was one of Money's sweetest, prettiest, and smartest, and deserved only the best in love and life.

So one late evening, as they kept company with one another and the moon winked and the stars blew kisses, Vernon T. got down on one knee, placed his granny's wedding ring on Helen's slender finger, and proposed. She replied, "Yes, Yes, Yes," each *yes* successively louder. They were married in her family's colorful living room that bloomed with an array of flowers and well wishes. Then he went into the bedroom she shared with the youngest sister and grabbed her two suitcases and happily trotted off to Chinaberry with his secret new bride.

"And said, Naked came I out of my mother's womb, and naked shall I return thither: the LORD gave, and the LORD hath taken away; blessed be the name of the LORD," The Rev recited.

Augustus let out a loud yawn. The Rev read on and on and on. Augustus turned over to look at the good Rev in his eyes, but their eyes didn't meet because the Rev never looked up, just kept delving deep into the scriptures within thin crinkly beige and gold trimmed silky pages of his time-tested family Bible.

Pearl reentered the room and told him, "I know Augustus appreciates you reading to him and all, but I think we had better let him get his rest."

"You might just be right, Sista Pearl. You know it's hard to stop me when I get going."

"Well, you know I know that. I'm right there each and every Sunday nodding off at your long sermons."

They both let out a hearty laugh. Augustus didn't want to hear any laughter. He closed his ears and eyes and searched for sleep and found it.

"Sista Pearl, you mean to tell me..."

"Shhh. I think Augustus done drifted off. Let's leave him to his rest."

The Rev shook his head in agreement and shut his Bible gingerly. Pearl tucked the sheets for Augustus' comfort and followed behind the Rev out the bedroom door, down the hall, past the room she shared with Patty Cake, past the Rev's and First Lady's room, and through the living room where Eye slept out in the humid night air where you could hear a chorus of waiting crickets. Eye was asleep on the couch and First Lady was out of the house spending the night at Sista William's house. Sista Williams had broken her hip and First Lady and others were taking turns nursing her until her daughter from Philadelphia could come home and stay with her. Patty Cake got to go with her as a reward for being a good girl that day, mainly by staying out her mama's way. Try as she might, Pearl just didn't have the patience for Patty Cake most of the time. Seems like First Lady took over nicely where Charles left off.

Pearl would have normally gone straight to her room to go to bed but she wasn't sleepy at all. She had been having trouble sleeping since the incident. But beyond this, she longed for conversation more than ever since

Augustus wasn't speaking and if there was one thing the Rev was, that was a talker. So she followed him to the porch.

Pearl was about to sit in the lone wooden chair with the floral tapestry cushion, but the Rev invited her to sit with him on the swing padded with a folded midnight blue quilt with a pattern of red and white stars. He welcomed her by tapping his hand at the empty space beside him. The swing could hold an average of three people, which was about right with the two of them, given Pearl's wide, child bearing hips and the weight of the Rev's stoutness and ego.

They slowly moved the squeaky swing without much trying and then their knees encouraged it with a slight yet synchronized, unconscious pumping. As they got a rhythm going, there was a rising in the squeaking, and soon the swing had a nice back and forth musical flow. But between them, there was quiet, each making their own contemplations, until Pearl swatted a bloodthirsty mosquito that had landed on the Rev's arm. Unfortunately, she missed the mosquito but whacked the Rev with a force so hard that a loud "Ouch" shook the porch.

"Well, my goodness Sista Pearl, you just gon beat me up. Now what I done did to you to deserve that?"

Pearl laughed. "I'm sorry. Guess I just don't know my own strength."

"Well if you don't know it, I shore do and in more ways than one."

Those simple words made Pearl's entire body smile and her ears perked up hoping he would expand on the notion.

"Look here, Sista Pearl, allow me to get real serious with you right here for a second. I can't claim I'd know what I'd do in your situation but what I do see is a strong woman and one that loves the Lord without a doubt. You alright in my book. Yes ma'am, you alright with me." In another chapter of that same book, he also saw a beautiful woman, fine as wine, and thick like he always liked them, but he didn't dare share that part out loud.

"Well I sure appreciate your kind words but I ain't done nothing special. I'm doing what I'm supposed to do and I know that the Lord don't give us no load we can't tote. Heard the old folks say it plenty of times and I reckon it's my turn to experience it for myself."

"Well, all the same, Imma stick to what I said. You're a strong woman if I ever seen one."

"And you're a good man, taking us in. You and First Lady both been so good to my family. I don't reckon we could ever pay you back." Pearl meant that from the bottom of her heart. Besides taking them in, both the Rev and First Lady had comforted her in different ways. It was the two of them that helped her get up the courage to go back over to the property after the fire to see the remains of the Rivers' home so she could accept the loss and find the strength to press onward. As she approached the void of home in the Rev's forest green Chevy, she felt a wound in her soul open up so big that she thought it might swallow her whole and eat her alive. Still she did not cry. The Rev got out the car first and walked around and opened the door to the backseat and helped her out and then he opened his wife's door. First Lady took one of her arms and the Rev took the other and arms-in-arms they marched with solemnity toward the center of destruction as if walking down the church aisle to view the open casket of a dearly departed one. Sadness covered her. Still she did not cry. No sunflowers. No daylilies. No summer. Still she did not cry. No steps. No porch. No chair. No house. No kitchen. No family. No life. It was all gone. Still she did not cry. She just stood there on a bed of ashes, hunched over with her hand covering her mouth to hold down the welling up of vomit. She was overcome with a deep sense of aloneness even though the couple was right there and she could faintly hear the Rev praying and First Lady whimpering.

All Pearl wanted was to feel the sensation of her husband's strong, steady hands. She needed Augustus by her side so he could mourn this loss with her, so she could bury herself in his chest, so they could spread the blues between them, he taking the greater share. She felt nothing but anger now. Still she did not cry. She longed to see and hear her children playing and fussing and running and fighting. Still she did not cry. She looked beyond the ashes to the trees, all still standing strong. At this moment, only they could bear witness to the depth of her pain because they had lived there along with the family and had heard every laugh and every cry and every other sound of love and life that had come from that home throughout the years. Pearl bent down and gathered up some of the ashes in her bare hands and walked over to the towering oak tree that she had looked upon with a smile countless days as she sat and sang on the porch in her chair, a chair that had survived many seasons just to suffer this ugly and sudden death. She closed her eyes and said a prayer and then sprinkled the ashes of her home at the trunk of the mighty oak. Then she couldn't help but to wrap her arms as far around the tree as she possibly could and when she did, she instantly felt the warmth of its embrace move through her body. She looked up in reverence at the tree's crown and its outstretched branches. Then she smiled a second before releasing tears of joy and gratitude. Even still she did not truly cry but she did come close to the edge. The Rev and First Lady waited at a respectable distance and let her feel her feelings, whatsoever they may be, as long as she needed and then they got back into the old Chevy and went home, together. Yes, to have the care of your pastor and best friend was indeed a blessing, Pearl would remark again and again.

"Pay us back? I might've been giving you too much credit because I think you done took to drinking."

Pearl tossed her head back and laughed. "Now, what on earth would make you say such foolishness?"

"Because you ain't gots to worry about paying nobody back. If you don't do another thing in your life, I have it on good authority that your ticket to heaven is paid in full. Matter fact, it's time for *you* to get paid back. All the good you done did. I have to watch my back with you. Before I can even get to the sick and shut-in list, you done already crossed off three, four names. I be coming behind you trying to eat up the trail of food you done left behind with your ministering." The Rev let out a deep belly laugh and made an army of mosquitoes switch directions.

"Hush now, Reverend Willis." Pearl was beaming and blushing. The initial awkwardness she felt sitting on the porch with the Rev with First Lady gone, was lifted. It felt like she was talking to a friend. It was a different experience but she wasn't minding it one bit. Laughter had been missing her on its day-to-day rounds.

"And that sanging. That there is another God-given talent you gots. If it was up to me, you'd get a solo every time I hit the pulpit. When God was handing out talents, what you do? Keep going back in line until one of them angels caught you and told on you?"

"You ought to quit that right now before you get struck down this very second," Pearl admonished, smiling wider.

"Well, If I'm lying, I'm dying. You just give so much of yourself and don't expect nothing in return. The God honest truth, I couldn't ask for a finer member of my flock. Me and First Lady considers y'all family and that includes that stubborn, crazy husband of yours."

"Now Rev, your kind words make me feel right nice and proud but I can't allow you to speak ill of my husband like that, especially while he ain't himself." Her voice took on a serious tone.

"You right, I probably shouldn't have said that but tell me this right here. What's wrong with him... *exactly*? Shore you know him better than anybody on this earth. But I ain't gon lie. I ain't never seen a man to just shut down altogether like that. He ain't the first one to get a raw deal and he shore ain't gon be the last. Almost to be expected for a colored man. Why he gots take it so harder than the next fellow?"

"Humph. I wonder if you so sleepy you done got beside yourself. It seems to me you mighty close to judging and you ain't no stranger to what the good book says about that."

"You right to say that but I guess I done got to the point where Augustus done begun to frustrate me and I'll tell you why. Because I can't stand to see no strain put on you whiles he's going through whatsoever he's going through."

"But don't forget what you said before. I'm a strong woman."

"Yes but you ain't stronger than I am as a man and as long as your husband can't take care of his business and do right by you and those youngins, I aim to take care of you and protect you and make sure you got everything you needs and I do mean *everything*."

On that note, Pearl jumped up and declared, "I think it's done got way past *both* our bedtime." Pearl tugged her dress downward although the hemline was already approaching her ankles. She couldn't get to the door fast enough; her body was talking in ways that made her want to hush it before it talked too much and let something slip out. When she reached the door, she turned around and wished the Rev a pleasant yet hurried, "Good night."

He raised his chin up and said good night with more bass in his voice than Pearl could recall him having. He then flashed her what looked to be a store-bought smile that was accompanied with a look that held a freshness to it. Even though it was just a hint, anybody could see it unless they were blind. Pearl not only saw it, she caught it, felt it, and couldn't deny it. Truth be told, the crickets, who had been in their business the moment Pearl stepped on the porch, stopped chirping and started whispering as soon as they saw it. The bright eyes of a thousand gossipy fireflies flickered with excitement. All of nearby nature was a witness to that look and there was no taking it back even if he wanted to, and he didn't want to.

As soon as Pearl cut the corner out of his sight, she looked up while grabbing her chest and said out loud, "Lawd have mercy, Augustus, you need to get up out that bed right now and say something!"

Later while lying in bed, Pearl would seek forgiveness for her body's response at the sound and command of a man's voice that was not meant for her. Her man's voice was silent in a bed down the hall. Her man's voice could not answer the call of her body down below and in between but her hand was eager to please. To comfort her, it instinctively massaged her where she stirred the most but this just served to intensify her longing. She pulled her hand away but it crept right back to where it left off in the middle of the sea. Her hand had a mind of its own and a mission. It wasn't distracted by her pining and trepidation. It stayed on course. It had its way. Was this feeling a sin? Her hand said no. Was it a shame? Her hand said no. It just kept loving on her until she couldn't fight it anymore. She let go. She surrendered to the pleasures of her hand in the quiet darkness of her room underneath the covers on a night too hot for covers. It felt like heaven. It felt like hell. It felt like heaven. It felt like hell. It felt good. Really good. Her hand made her jerk and then a moan above a whisper escaped. As she tried to cover her mouth with her other hand, she saw the face of her husband. Then she saw the face of the Rev. Before she could will the Rev's face away, she saw the faces of a thousand angels. Then she saw the sweet face of baby Jesus! Her body screamed. She released out an *ahhh* and pulled her hand away in both satisfaction and indignation and rolled over on the bed. Once she caught her breath, she got up to wash the sins of her hand away. Then she returned to bed and prayed long and hard. She prayed that she could make peace with Augustus' silence as long as it had to be. She kept faith that it could all change for the better the next day. Her man's voice could come back and he could be the one to take care of their family's needs and all of her needs. She closed her eyes to hurry the possibility.

13

Augustus woke up early to the sounds of the chickens and other lords of the morning and waited for the sun's rays to make their way to Chinaberry's part of the sky. He was accustomed to getting up at the break of dawn all his life to work in the fields. Waking up early was the only thing left of what had been his daily routine. Now his existence consisted of Pearl serving him meals in between visitors sitting and talking at him and him staring blankly or watching the wall. Today would likely be no different than yesterday. He stretched and yawned and looked as far out the window as he could. He hadn't seen a horizon since the incident, just the light blue of the sky checkered with the branches of a tree beside the house. He caught a flicker of movement out the corner of his right eye and he quickly darted his head toward the wall. He squinted and the hazy picture he saw slowly came into focus after a few rapid blinks.

The scene was in vivid color this time. Augustus saw himself as a little boy. He was no more than four years old. He was lying down and curving his thin little body toward his mama while she lay down on the bed on her back with her legs stretched out straight and stiff before her like parallel lines. She was staring in the direction of the door like she was anticipating someone would walk through it at any moment. Her hands crossed and rested on her stomach. Her body seemed to form a locked gate that Augustus was not permitted to enter. Augustus didn't read body talk so he pushed up against her as much as he could anyway. He was sensitive to smells and sounds. He pressed his nose into her arm. Every few seconds in between breaths, he would deeply inhale his mother's natural scent as if he was trying to take some of his mama and make it a part him. And then there was her heartbeat that had first soothed him when he was still in the womb. It beat stronger than his. He noticed that sometimes their hearts beat as one in complete harmony and other times, her beat was too frantic and unpredictable for him to join in. Today was a frantic day and he couldn't keep pace but he still listened intently. This rhythm that bothered him as a baby no longer did. He accepted and appreciated all of his mama's heartsongs.

Then the door creaked open and a tall, heavy-set, salt and pepper-bearded white man appeared. Augustus grabbed onto his mother's arm and held it tight. The man could visibly see the fear in Augustus and it amused him to the point of laughter.

"Boy, what you afraid of? I ain't gonna bite ya," He laughed and roared. The smell of alcohol shot out of his mouth and poured out of his skin. He dominated the room with his smell, voice, body, command, and sense of ownership. Then his voice moved away from an attempt at lightheartedness to a definite sternness. "Ursula, I thought I told you to make sure nobody was here. You think I wasn't talking about this here youngin? Now tell him to get so I can get what I come for."

Ursula tried to loosen Augustus from her arm but he grabbed her tighter.

The man's name was Bruce Calloway. He was the overseer of the plantation. He was a short, stout man but had broad shoulders and a thick torso that made him seem chopped off and in wanting of that part that could have given him the height he assumed. He had a venomous attitude that evoked fear even when he was in a good mood. His eyes were wild and almost always red and their intensity made you figure he was a blink away from destroying something, someone, or himself. As soon as he had seen Ursula standing next to her husband that first day looking for work and shelter, he claimed her as one he would have in every way. He kept his promise to himself.

Calloway looked down at Augustus' round eyes and saw him as a nuisance.

"Oh, looks like we got a mama's boy. Alright, you need to learn you can't be up under your mama. Ursula, get him under the bed out of my sight." Ursula hesitated.

"Now!" Calloway raised his voice.

Ursula directed Augustus through motions that forced him under the bed. He laid there quiet and afraid. The bed above squeaked with each move as Calloway had his way with Ursula. He heard noises from his mama somewhere between moaning and crying and heavy breathing. He'd heard something similar before but not this loud. He wanted the noise to stop and the scary man to leave. He didn't understand this. Was Calloway another daddy? Did he have two? He hated the dark. He wanted to be on the bed and not under it. He did not like this game. The noises got louder and louder. Finally, he heard a loud groan then growl then grunt that came from the man and then the bed became still. He did not hear his mama. Was the game over? A weight was lifted above him. There were no words. Seconds later, he heard the door slam. He wanted to see his mama and hug her but he stayed put. Then he heard her call his name.

"Augustus, come on out from under there."

He crawled from under the bed and got back on top and lay next to his mama real close. She hugged him tight both to console him and to bring back a tender love to her body that she was incapable of doing for herself in that moment. Augustus didn't like the smell of her now but he still pressed his face into the side of her bosom and listened for her heartbeat. It had slowed down so he focused on slowing his down by relaxing his breathing to bring their heartbeats into harmony. Just as they matched rhythms, she unloosened herself from him to go and wash away Calloway.

She climbed back into bed and Augustus climbed back into her. She had not been able to cleanse away the filth of Calloway that had formed around her heart. She had tried to fight him off the first time, less and less the many times after. Her spirit had died a slow death and her body had lost much of its fight. Now, she was struggling to find a place to put her pain out of reach so she could go about her chores.

She looked down into Augustus' eyes and he smiled at her. She felt some of the pain release. She looked deeper and deeper and deeper into his eyes until a song came to her. She couldn't see or hear the words so she began humming it just above a whisper and it was so angelic and beautiful that every nearby living thing with wings, from flies to bees to butterflies to wasps to mosquitoes, that could gain entry through the cracks of the shack flew in closer to hear. The rest hovered at and about the door and window, even birds of different feathers pressed their beaks against the outside of the shack, not wanting to be left out of the majesty taking place inside. She sounded so sweet holding the charm of an innocent child in that hum that stretched across the expanse of her soul and spilled into a glimpse of light. The living things circling about left their nature and never once landed on nor disturbed her, just buzzed and flapped their wings as quietly as they could. They were so delighted by her song. Suddenly made aware that she had attracted an audience, she hummed louder with greater virtuosity. Then out of the hum came a thought that added a smile to the hum.

Then Augustus, who had fallen asleep in the embrace of the song and in his mama's arms, shifted his body ever so slightly but enough to take her out of her thoughts and out of her song and back into her pain. Ursula looked back down at him and frowned. She then unwrapped him from her and rolled over on her side, facing the opposite direction. A fly landed on her cheek and she shooed it away. She moved further away from her son in the shabby bed. She wanted to be completely free from his touch, free from his eyes, and free from all of his reminders. She felt the same way about his father who would be coming home soon. She would save some pain for him.

He looked at the wall and saw his mama in so much pain. Augustus wished this memory had remained buried, all but that beautiful song.

14

The Rev, typically known for his snazzy threads, was sitting on his porch relaxing, dressed comfortably in denim and a white tee-shirt with a hole that was only noticeable if he lifted his left arm. He was minding his own business, preparing for his next Sunday sermon and deep into the chapter of Psalms, when he heard the crack and pop and sizzle of gravel getting louder and louder. He looked up quickly and tore his glasses off because surely they must be lying to his unbelieving eyes. He leaned in and squinted. Did he really just see a light blue Ford pickup with a dent on the driver's side door pull up in front of his house and its passenger nonchalantly get out of the vehicle as if he was a long-awaited guest just arriving for supper? Surely not. The Rev had no choice but to rise to his feet. He stood there and tried to look like he didn't just such see a ghost—even though the unexpected guest did look kind of ghostly. It was a pale, scrawny version of David Duncan standing there before him, smiling with a whole heap of audacity and matter-of-factness circling all around him. The Rev shook his head from side to side, let out an inner sigh, and readied himself the best he could for the peculiar ways of white folks.

"Howdy, Vernon."

The Rev forced out a measured, "Mista David" for a greeting, as he boiled inside at the mere sight of him.

David sensed uneasiness. "Right off, I need to let you know I didn't come here for no trouble. I know what happened to Gusty but trust me, I didn't have nothing to do with it. I'm just here as a friend. I wanna offer up my condolences like any friend would."

"I ain't shore if Augustus or his missus consider you as friends at this juncture. Besides, it's been a whole month. What makes you come now?"

"I can see how you would think that but that'll be up to Gusty to decide on. Right now, I just wanna see him and talk with him. As for why now, all I can say is it was just time."

The Rev looked down at the Bible he was still holding and squeezed it against his side. He closed his eyes and recited two verses of Psalm 27. Then he opened his eyes and said, "I guess it ain't no harm in letting you see him but there won't be no talking with him, least ways not on his part. Thought everybody knew. Augustus ain't spoke nary a word since he come here."

"Not a one?" David had heard that but could hardly believe it. He still felt confident that if anyone could get him to talk, he could.

"No sah. He definitely ain't himself but I'm gon allow you to see for yourself. I've always known you to be a fair man so I'm trusting you come here in good faith. This family has had its fair share of troubles and I don't reckon you plan to bring them no more."

"Couldn't agree with you more," David said as he extended his hand to the Rev. The Rev returned the gesture and determined that David was likely sincere by signs he read in the handshake and what he knew about him as far as reputation. From talk, he heard that it was David who punched Peter clean out once he heard what he had done and told him that enough was enough, to spare the Rivers from his venom. David was his mama's son, not his father's. The Rev's granny had taken in laundry from Irene Duncan before they both passed on. Miss Irene had been kind and did right by his granny as far as he knew. He prayed her spirit was with her son now and not his father's.

Then the Rev led David to Augustus' room. David tried to keep pace as he looked all around. Once they arrived, the Rev didn't announce him. He left him on his own. David pushed against the slightly ajar door, entered, and approached Augustus. The room smelled of flowers, herbs, and melancholy to him.

"Gusty? It's me, David. I come to check on ya. What's this I hear about you not talking? I had to come see this for myself. Nah, I don't believe this. You always got plenty to say. Even when you humming, you got your guitar to talk for ya. Don't tell me you done give up on going to Chicago. That's where a blues great like you supposed to be. What about you playing with Muddy Waters or Howling Wolf or Alvin King even? Pretty sure you could teach them a thing or two. Don't tell me you gon spend the rest of your life in this here bed. Where you keeping that nice Gibson I last saw you with?" David looked around the room to see if he could spot the guitar but didn't see it.

Augustus took his eyes off the wall, laid flat down and rolled over and away from David's direction.

David took a deep breath. The room seemed to close in on him and it felt way smaller than when he first entered. Seeing Augustus like this was hard for him to take but he pressed on in hopes to get him to say something, anything at all before he left. He felt awkward standing so he pulled the rocking chair in closer to the bed, sat down, and continued.

"Now I don't know what you been thinking or what folks been telling you, but I swear before God and on my mother's grave that I didn't have nothing to do with what happened and that goes for your house too. I wouldn't do that to you, Gusty. You got to know that. And I'm making sure that Vernon's house or the church won't be touched. That's a promise. We been friends for the longest. You're special and you know that. You not like any colored in this whole town. Sometimes, I even forget you colored. You like family to me, like a brother. I can't make no excuses for other folks but I think you know deep in your heart I wouldn't do nothing like that. That goes for your family too. I don't want you to throw me in the same pile with the rest of 'em just like I don't throw you in the pile with the rest of the coloreds. Now, what's done is done and ain't nothing we can do about it now. But Gusty, you gots to get up from here and go on with your life. Y'all did good to send your middle boy out of here. There are folks that just don't see things the way I do. No changing that. But listen up, Gusty, I didn't have nothing, I repeat nothing to do with what happened. My brother Peter was just obsessed with getting your land. I reckon for the timber. That's the God honest truth. I shore hope you can hear me because I need you to wake up and fight and put a claim on what belongs to you. I can't help you none outside of this here room. It's all up to you. Now, please talk Gusty. Say something. Let me know you hear me."

Augustus sat back up in the bed. He didn't face his visitor but David caught a glimpse of life in his eyes and got excited. He sensed he'd heard him and was on the verge of speaking. He went and stood beside him on the bed. He determined that all he needed to do was talk about their love of music and he would bring him back.

"Gusty, did you know you the only person who has ever seen me cry? Not even my wife, much less Peter, can say they seen that. Remember when my mama died? I sat right on your porch while you played out my emotions on that guitar for me till I joined in and cried my eyes out just like a baby. You just kept playing and singing and I kept crying and crying till I just couldn't cry no more. Well Gusty, when I thought you was shot dead, I went into the woods and damn if I didn't cry just like I did that day, except you weren't there but then again maybe you was because all I could hear was you singing and playing the guitar. Gusty, you know what? I think I may have had the blues. Can whites have the blues? Imma have to say yes, Hummin' Gusty. Matter fact, I'm gon have the blues till I see you out this room playing your guitar again like you meant to. Dammit, I got the blues myself. Are you listening, Gusty? I got the goddamn blues."

After a few moments of watching Augustus stare at the wall in silence, David decided that it was time for him to leave. He had given his all and failed. He squeezed Augustus' shoulder and told him, "It's OK. I'll be back to see you again. Take care now, my friend."

Then he left the room with his head lowered and thanked the Rev for his hospitality. He felt like he was being punished. He knew he had not been a true friend to Augustus when he was with his family and friends, when it truly mattered. But beyond that, something else was on his mind. He knew that he had not been a good husband either. But most importantly, he had not been a father at all to the son he had conceived out of wedlock. How many times had he passed his own flesh and blood, the spitting image of both him and Peter, on the road and here and there in Chinaberry and had not acknowledged him or even his mama for that matter? Countless. It was Augustus that he entrusted to provide for them on his behalf. And now that Augustus couldn't deliver the money and food for them, he had not done it himself. He could not bear to face a child he would never claim and the woman who was a reminder of his betrayal to his wife. With the weight of the world on his shoulders, David drove down the bumpy road headed toward the diner. He was convinced that he definitely had the blues but since there would be no Hummin' Gusty with his guitar waiting for him in the back room to chase them away, he hoped to find a whiskey barrel.

In the meanwhile, Augustus was alone again in his room. He may have been dead to David but his ears had been very much alive and they twitched and burned.

15

While Pearl made her way home, Augustus sat up in his bed and searched for more puzzle pieces on the wall and then as plain as day, he saw Callie, but not the grown-up Callie, the twelve-year-old Callie and she was smiling at the nine-year-old him. Perhaps her thoughts all the way from the Reynolds' General Store to the Willis' house had been strong enough to conjure her up or maybe it was his thoughts on her all the way from the house to the store. No matter.

All that mattered is his mama had said yes and he was excited. Ursula said he could follow her to work at the Reynolds' house to help her with her cleaning duties. He didn't mind helping with chores at all because it meant that he could both be up under her and he could get the chance to see his best friend, Callie. And the lady of the house, Abigail Reynolds, didn't mind either—four busy colored hands for the meager price of two while she helped her husband mind their new store that was doing quite well.

Ursula lost herself in her work and song while Augustus and Callie played in the closet and on the far side of beds and under their house made with tree branches against the fence and behind the barn and in the barn and deep in the woods and in their dreams and other colorful worlds they created free from the mean, dangerous black and white world where good little black and white children were forbidden to play. They knew better but what could be wrong about fun and being best friends and having secrets and feeling good and tickles and hugs and whispers and quick embraces and passing years and bigger feelings and longer embraces and soft kisses and hands wandering in places and passing years and budding bodies and hands lingering in places and special moments and I love yous and vanquished fear and insanity of the heart.

They decided that nothing could be wrong as long as they didn't get caught. And then one day Callie was sixteen and Augustus was thirteen and she whispered to him that when he saw a red rose on the whitewashed rocking chair on the porch, he should meet her in the barn for a special surprise. Every chance he could, he rushed there, looking for that rose. On the fourth visit, he spotted it. He felt a rise in his overalls, something he had never felt quite like that before. That excited feeling lifted him off the ground and carried him down a dusty path to the old barn that was now used for storage.

He used his determined muscles to push the big, heavy door open. The loud creak refused to let him keep his secret entrance quiet. He looked all around until a sweet hissing sound pulled him in the direction of Callie in the back corner, sitting down near several bales of hay. She flashed a big, toothy smile at him and patted the ground next to her, letting him know he should sit there. Beads of sweat started to form at Augustus' temple and he felt his lower thing bulge even more than before as it wiggled and stretched out the inside crotch of his overalls. He tried to will it to be still. He hoped that Callie hadn't noticed it but not only had she noticed it, her eyes rested there until she finally got up the nerve to touch it, which startled Augustus. Was he dreaming? She then took her hand and began kneading his thing like he had seen his mama do bread dough many times before. They didn't speak. He followed her lead. His body was tingling and growing hotter and hotter. She pushed his back down onto the ground bed, lifted her dress and climbed on top of this thing whose sole purpose before this moment was to pee. Now this thing was bigger and hard and felt magical and powerful. She bent her upper body toward him and started to roll her hips and grind the inside of her legs in a perfect circle over and over again as if she was trying to mesh her body into his, to become one. She reached a definite rhythm that moved into a wild hump and Augustus matched it with his movement and breathing the best he could. His heart was beating fast and he felt as if every part of him was rushing into the tip of this thing that Callie was riding through her bloomers and his overalls. She let out moans that had replaced the giggles he was used to hearing and he wondered if the devil had gotten into her or was the devil in this thing? If he could just push the river building inside of him out, he would be free from this feeling of good mixed with fear and the whole thing would be over. He promised himself right then and there that he would never go back to the barn again.

At some point, Augustus had nailed his eyes shut to focus on forcing the river out but then he felt something like a strong spirit force them open. He thrust his eyes open and looked up and just over Callie's bobbing head was his mama locking eyes with him. He let out a scream and at the same time, the river gushed out of his thing and Callie jumped off him, stood up, saw Ursula and ran out the barn, almost stumbling. Augustus' mama stared at him expressionless and didn't speak a word for what seemed like an eternity. Finally, she turned away, walking, and looked back at him with a contorted face that had aged since she entered. Augustus heard the door creak again and then slam shut.

Scared Ursula would tell on them and get her in trouble, Callie ran and told her mama that she caught Augustus staring at her as if to look beneath her dress. Abigail had a fit. She called for Ursula and told her to leave immediately with Augustus but Ursula pleaded with her to let her keep her work. She responded that she should let her go but out of the kindness of her heart she wouldn't, but instructed her to bring Augustus to the house. Ursula went and found him in the barn curled up in a corner crying. She admonished him to stop crying and be a man since he thought he was one and then she marched him in silence back to the house. For Augustus, it seemed to be the longest walk he had ever taken.

Augustus stood before Mrs. Reynolds, his mama, and Callie. He looked at Callie but she looked away.

"Now tell him what a dirty boy he is." Ursula was silent.

"Ursie! Tell him now."

"You are a dirty boy."

"And needs to be punished."

"And need to be punished," Ursula repeated.

"Now whip him for his own good or I'll have my husband do it. Do you want me to tell Mr. Reynolds what your dirty boy did?"

"No ma'am."

"If you don't want me to breathe a word, whip him, Ursie."

Ursula took the leather belt from Mrs. Reynolds and she did it. Slowly and restrained at first but then something came over her and she let loose and with every strike she saw red and no longer her son. She emptied her pain into him until he lay limp on the floor.

"That'll teach you to disrespect my daughter. Such a disappointment after all I've done for you and your dear mama. Humph, you can't even trust nigger children. Now Ursie, get him home and make sure you don't bring him around here ever again around my sweet, precious Callie!"

Augustus held back his tears but felt waves of them thrashing about his body on the inside. He took his whipping for the honor of Callie. In his mind, it was his mama who had betrayed him, ripped out his heart, and made sure that he and Callie would never have a chance to be together. How was he going to get back to that feeling that made him feel as powerful as a king and then weak as a baby? How was he going to ever get back to what must be love?

The Rev had accomplished a miracle with Pearl, something Augustus hadn't even bothered to try. He had taught her how to drive. Not only that, he had taught her how to drive Augustus' pickup, which had its own special rules. Pearl was grateful for her newfound freedom, couldn't believe she could have been driving all along instead of depending on Augustus and others. It never failed. She'd be cooking, and would discover she was out of something that she could only get from the store. Mind you, she knew how to improvise and still make the dish just as good; anybody would assume it was supposed to be just like that—missing ingredient and all. But now she could just go and get what she needed. She had even been driving to work instead of hitching a ride with the other ladies that worked as domestics near her work. Life was easier in this respect, but she did miss Augustus and the ways he took care of certain things like only a man could in her view.

Pearl needed some potatoes for a casserole she planned to make so she threw on a peachy orange and cream cotton dress suitable for going to town, and hopped in the truck and headed to the Reynolds' General

Store. She had to travel about five miles to get to the main road, which consisted of the grocery store, feed store, post office, a diner, filling station, dress shop, tailor, barber, beauty shop, blacksmith and a few other shops that provided the essentials. Since each had their own specialty, one didn't present any competition to the others. Halfway through the ride, Pearl had to go across that rickety little bridge. This bridge scared Pearl so much she actually closed her eyes when traveling across it in the past, but since she learned how to drive, she wasn't about to let fear stop her from getting where she wanted or needed to be.

She arrived at her destination and parked where the colored folks were accustomed to parking and began walking the distance to the main street, the hub of Chinaberry's activity. She shared a "howdy do" with each person she passed walking directly past her, across the street, and even cars passing by. Everybody knew each other and it was customary to speak to everybody. She came across her dear friend, Little Bits, who stood four foot eleven, five foot two if you counted the beehive hairdo she was known for. Little Bits also wore bright colors and talked loud to give herself some height—said high heels hurt her feet. They exchanged a tight, warm hug. Little Bits was happy to run into Pearl because she had something for her that was burning a hole in her black patent leather pocketbook—thirty-six dollars she and the quilting bee ladies had collected to give the Rivers family. She gave it to Pearl, then palmed her hand over Pearl's hand and squeezed. Pearl was overwhelmed with gratitude. She wouldn't dare turn this gesture down. Being proud had no place amongst friends. She hugged her again and thanked her heartily and continued on her journey, full of emotion.

Pearl caught a whiff of fried chicken floating in the air. She looked across the street and saw the Duncan Diner was open for business as usual. The gleeful moment she had found disappeared. This diner was the only place you could go to in Chinaberry to buy some already cooked food unless you counted the fish fry at No Ways Tired Baptist Church on every first and third Friday, where Pearl's buttery pound cakes and pecan pies were staples for dessert. One day the church's building fund was bound to be paid off through offerings and the popular fish fries. A good sampling of folks started Friday evening in the church's dining hall getting a nice hot plate, covered with shiny, crinkly tin foil if there wasn't time for fellowshipping but ended Friday getting a drink or two or three at the juke joint. They figured that the line from gospel to the blues may be a crooked one, but it was a line worth taking and neither the sun nor the moon sat in judgment; on the contrary, they divided up the glory the first morning blush of Sunday.

Everyone was glad that the Duncans had sense enough to get Patsy Washington to cook the food when they realized two weeks after opening up the new establishment that the colored folks weren't patronizing the diner with Lizzie Duncan in the kitchen. The town wasn't big enough to have a business where Negroes didn't frequent or were refused service. Lizzie Duncan couldn't "cook a lick" was the general consensus but Miss Patsy sure enough could "throw down." Pearl could admit that Miss Patsy's cooking could almost hold a candle to hers if you didn't include her desserts. Plus, since the colored folks couldn't eat in the diner but picked their food up from the back porch off the kitchen, they observed through the window that Miss Lizzie kept a nice nasty kitchen, everything strewn everywhere, messy, disorganized countertops, and dirty floors made for all-around suspect food and this couldn't be overlooked for that pickle they boasted with a sign that read, Home of the Best Fried Chicken in the South, Free Crisp, Juicy Pickle with Every Meal. Even white folks might not have eaten there if they had the privilege to see all that was going on behind doors. That all changed under the management of Miss Patsy, who ran a tight ship and had a cook and clean as you go policy that was strictly enforced in her kitchen.

Well after the Augustus shooting, all the Negroes of the town got together, not in a room but in the mind, and decided that they would not give any more business to the Duncan Diner. But when the Duncans let Miss Patsy go—Miss Patsy, who had four mouths to feed all by herself after her husband left to lay up with some young gal in the next town, that's when Pearl put the word out that it was alright to go back to the Duncan Diner. Miss Patsy needed to make a living and where folks filled their belly or didn't fill their belly wasn't going to bring Augustus back to himself or her house back. Besides all that, the Duncans also owned the only filling station in town and nobody with a car or in need of a ride was going to protest that—you'd be out of gas trying to get to the next closest filling station, and what kind of sense did that make? All the same, Pearl appreciated the solidarity among her people shown to her family in their protest. She had earned every bit of this love over the years and Augustus had just piggybacked on it all.

Pearl kept walking and as she neared the store, she felt angst. She hoped with all hope that Callie wasn't the one overseeing the store. That was another white woman, besides Miss Perry, who annoyed her to no end. She reckoned that they all got on her nerves to some degree, hadn't ever met one that didn't, even the relatively nice ones, because of how they looked down on her, past her, or didn't see her at all. She felt they were no better than her and wondered what lengths they had to go to convince themselves otherwise. She resented that she was forced to help them along on their journey.

If she had to go to the store, she much preferred Callie's father, who gave her special attention, at least when no one else was around—better cuts of meat in quality and quantity, an undercharge every now and again, and always a hand full of free butterscotch candies slipped into her bag with a wink. Pearl just winked back with a smile and he returned that with a wider smile. Figured it all was innocent enough. But that Callie, she couldn't stand her. Her Christian walk just about stumbled every time she came into her presence. Callie was always real short with her and her nose seemed to be pulled into the air with an imaginary string. And Pearl wasn't blind. She had picked up over the years, based on this and that and whisperings that Augustus had some kind of thing for this woman, but she also knew that he didn't have a death wish so he wasn't fool enough to act on it. She also had a feeling that Callie would have got with her husband if she could but she couldn't and wouldn't under any circumstances. Pearl didn't like knowing this. In fact, she hated it. It pinched her spirit every time she thought about it. She wrestled with it but she figured that there wasn't any use in confronting Augustus with something he could so easily deny. Nope, didn't see what good that would do. She had plenty of other pieces of life to deal with on the day to day.

Pearl said a prayer and entered the store. She didn't have any luck. Callie was there and her loud French perfume instantly replaced the aroma of Miss Patsy's fried chicken. Pearl sneezed, "Achoo."

"Well God bless you, Pearl," Callie said with a big smile that looked like she had spent a good while holding it for the next person that walked through the door.

"Howdy do, Miss Callie."

"Look at you. I take it you drove down here all by yourself. That's right. I heard you driving now. My goodness, I haven't even got up the nerve yet."

Pearl figured right away she was being friendlier because of Augustus' situation and she tried to mirror her friendliness back the best she could.

"Ain't really nothing to it once you do it," Pearl said proudly, feeling pretty good to have yet another up on her.

"Well good for you. Now, do tell me. How's Gusty?"

Pearl also hated how she and other white folks called her husband Gusty, let alone, Hummin' Gusty.

"Pretty much the same," she responded.

"Is it true what they saying? He hasn't spoken nary a word since the accident?"

"No ma'am. Afraid not." *Accident?*

"Well, that's just awful. And with your house burned down—how on earth are y'all making out? So much for one family to bear. Just breaks my heart."

"We are doing the best we can." *Lawd, let me hurry up and get what I came for. I can't take too much more of this.*

Pearl gathered up the potatoes quickly and brought them to the counter. She asked Callie to add some chewing tobacco from the shelf behind her. Callie obliged and added up the total with a pen and pad.

"Now Pearl, should I put this on your credit?"

"No. I can pay you right now." Pearl pulled out a handkerchief from her bosom that contained the several nicely folded dollar bills she had just got from Little Bits. She counted out the amount owed and was happy to hand it to Callie, thanks to the generosity of the quilting bee ladies. Pearl wanted to say, "*That's right. I don't need your credit today and you can put that in your pipe and smoke it.*" Instead, she said. "Thank you kindly," as she accepted her change and turned toward the door.

As soon as Pearl set foot out the store, Callie ran over with a big brown paper sack full of shiny red apples. "Pearl, please give these to Gusty. You know how much he loves apples."

Pearl accepted the apples graciously and immediately made plans to make some fried apple pies for dessert, thinking to herself she never knew Augustus to favor any fruit over another.

"Oh and Pearl, I hope you don't mind me asking but would it be alright if I come and visit Gusty. I just feel so bad about what happened and well, I consider him a friend and just wanna check on him. You know, we grew up together. His dear mama was with our family for nearly twenty years. Why, Gusty is almost like family to me. Of course, my husband mustn't know. He wouldn't really understand and it's no secret he and the Duncan brothers been best friends forever and there is just so much bad blood about this thing that happened and all. It just wouldn't be a good idea if he found out. So what do you say Pearl, is it alright with you? I mean I'll understand if you say no, but I'm hoping you'll say yes."

Pearl clenched her teeth and gave Callie a blank stare she realized must have gone too long when she heard Callie call her name.

"Pearl?"

Pearl took a deep breath and exhaled into a slight smile. Then in a lowered, monotone voice devoid of energy, she finally answered, "No, Miss Callie. It's fine. That's mighty nice of you. Sure Augustus wouldn't mind seeing some new faces. I'll let the Willis' know you plan to come calling."

"Alrighty then! I will close up the store around noontime and make it over tomorrow before my husband gets back in town. My helper, Jeremiah, can give me a ride. Don't tell Gusty now. I wanna surprise him," she squealed and smiled, bringing her hands together under her chin, already feeling confident that she could get Augustus to talk without a problem.

Pearl had no parting words for Callie but mustered up one last fake smile. As far as she was concerned, Callie knew good and well that her husband was very likely to have been amongst the ones that burned down her house. What nerve! What disregard and disrespect for her family! As for being like family to Augustus, that was just plain crazy. Bet Callie wouldn't say that nonsense around another white soul, Pearl thought. As she climbed back in the truck, she said to herself, "*I declare if that that Negro opens up his mouth and talks to that heifer, I will make sure it's the last words he speaks in this lifetime for real.*"

16

The peacock blue walls of the Willis' kitchen enveloped Pearl and provided her a measure of calm as she sliced the last of the red potatoes needed for her beef and potato casserole. She put them in a good-sized pot to cook and added a pinch of salt. Next, she reached for a big delightful sweet onion to chop. She paused for a second to look out the window hugged by lemon drop- colored curtains. They were the closest thing to sunshine on an otherwise dreary day expecting rain. She returned to chopping, this time entering a frenzy. It was a way to release the frustrations that had built up over the course of a lifetime. A baby square from the onion fell to the floor and she rushed to pick it up. It pained her to see even a minutia of a crumb on the spotless black and white checkered linoleum floors. Pearl always wanted this pattern for her own kitchen but First Lady got it first and she hadn't wanted to be a copycat nor could she afford to be.

She certainly missed the flow of her kitchen but was enjoying cooking in this one much better. From the white cupboards and appliances with shiny silver handles to the white-topped, oblong table pushed to the wall with its chrome frame to the teal, vinyl chairs speckled with glitter, everything just sparkled. All it needed was her and it had her for the time being.

No matter how much she cleaned her old kitchen, the oldness of everything in it seemed to dull its brilliance. Nevertheless, she had been the soul of the kitchen and therefore its light. She carried its spirit within her and celebrated its memory with each dish prepared in love in this new kitchen and avenged its tragic death with each deliberate chop.

While the potatoes continued to boil, she combined the beef and onion to cook over medium heat. It was soon after that First Lady entered the house, wearing a lemon-drop yellow colored dress that coincidentally matched the color of the cotton fabric of the curtains.

"Howdy do, Sista Helen," Pearl delivered, admiring the over-sized, frilly white bow flowing from the round collar of First Lady's dress. She wished she had such pretty dresses as First Lady did or at least had the time and fabric to make some. She noticed the straw pocketbook First Lady was toting. From there, she quickly moved her eyes down to her kitty heeled pumps to confirm that they, both being beige, did indeed match perfectly as well.

"I'm blessed," First Lady responded, admiring Pearl's ruffled pink and strawberry red apron with the elaborate circle pattern. Was she mistaken or did Pearl seem to wear a new apron daily as if it was a fashion choice? She only owned two aprons, one a gift from her mama and the other, a gift from the Rev, a hint he soon after regretted. She had only worn them a few times since one generally wears an apron while cooking, which she rarely did. Every blue moon, she would attempt a dish but mostly the Rev did the cooking or he'd bring plates home from his many rounds of performing his pastoral duties.

"And how *you* doing?" First Lady continued.

"Fair to middling," was Pearl's response.

"Fair to middling? You ain't gonna win no prize with that." First Lady put her pocketbook down on the table, sat down, discreetly eased her right shoe off and started massaging it. She had discovered that the cute shoes were only comfortable for the first three hours of wear. "Why don't you come here and sit down with me for a little bit. Can you just stop doing for a minute? Lawd have mercy, do you ever sit down?"

Pearl laughed. "Chile, you know I can't sit still. I gots to be doing something or another to keep my mind right."

"Keep your mind right? You mean to tell me that your mind ain't right unless you up doing something? Well I reckon my mind is wrong most of the time if that's the case!"

Pearl chuckled. She hadn't meant to imply any such thing.

"Seriously, I don't make a living around this house and I ain't got no babies to run behind." God, rest Phillip and Phoebe's souls. *The Rev and First Lady had twins that were stillborn.* With all your doing, you starting to make me look right lazy. And, honest to goodness, since you been here, me and the Rev done ate better than we ever ate on a day to day. What in the world we gon do when you leave? You done messed around and got my husband use to something I ain't gon be able to keep up," First Lady said in jest but the thought had seriously crossed her mind more times that she cared to admit to herself, let alone to anybody else. Truth was, having Pearl there was a mixed blessing. Who wouldn't want to help out a dear friend, especially one as dear as Pearl? Who wouldn't want to have daily girlfriend talks as you devoured sweet, buttered, well-seasoned dishes prepared by the generous, gifted hands of that dear friend? Then again, who would want all that loveliness in the reach of their husband whose greatest weakness had shifted from the sinner woman to the sanctified woman? First Lady tried to shake all these un-Christian like thoughts from her head.

"Chile, you keep me in stitches. You sounding like you a no-account, good for nothing and I won't have any of that. You do a lot more than look pretty up on the front pew, helping Pastor with all the church business, teaching Sunday school, knitting all those pretty baby clothes and blankets for every baby born this side of the river. You live a more charmed life than most with boxes full of fancy hats to prove it, but you do more than your fair share as First lady, a wife, and good friend."

"Aw...that's real sweet of you to say, but tell the truth and shame the devil. I can't cook worth a damn, can I?"

"Helen! I know I didn't just hear you cuss but what can I say? You ain't never lied about that!" They burst out in laughter.

"So all of that and I still can't convince you to sit down and rest. There ain't no rush in supper, you know. I know you got to be tired from fooling with Miss Perry all day."

"She is a handful but cooking ain't a chore. It's my peace just like knitting is yours. Now cleaning, you can keep that so be ready to wash these dishes." More laughter was shared between them.

Just as Pearl put her dish in the stove and closed its door, in sauntered Patty Cake. First Lady saw her first.

"Come here, little girl. What you moping around here about? Sweet little girl with all this here pretty hair shouldn't be looking so sad. Who messing with you? Did you have a bad dream? You gon tell Miss Helen?"

Patty Cake started whimpering and Pearl whipped her head around, momentarily taking her attention away from adding the potatoes, beef, and remaining ingredients together in the casserole dish. "You gon go and spoil that child. Patty Cake, now hush up that crying, chile."

Patty Cake took big gulps of air and sniffed hard, trying her best to pull her crying back in. First Lady pulled a handkerchief out of her pocketbook and handed it to Patty Cake to dry her eyes.

Then she asked her again, "So what's the matter, baby?"

Pearl chimed in before Patty Cake could gather her words from her heart and place them in her mouth. "She misses her brother and rightly so. The two of them always been thick as thieves. If he didn't do nothing else, he would always watch out for his baby sister. Eye never paid her no mind but I can't fault him. He is into his books and that's what he supposed to do if he wants to be a lawyer one day like his cousin Esquire."

First Lady didn't really see the sense in what Pearl had just said. She returned to Patty Cake, "Is that it, pretty girl? You miss Charles?"

"Yes ma'am," Patty Cake answered with her head still lowered.

"Well. I bet he misses you too. How would you like to write him a letter?"

Pearl laughed as she cleaned the counter off. She knew better than to count on Helen to do it to her liking. It was clear that the Rev's and First Lady's kitchen belonged to her as long as she was there and neither one of them would dispute her on this if they wanted to eat. "Patty Cake barely know her ABCs. How she gon write a letter?"

"From the heart. I been thinking on what you said before. Jesus give us each a special peace. He gives you peace in cooking. He gives me peace in knitting. Down the road, it might be something else. He ain't stingy with the peace giving. Patty Cake got something too. We just got to find out what it is because if all your peace is wrapped up in a person or something outside of what's been given special to you, you setting yourself up for heartache in this life."

Pearl thought for a second. "You're a wise woman. I wouldn't be surprised none if I looked up Sunday and saw you in that pulpit in place of your husband."

Over First Lady's laughter, Pearl shouted, "Eye, come here baby!"

"Here I come, mama!" Eye answered as he jogged into the kitchen. "How you, Miss Willis?"

"I'm just fine. I think you grow an inch every time I see you. Looking almost as tall as your daddy."

Eye forced a smile and went up to Pearl washing dishes in the sink and gave her a hug from behind.

"And what can I do for you, Queen Mama?"

Pearl blushed. "Boy, go on away from here with that talk. Don't know what you trying to butter me up for. I ain't got nothing for ya but there is something you can do for me."

"What mama? I done did all my chores."

"I know and without even asking. I appreciate that but what I want from you is for you to go in there and spend some time with your daddy."

Eye pulled away. "Mama, what for?" he whined.

"What you mean what for?"

"I feel funny going in there when he ain't saying nothing. What's the point? What good is that gon do, mama?"

"A whole lot of good. He needs to see his family."

"Alright. Send Patty Cake in there then."

"Don't worry about Patty Cake. We talking about you right now. Since you always in your books, why don't you read to him? Yes, that's what you can do. Show him how smart you are."

"Mama, he ain't gon wanna listen to me read."

"How you know? You don't. Tell mama what you reading now anyhow."

Eye let out a big sigh. "*The Souls of Black Folk.*"

"Hmm...I like the name of it. Who is that by?"

"W.E.B. Du Bois."

"I bet Cousin Esquire sent you that one."

"Yes ma'am."

"OK then. Go read that."

"But mama..."

"Boy, I'm tired of talking to you. Go on and do what I say. By the time you read a good bit, dinner be ready. I gots to bake a German chocolate cake for Sista Hayes. I might just make you a special sample."

Eye smiled with all thirty-two of his sweet teeth.

First Lady, who had been braiding Patty Cake's hair and listening to mother and son, chimed in where she saw an opening. "Eye, you are doing a good thing. Remember to always honor your parents so that your days may be lengthened. You bound to receive a blessing for taking care of your daddy whiles he can't do for himself. Plus, all that knowledge in your head don't do nobody no good just sitting in there. You suppose to share what you know. You understand?"

"Yes ma'am."

"Alright now, go on. You know your mama and I wouldn't steer you wrong, much as we love you."

"Yes ma'am."

With Eye off to read to his daddy and Patty off to an adventure with her tears dried up, First Lady hopped out of her seat and came up behind Pearl and untied her apron, to Pearl's surprise. "Go sit down. I can finish this dinner from here on out."

Pearl obeyed with a smile, knowing full well that there wasn't anything left to be done. She appreciated her friend's gesture though.

First Lady turned the fire under the pot of green beans to a simmering low. To be warmed up was all they needed. She then opened the stove to check on the casserole just to be doing something since it was not nearing done. Finally, she grabbed the broom from the far corner and began to sweep. Pearl sat back, smiling, and wondered if First Lady would double back and sweep up that missed crumb by the stove that she, herself, could see clear as day from where she was sitting.

Eye went and got the book and headed to Augustus' room. He went to sit down in the rocking chair which hadn't received so much attention in all its days before it did duty for Augustus' visitors. He sighed. This was the last thing he wanted to be doing. What good was it going to do? He probably wasn't ever going to speak again anyway. As a matter of fact, he didn't really care if he did. His daddy never had any time for him and he had lost respect for him long ago. He understood what shucking and jiving was and as far as he was concerned, that's exactly what his daddy did whenever he was around white folks. Besides all that, he got everything he wanted and needed from his mama. All he had to do was be smart and that came easy. Whatever didn't come easy, he taught himself in books. One day he planned to make his mama proud and become a lawyer. He would move her away from Chinaberry and build her a great big house like she deserved. He and his beautiful wife would live in a house right beside hers. Daddy could stay right there in that bed forever. Charles would take care of Patty Cake. Maybe she would move to Little Rock to be with him. That wasn't his problem.

"Daddy, mama want me to come read to you so that's what I'm doing. I won't do it long. You can let me know if you want me to stop somehow."

He opened the book with a bookmark made out of a twisted strip of brown paper sack, just like what First Lady used to curl her hair at night by wrapping her strands. Then he straightened his back and gripped the book tight. Finally, after clearing his throat, he placed as much bass in his voice as he could and began to read the words of W.E.B. Du Bois.

It is a peculiar sensation, this double consciousness, this sense of always looking at one's self through the eyes of others, of measuring one's soul by the tape of a world that looks on in amused contempt and pity. One ever feels his two-ness, --an American, a Negro, two souls, two thoughts, two unreconciled strivings; two warring ideals in one dark body, whose dogged strength alone keeps it from being torn asunder.

Eye took a deep breath and read on.

The history of the American Negro is the history of this strife,--this longing to attain selfconscious manhood, to merge his double self into a better and truer self. In this merging he wishes neither of the older selves to be lost. He would not Africanize America, for America has too much to teach the world and Africa. He would not bleach his Negro soul in a flood of white Americanism, for he knows that Negro blood has a message for the world.

Eye looked up to see if Augustus was looking in his direction. He was not. He kept reading anyway. He liked how he sounded reading out loud. He had never done it before. His imagination wandered to visions of him being a lawyer talking to a judge in a packed courtroom someday, but still he kept on reading.

He simply wishes to make it possible for a man to be both a Negro and an American, without being cursed and spit upon by his fellows, without having the doors of Opportunity closed roughly in his face.

With that, Eye shut the book, making a loud thud. He looked over at Augustus and their eyes actually met. Augustus curled up the corners of his mouth. He was about twenty-five steps from a smile but it was enough for Eye. His smile finished where Augustus' would-be smile left off.

Just then Pearl walked in the room in time to see the smile on Eye and the would-be smile on Augustus.

"Mama, daddy smiled. I saw it. It wasn't big but I saw it."

"Ain't that fine, son. Your mama knows what she be talking about. Seems like you ought to listen more."

"I think he enjoyed me reading to him."

Pearl went over and hugged Eye. "Of course, he did. I want you to keep it up too. Don't let this be the last time."

"Hmm... can I get a whole chocolate cake all to myself?"

Pearl laughed. "I ought to give you a pound cake," she said as she thumped him on his head.

By then, Augustus was facing the wall again. Pearl and Eye left him to it, feeling the joy of a gesture that was enough to call a victory.

17

Charles sat on the side of his bed and squeezed one of the big, fluffy, snow white, lace pillows with scallop embroidered hems. The pillow was a comfort to his loneliness and melancholy. After being lost in his thoughts for a while, he propped the pillow up against the headboard, leaned against it and thought some more in a new position. He had plenty of time for thinking. His thoughts turned to how comfortable this bed felt to him. The mattress was much firmer than he was used to back home yet somehow it felt softer too. He wondered if this was what it felt like to lay on a cloud. He stretched out legs that seemed to be getting longer day by day. As he did so, he couldn't help but think that this bed was awfully big for just him and it was hard to get used to being able to roll around all over it without having to be squished into the wall while Eye hogged the lion's share. As a matter of fact, the bed wasn't even by a wall. There was plenty enough room to have a little table on both sides with lamps. This bed also had a wood headboard and a footboard. He liked to trace his fingers through the carved wood of the headboard like he was following along in a river. And to think, Cousin Gloria said this was what she called a guest room. He didn't understand how you could have a room all made up with no one sleeping in it, just waiting on somebody to show up to put it to use. Thinking on such things to avoid thinking on other things, he curled up and drifted to sleep.

Even though two months had passed, Charles was still finding it hard to enjoy his new life. Everyone kept calling him a hero but he couldn't help but dwell on the fact that the only reason his daddy was on those white folks' land was because of him. If he hadn't got such a bad report card, his daddy wouldn't have taken him fishing after his mama took Eye. And now not only was his daddy not playing his guitar, he wasn't talking either. And to top that off, their house burned down and Patty Cake didn't have him around to watch out for her. All of it was his fault in his mind. And here he was living in a nice home with nice folks doing nice things for him. He thought maybe he had wished too much to leave Chinaberry and this was his punishment. As for Cousin Gloria, he figured she was an angel and would somehow eventually make it all better.

The Carters had created a good life deeply involved in the uplifting of their community and being on the frontlines of the freedom fight. The couple didn't have any children and had plenty of room to spare. They were happy to take in Charles given the circumstances.

Cousin Gloria, a petite woman, wore tight curls, fashionable cat-eye glasses, pretty dresses with subtle patterns and matching jewelry sets and pumps every day, not just on Sunday. Well actually, she and Esquire hadn't gone to church since Charles had arrived and a long time before then. She was an assured woman, confident and pushy in a sweet way and proud not only to be a lawyer's wife but to be herself, a popular English professor, a contributing writer to the *Arkansas Black Press* newspaper, a pianist, an active member in the N. Double A.C.P., and an all-around fighter for civil rights and justice along with her husband. And now she was someone in between a mother and an auntie to Charles, and although her biggest challenge yet, this new role fit her just fine.

She walked in through the open door of Charles' room and found him lying on the bed, facedown with the pillow over his head, already in deep sleep.

"Charles. Wake up, sweetie. Charles!"

Charles jumped up to a sitting position. He rubbed his eyes and muttered, "Yes ma'am" to cover all grounds until he could figure out where he was and who it was talking to him.

"You shouldn't be sleeping in broad daylight or you will never get to sleep tonight when you're supposed to. I sure do wish you would stop moping around here. It's not that bad, is it? Don't you like your new room? It's all to yourself. What about your new clothes? You've been looking really dapper. I bet all the girls have been checking out the new fellow in town. And you told me yourself, you're making good friends with Rutherford and Smitty across the street. You've got everything you need, don't you? If not, we can go over to..."

Charles, now fully alert, interrupted Cousin Gloria, "Yes ma'am. I have everything I need and I thanks you and Cousin Esquire for all y'all give me." He definitely didn't want her to think he wasn't grateful. He thought back to how the evening he left Chinaberry, when his mama reminded him of everything he was taught during the course of his young life. Charles took it all in the best he could but it was the words that his mama whispered in his ear that stayed with him the longest—"I love you." He had never heard her say that before or anyone else for that matter. He also remembered her sweet scent that smelled like honeysuckle when she hugged him tight, and the tiny smile she forced through tears as she placed three butterscotch candies into his shaking hands and closed them tight before letting him go. He would throw one to a crying Patty Cake out of the window as they drove away, eat one on the long bumpy ride to Little Rock, and save the last one for when he really, really needed it. He still had it even though he had been tempted to eat it several times, all day, every day, really. It was in the bottom drawer of the rosewood dresser he had all to himself, full of clothes that fit and smelled good.

"So you're just missing home, aren't you, your mama, daddy, sister, and brother, huh? I know you and Ruby Lee are really close. That's what your mama told me. Are you homesick?"

"Yes ma'am."

"Is that all you know how to say? Yes, ma'am?"

"Yes ma'am. I mean, no ma'am."

"Oh Charles, so tell me. What are your hobbies?"

"Hobbies? What's that, ma'am?"

"You know the things you like to do for fun. You play sports?"

"No ma'am. Eye is good at sports."

"That's Isaiah. I asked about you. What do *you* like to do?" she inquired as she took a seat in front of the mahogany vanity and looked in the mirror and twirled a curl. She thought about moving the vanity from his room; too feminine, she concluded, for a young boy to have in the way. She turned back in time to hear Charles' answer.

"I use to like fishing but not no more."

"Well, considering, that's surely understandable. How about music? Did your daddy teach you how to play the guitar?"

152

"No ma'am and now he don't play no more." Charles lowered his voice.

"Doesn't play anymore, Charles," she said to correct him. "So, young man, do you like music?"

"Yes ma'am. I like music."

"You do? Fantastic. That's a start. What kind of music do you like?"

"The kind my mama sing around the house and in church and the kind my daddy use to play, I reckon. You know, the blues. I use to listen to him play all the time."

"Well, would you like to learn how to play an instrument?"

"I guess so."

"Well, I play the piano so I'm going to give you your first lesson this evening after supper. How's that?"

"Okay." Charles perked up inside but he didn't let Cousin Gloria see on the outside. He didn't want to be disappointed if she changed her mind.

"Now would you like to help me finish preparing dinner?"

"No ma'am."

"There you go again with the *no ma'ams*." They both laughed.

"So I hear your mama is a really great cook. How does my cooking compare to hers?" Charles just smiled; he thought it was best not to respond.

"Humph. Cat got your tongue? Well, we will see how well you do with washing the dishes."

"I meant to say you cook real good," Charles said quickly with a giggle.

"That's what I thought. You sound like my husband now. Flattering me will get you everywhere."

"Flattering?"

"Telling me sweet things." *I have to work on improving his vocabulary,* Cousin Gloria proclaimed to herself.

"Oh yes ma'am. Where is Cousin Esquire? He usually be here by now."

"He's over at the college in a meeting, trying to make arrangements so that some of us professors can teach the children trying to attend Central High while they work things out. Did you know that your cousin and I met as students when we were in college together? He is a very important alumnus there. An alumnus is someone that has graduated from college."

"Oh. That's nice. Do you reckon they gon let those colored kids go to school with them white kids?"

"Yes I do. They will have to. It's the right thing to do, not to mention, it's the law."

"It shore didn't look like they cared about that none when we was watching it on the television. Seem like a whole lot of white folks yelling at them and blocking them from getting in."

"True. I agree that right now it doesn't look promising." Cousin Gloria was delighted that Charles had warmed up and was talking way more now and holding a very intelligent conversation too. She continued. "I never would have thought they could be so cruel to children who just want to go to school and learn and get the same education and opportunities the white children receive."

"I don't think colored kids ain't never gon go to school with white folks, Cousin Gloria."

"You mustn't think like that, Charles. Eventually, it's going to happen. There's a lot of foot soldiers like my husband and my friend, a feisty woman by the name of Daisy Bates, fighting to make it happen. And trust me, Ms. Bates is a fighter and I know she won't stop until those babies are receiving the same education as anyone else, and that includes you too."

"Did you know that I don't do good in school?"

"You mean you don't do very well. Start again."

Clearing throat, "I don't do very well in school. My brother Eye is the smart one."

"And which one are you?"

"Not sure."

"Well it's time you knew. I can help you with your school work and teach you the piano, too. Before long, you will be the smart *and* talented. Do you believe me?"

"Yes ma'am. I guess so."

"You guess so? I know so! Wait...what's that smell?"

"Smells like something burning to me."

"My rolls!

"You still cook good."

"Aw thank you but it's you cook *well*."

"But I don't cook."

Cousin Gloria giggled. Just then Esquire entered the room, walked over his wife and gave her a kiss and asked, "What in the world is that smell?"

Cousin Gloria and Charles looked at each other and let out deep belly laughs. Then they followed the smoke into the kitchen together.

18

Pearl invited First Lady to sit outside on the swing to get some fresh air. They sat there awhile and just watched Patty Cake color on the porch until she laid her head down on her coloring book as if it were a pillow. That's when Pearl called her name and told her to get up and to go lay down. For a change, she listened and stumbled off inside.

Then First Lady got up the nerve to ask Pearl something that she had been curious about. "Pearl, my dear friend, can I please ask you something?"

"Why shore you can. What's on your mind, pretty lady?"

"Lawd knows it ain't none of my business and really you don't have to answer if I'm out of bounds. Even though we're friends, there's just some things..."

"Girl, just ask. Just ask. I got sense enough to not answer if I don't want to."

"Alright, since you insisting. I'm just wondering... Since Augustus took sick, do you miss being with him?"

"If you mean the companionship, not a day goes by..."

"No I mean...*being* with him?"

"Oh *being* with him? Do I miss him that kind of way? Why yes, yes I do, something awful. But to tell you the truth even before he shut down, he could hardly keep up with me. Don't let my Sunday dinner fool you. My husband is privy to the fact that some of my best cooking take place on Saturday night."

"Oh Pearl, hush your mouth. You just too much. So tell me this. Do you like everything about it?"

"You mean everything about making love?"

"Yes ma'am."

"Well, honey, what's not to like? It wakes up everything you ever felt and could ever feel all at once, puts you right up there amongst the sun, the moon, and the stars. And at the peak of it, well that's a piece of heaven right here that you just wanna hold on to forever. Everything bottled up inside you just pours out, then you just kind of floats like you on a cloud until you reach back to earth again. And that's when you just lie there in a daze feeling mighty special and loved like you ain't got a care in the world. That's why I reckon they call it making love because you feel like you and your man just got through cooking up some good love together and nothing or no one can partake in that feeling but y'all."

"Oh my, Pearl, that was beautiful. So that's what you feel every single time?"

"Well, maybe not *every* single time, but it shore is worth the try every single time, you know, just in case."

"I see."

"That ain't what you feel?"

"Can't say that I do."

"Well what is it that you feel?"

"Some moving around, some messiness, and a whole lot of nothing is all I feel."

"Oh my!" Pearl gasped. "Well that don't seem right a 'tall. This something your husband knows about?"

"Heavens no. By the time he rolls over and starts snoring, I reckon he done convinced himself that he done something."

"Girl stop, don't tell me no more. You gon have me looking at the Rev funny."

"Well it ain't no secret that my husband was a real ladies' man before he started courting me. And I'm talking about after he was saved. I shudder to think about his ways *before* he was saved. I gather from the trail of broken hearts behind him, he must've known a thing or two about making love or whatsoever it's called outside of wedlock but I feels like whatever he was giving them heifers, he must've run out by the time he got to me. I wanna feel what you describing. I want some of that sun, moon, and stars. Problem is, he always have put me on a pedestal and even more so, after we lost our babies—God rest their precious souls. He treats me like I'm gon break to pieces even if I lift just one finger."

"Please tell me it's bigger than an iddy biddy finger."

"Pearl, I declare. You crazy. Don't know why I even bother with you. Glory be!"

"Because I'm your best friend and you know I ain't gon judge you one bit. Now first off, there's a whole heap of women that would appreciate being placed on a pedestal by their husband and a good Christian man at that, so that's a blessing indeed. Of course, it ain't nothing you don't deserve. You're a good wife. Looks like to me, you might need to tell him what you want, what you need to liven things up between you."

"Oh I could never do that. I don't wanna disrespect him no way. You know it's easy to get in these menfolk's feelings."

"Ain't that the truth. Well, if you can't find the words, I reckon you gon have to show him. You gon have to put a spell on him," Pearl said with a mischievous grin.

That's when they heard the car door slam and saw the Rev approaching the porch. They quickly tucked their conversation away for safekeeping.

"Good afternoon ladies," the Rev said with a big clueless grin, unaware that he had just been the topic of conversation.

Pearl and First lady responded in unison. Then they looked at each other and giggled as good girlfriends do. And Pearl thought to herself, the grass is always greener until you know the secret. Now if she could just put a spell on her own husband, maybe he would get up and take care of her needs.

19

Callie had never set foot in a colored family's house before, yet there she was sitting in the Willis' living room on a gold tweed couch with three matching pillows, being offered tea from First Lady and a slice of apple pie from Pearl, both of which she graciously declined.

"Oh no, thank you, mighty kind of you to offer."

"Well, is it anything thing else I can get you, nice tall glass of ice water. That sun is something fierce out there today."

"Now that is true and that is really just so kind of you but no thank you," Callie responded in a nervous chuckle. "I really must get back to the store soon, plus Jeremiah is out there waiting on me."

First Lady and Pearl looked at one another and shared a little smile. They had both forgotten for a second why Callie was in the house in the first place.

First Lady got up from where she was sitting. Pearl had never sat down.

"Oh that's right. You here to see Augustus. Of course, you are. I'll show you right to his room now," Pearl said.

Pearl led Callie down the hall. Right when she got to the door, she warned her.

"Now Miss Callie, I think I need to remind you that Augustus don't speak at all—not nary a word, but I reckon he understands folks talking to him. Least ways, I pray he does, much talking I and other ones do."

"Oh yes, Pearl. I understand. I just wanna check on him for a little bit all the same. Gusty like family, you know."

"Oh yes," Pearl said but thought to herself, *Lady, if you say that one more time.*

Pearl slowly opened the door. Augustus was staring at the wall with a blank face, something Pearl had come to expect.

"Augustus, you have a visitor here. Look who done come to see you. It's Miss Callie. She just wants to visit with you a spell."

Pearl looked at Callie and gave her a nod and a smile to let her know it was alright to proceed in. Leaving the two of them behind, she then closed her eyes, took a long, deep breath, and prayed that Augustus would not talk to that woman!

Callie wore a baby blue dress. Years ago, Augustus had told her she looked nice in that color. She remembered. There were so many things about Augustus that she had tried desperately to forget but just couldn't. She was taken back when she saw him lying in the bed, something she never even imagined that she would ever see. And suddenly it was her that couldn't speak.

Augustus turned from the wall and their eyes met for what seemed like an eternity to Callie.

Callie looked away. There was something piercing in his eyes that she couldn't bear. They held the weight of too many different emotions—deep sadness, rage, happiness, weariness, longing, love, hate. These eyes were new occupants on Augustus' strong, chiseled face, softened by smooth, flawless chocolate skin. These eyes seemed to see right through to Callie. This is what she felt. But here she was. She didn't know whether to sit or take on those eyes up close. Despite the fear she felt, she was moved toward the bed. She stood right next to him. She found it odd that he was under the covers when it was so warm in the house. His strong, long arms rested comfortably outside the covers. She noticed his muscles and felt guilty that she would be lusting after him at this time.

"Well hello there, Gusty. Howdy do? Now what's this I hear about you not talking? I told Pearl I didn't believe it—couldn't believe it, and I would just have to come out here to see for myself."

Augustus was no longer looking in Callie's direction. As a matter of fact, he had turned his head in the opposite direction. He closed his eyes but they fluttered and his mouth quivered. Callie noticed the rocking chair. She sat down on the edge and leaned forward toward Augustus.

"Oh, Gusty. Why don't you talk? You always full of so much to say. You know I miss you coming in the store bringing me this and that from the garden, especially those nice plump tomatoes you grow so well. I know things are hard on you right now but you're one of the strongest people I know. Your family needs you, Gusty, and when you gon play that guitar again? Everybody say they miss that guitar playing of yours. You are so talented Gusty but I don't have to tell you that. Nobody does."

Augustus stared at the wall. He saw him and Callie in the barn, her sitting on him, her grinding on him. He could hear her moaning and his own heavy breathing.

Callie looked at the door to confirm that it was closed, then she slowly got up and moved back to the bed. This time she found space to sit on the edge. Augustus looked at her in a way that anyone would interpret as shock but he quickly released his face back to its blank state.

"Gusty, it pains me to see you this way. Now, you know we have known each other ever since we were as young as our youngest babies. And we remained friends even after what happened."

Callie then took his chin and positioned his face to look directly at hers.

"Gusty, I am so very sorry. I wish I could erase everything about that day all except the moment you found me in that barn. Do you remember smiling at me? Seeing you made me feel so happy. You brought me the rose petals that I left for you and you blew them on me. Remember, Gusty. I didn't care about anything. Finally, we were alone away from the house. I felt safe and I kept right on being happy right up until your mama came through that door. I was so scared she would tell my mama. I had to make sure that didn't happen. Gusty, I'm sorry. Do you hear me? I am so sorry. I told my mama that you had looked at me in a way. I knew that would be the end of everything, but that look on Aunty Ursie's face made me feel so ashamed. I just didn't know what to do. I knew it could get you in trouble but I-I-I..."

Callie started to whimper. She looked deep into Augustus' eyes through her tears, hoping they would look loving and forgiving, but she could not see any meaning in them. She longed for Augustus to say something. He didn't. The nothingness of it all told her she should leave but she was not ready. She didn't know when she would ever see him again. She certainly could not be a regular visitor. And if she stayed too long, that would not look good. She saw Augustus' eyes widen as if he had seen a ghost. She thought it was a sign he was going to talk. She called his name but again he didn't respond. There was life in his eyes but they were not looking at her. They were looking at the wall.

Augustus was too busy looking at his mama, who had joined them in the room on the wall. She had died from pneumonia the week after he married Pearl. There she was before him, on the wall as plain as day, dressed in the same dress she wore to his wedding, a long, cream-colored dress with flared sleeves that made her look like she had wings. Her eyes fixated on Augustus, but it was a soft look returned by Augustus' hard look on her.

Things had changed between them after that day in the barn. He began to speak hatred against her in his mind. He tried to hold a light and easy feeling for her as he held before, but all he felt was a heaviness and anger. Sometimes, he even wished her dead but he would shake the thought away. They never spoke of what happened. It was a secret between them.

For many months, at night, he would think of Callie and long for her, wishing things had been different that day. Wishing his mother had never shown up in that barn and in fact wishing that she never existed. When he closed his eyes real tight, he could see Callie, and each time he did that, he found his thing thickening below in his pants to a hardness. He wanted to touch it to make it go soft again but he didn't dare, because he feared the evil river would overcome him again. So he had no choice but to twist and turn until he would wear himself out and fall asleep. After a while, he gained better control of his thing until he reached a point where the moment he would feel the slow swelling, he could make it stop and go limp if he concentrated hard enough. And the years passed and he grew taller, stronger, and his manhood got bigger and bigger and he could no longer contain it as before. He stopped fighting it but he never quite made peace with it and it seemed to have moods outside of him, like it was a whole separate person to be reckoned with. He grew to believe that his mother could see under his clothes. He always felt naked and ashamed around her. When she died, he did not mourn her death; he was happy to be free from her and what she saw or what he thought she saw.

Callie had to face that Augustus was not going to talk to her. She was not going to be his miracle. She dried her tears with the skin of her hand. She stood up. She took a deep breath to prepare herself for what she planned to do. Then she lowered down and pressed her lips against his forehead and then whispered in his ear, "Gusty, I love you," and immediately turned to leave the room.

But it was not Callie's "I love you" Augustus heard. It was that of his mother that echoed off the wall and shook the room.

20

E ye sat on the floor against the freshly washed (*thanks to Pearl*) wood-paneled walls in the corner of the Willis' living room. He and Patty Cake were no longer allowed to sit on the furniture in the living room after Patty Cake soiled the sofa with her sticky little fingers. His bed was a pallet made in front of the sofa each night. First Lady didn't mind where they sat or slept, but Pearl did. She didn't want to chance messing up anything in that house while they were there as guests, even though they had been told time and time again by the Rev and First Lady alike that they were not guests and to make themselves completely at home. Eye hated rules but didn't care about having to follow this one. He was in his most comfortable position, with his knees and toes pointed to the ceiling and

167

his curly-top head buried into a book. He curved his back and neck into the beginning chapters of *War and Peace* by Leo Tolstoy. Cozy corners were perfect for reading and his cherished solitude coupled with the respectfully quiet squeaks of the house helped him focus on the people he was meeting along the way in his and Tolstoy's overlapping world.

Just as he went deeper into his journey, he heard approaching footsteps on the porch and then a loud knock on the unlocked front door. His whole being sighed at the interruption. He laid the thick book down wide open on the floor to save his place among the thousand plus pages. He made his way to the door in hopes that this person disturbing his peace or in this case, his war and peace, was at least somebody visiting with something good to eat. Coming out of the trance of good reading, he was suddenly made aware of his hunger. His mouth watered as he counted his eggs before they hatched in anticipation of a treat. Maybe this visitor had arrived with some juicy peaches for Pearl, an angel food cake for the Rev, fresh buttered rolls for the family, or some treats for him and Patty Cake. Pearl, Patty Cake, and Charles favored butterscotch candies but he, with an overactive sweet tooth, loved each and every one of the penny candies at Reynolds' General Store—apple red and ink black licorice, Bazooka bubble gum, chewy Tootsie Rolls, Pixy Stix in every flavor but especially grape, sticky rainbow-swirled suckers, jaw- breaking jawbreakers, orange flavored Tootsie Pops, Mike & Ikes, peanut buttery coconut, crunchy Chick-O-Sticks, powdery-covered candy cigarettes, tangy SweeTarts, rolls of Smarties, and more. Gifts of candy replaced comforting words.

It wasn't always candy though. Besides edible treats, sometimes they brought Patty Cake toys missing paint, a limb, wheels, horns, or clothes worn but infused with love, and they brought Eye "borrowed" books from the houses of the white folks they worked for in one capacity or another.

Eye whistled as he walked. Then his thoughts were interrupted. He and the whistle stopped in his tracks in a panic when he saw that it was Peter Duncan standing at the door, gnawing on a stalk of sugarcane with an aura of darkness hovering all around him. Their eyes met and Peter flashed his half-smile. Eye did not regard it as friendly at all. Both Eye's head and heart raced. He wanted to call out his daddy's name so he would come running. He needed his daddy to get out of that bed to address this white man. Why was he here? What did he want? And where was the Rev? Even he would do for the moment. His mama? First Lady? He wanted to leap back into Tolstoy's Russia to avoid talking to this man.

"How you doing in there," Peter called out to pull Eye toward the door. He was trying to give him a chance to open it before he just walked in. "You Gusty's oldest youngin, ain't you? You and that brother look so much alike."

Eye forced a tiny smile. *What is he talking about? We don't look anything alike.*

"Is your mammy home?"

"No sir." *Did he just say mammy?*

"What about Vernon or his missus?"

"No sir." *That's Reverend Willis.*

"Mean to tell me, you here all by yourself? Where your brother and sister?"

"Gone." *None of your damn business.*

"Gone? What boy?"

"Gone, sir." *Sigh.*

"Good. I know your mammy and pappy raised you better than that. Ain't that right?"

"Yes sir." *What do you want?*

Then Peter walked right on in the house, since Eye hadn't taken one step toward the door to open and welcome him in.

"You got way better sense than your brother. You know the difference between right and wrong, don't ya?" Peter looked around the house in serious curiosity. He observed that everything was extremely neat and took in a combination of scents that together smelled like something good to eat.

"Yes sir," Eye responded as he intuitively inched backward away from Peter and his aura. Eye sized Peter up as he would any adversary. He concluded that he could overcome him easily in a fight with bare strength or even with words. As the thought crystallized, it gained speed and spread through his body. A layer of fear rolled off of him. He understood that the opportunity to demonstrate his prowess in either of those ways would never present itself, but he gained strength by simply knowing he had already defeated Peter with the potency of his thoughts. He reckoned Peter knew he lost too but had to pretend he hadn't. What Eye might not have known was, in the end, the greatest battle wasn't a battle of physical or verbal wills but one of soul and in this regard, he too, had the upper hand.

"And maybe more than Hummin' Gusty too. Don't know what got into that pappy of yours that made him trespass on my family's land. Just can't go on folks' land without permission and expect not to be run off or punished. You understand that don't you, boy?"

"Yes sir." Eye wished that the Rev would walk through that door or better yet, that his daddy would get up and get this man out of this house.

Hearing that last "Yes sir" from Eye, it dawned on Peter that he didn't like the way Eye said the word "sir". It sounded uppity like he had heard the coloreds talk on TV, the agitators always wearing suits and ties better than he could even afford, the kind that like to stir up trouble. In his world, there was nothing worse than a colored that didn't know his proper place.

170

"That's a good boy. Now let me go see Gusty. Heard cat got his tongue. I betcha I can make him talk."

Eye stood frozen. He wanted to climb into a book and be anywhere but where he was.

"You hear me boy, show me the way to your pappy."

Eye didn't know what else to do; he did as he was told. He hated having to listen to Peter. He hated having power but being powerless. He wasn't afraid though. No, he was angry. He walked slowly to his daddy's room. He was a man. He could take care of himself and protect his father. He didn't need anyone. With each step, his anger increased to rage. He wanted to turn around and jump on Peter and beat him up for himself, his father, and his whole family. His nostrils flared and he was breathing heavy. Then they were standing at the entrance of the room and Eye pointed to Augustus lying on the bed staring at the wall. Peter walked in as if he had done so many times before. Eye stood on guard by the door.

Augustus didn't look in Peter's direction, even though Peter called his name three loud times.

"Humph. Ain't this something. Never thought I'd see the day. The famous Hummin' Gusty ain't even humming no more. Well, maybe that's for the best. Your closed mouth is almost as good as you dead. Yep, that's best. Just lie in this bed and don't say a word because if you start running your mouth, reckon I'd have to cut that tongue out. When the time is right, you will meet your maker. No rush just yet. Seeing you hauled up in this bed is enough for me right now. Maybe not for my pa though. You know I could burn this house down with the flick of a match."

Then Peter got right in Augustus' face and pushed his hand against his forehead. Augustus remained still and expressionless but his hands burned and trembled under the covers and his heart pounded against his lungs.

"Can't even open that mouth to sing me a tune like a good boy."

When Eye, who had stood by the door out of sight, heard that, he stepped into the room and said, "I think my daddy is tired. *Sir.*"

Peter abruptly turned towards Eye. "I reckon he is tired at that. I was just getting ready to leave him so he can get all the rest he need."

Eye followed Peter to the door. As soon as the screen door swung shut behind him, words he'd seen before but hadn't paid any mind flashed before him. He rushed back to his reading corner in the living room where First Lady let him keep a small stack of books on a side table. He was in search of his favorite book by W.E.B. Du Bois that Esquire had given him. He found it. He kept up with the energy racing through him. He flipped through the pages. Then he shook it until a yellowed, frayed piece of paper fell out. It was a typewritten poem by Paul Laurence Dunbar.

Eye read the poem to himself and then went to his father's room holding it still in his hands. He stood above his father, who appeared to be sleeping soundly. He continued to stand and recited the poem out loud to Augustus:

> *WE wear the mask that grins and lies,*
> *It hides our cheeks and shades our eyes,—*
> *This debt we pay to human guile;*
> *With torn and bleeding hearts we smile,*
> *And mouth with myriad subtleties.*
>
> > *Why should the world be over-wise,*
> *In counting all our tears and sighs?*
> *Nay, let them only see us, while*
> > *We wear the mask.*
> *We smile, but, O great Christ, our cries*
> *To thee from tortured souls arise.*
> *We sing, but oh the clay is vile*

Beneath our feet, and long the mile;
But let the world dream otherwise,
We wear the mask!

Then he sat down in the rocking chair and held his head high and waited. He wanted his mama to find him there. He wanted to make her proud. He also prayed for his father. He prayed that he would wake up and make him proud.

21

First Lady, with her signature hairdo, a side part, a swoop of bangs, and the rest brushed smoothly into a neat bun at the nape of her neck was wearing a cream, button-down blouse with ruffles flowing down the center, and a black pencil skirt that hugged her slender, hourglass figure. She stood at the entrance of the seeing room and peered in at Augustus laying in the bed staring blankly at the wall like he spent most of the day since the shooting.

The door was open so she did an imaginary knock. "Knock. Knock. Howdy do, Augustus? Hope you up for visitors because you got a couple of them right here and one of them got you a real nice gift."

First Lady stepped aside to reveal Patty Cake, who had followed close behind in an attempt to hide. She was wearing a pink, burgundy, and gray plaid, short-sleeved dress that started with a rounded white, lace-trimmed collar and ended with a white, lace-trimmed flare at the bottom, wide and dainty. First Lady had bought it for her to wear to church for Pastor's anniversary. For three days straight, she had worn this dress, her first store-bought dress. To her, it was the first gift she had ever received besides the cardboard boxes filled with apples, oranges, peppermint, and nuts her mama gave her on Christmas. She had been so happy the moment she slid that soft cotton dress over her satiny, pearl-colored slip that felt cool against her skin. She was also wearing matching white, lace-trimmed bobby socks that hugged her ankles placed in her shiny new, black patent leather shoes. Patty Cake could hardly sit still while First Lady combed her thick hair in four sections, holding each section together with big, cottony, pink ribbons at the top and at the end of the long jet black twists. For finishing touches, she gently brushed the fine hair that formed at Patty Cake's hairline downward at a diagonal on each side of her forehead before kissing her to seal the rules. She reminded Patty Cake a third time that she must sit still like a little lady at church with her legs crossed at the ankles and hands placed on her lap and she forbade her to run around after service was over. She mustn't do anything to get her special dress wrinkled or soiled or ripped she told her. Patty Cake said "Yes ma'am," eyes twinkling. Then First Lady gave her a tight hug, leaving a hint of her fragrance on Patty Cake which blended with her fresh, baby powder scent.

Later at church, First Lady would let Patty Cake sit right up front in a seat next to her and the Rev, who were seated facing the pulpit in their special anniversary chairs decorated in starched, white slipcovers. She silently dared anybody to say that she didn't belong up there with them. And Pearl didn't take her eyes off Patty Cake as she looked down from the choir. She held "the look" on standby in case Patty Cake moved one inch but she never did, even throughout the numerous tributes by the congregation in honor of the First Couple's five years of service, the long-winded yet inspired sermon by the guest preacher, Reverend Jefferson Roberts with his stuttering, and the A and B and C and D hymn selections. She followed every rule First Lady told her that day and the many told to her on many other occasions by her mama and her Sunday school teacher Sista Ruthie. The only time she tossed the rules aside was when she clapped and sang along during her mama's signature solo, "I'll Fly Away," the Rev's favorite song. With Patty Cake singing so loud, it might as well have been a mama and daughter duet, but nobody minded her catching the Spirit in the way that only a precious little girl could. As a matter of fact, the whole church was moved out of their seats and fans and handkerchiefs were flying as folks stepped side-to-side and clapped to the rhythm and melody of a song they could feel deep down in their soul, *"Some glad morning when this life is o'er, I'll fly away; To a home on God's celestial shore, I'll fly away (I'll fly away). I'll fly away, Oh Glory I'll fly away; (in the morning) When I die, Hallelujah, by and by, I'll fly away (I'll fly away)."*

When the service was over, everyone doted on Patty Cake and called her a princess. Her beaming smile nearly leapt off her round face. In just a few hours of wearing the dress, the sunshine undertones had returned to her skin and the fullness had returned to cheeks that had begun to sink in more and more day by day after the loss of her big brother. The dress tickled her and made her laugh. One of the ushers, Sista Robbins, taught her how to curtsy in it and told her she was going to give her some white lace gloves to wear the next time she saw her. Cousin Rita gave her a butterscotch candy and Deacon Mathis placed a quarter in her hand, closed it, and winked at her. Eventually, the fellowshipping came to a close and it was time to go home.

When they arrived back at the house, Pearl told her to take off the dress and change into an old sundress but between twirling and curtsying, Patty Cake refused to take it off. Pearl yelled at her to mind and go take off the dress and threatened to whip her, but Patty Cake started wailing at the top her lungs. Pearl let out a huge, heavy sigh, not wanting to be bothered with Patty Cake. She didn't even have the strength to carry out any threats or to even say another word on the matter. So First Lady stepped in to calm the situation. Throwing her hands up, Pearl left and went into the kitchen to finish warming dinner. First Lady sat Patty Cake down on the couch and quieted her. She then went and got an apron for her and gently tied it around her neck to create a giant bib that would protect the dress while she ate. Dinner was served and the house was quiet except for the smacking and slurping noise Patty Cake made as she ate her mama's pork chops smothered with syrup instead of gravy like she liked them. Drops of syrup and biscuit crumbs fell on the orange and yellow flowered apron but the dress was spared.

Now, days later and still wearing the dress, Patty Cake dashed from behind First Lady and pranced right over to her daddy lying still on the bed. Patty Cake, oblivious to the lack of a greeting or a welcome gesture, plopped right down next to him, forcing Augustus to give her space by scooting over some. She held a piece of paper in her hand and with the other hand, she gently shook Augustus' arm.

"Wake up, daddy. See my dress. Miss Helen give it to me. Look daddy. Daddy." She shook his shoulder but Augustus remained expressionless. Daddy."

Patty Cake turned to First Lady. "Miss Helen, can't he see me? Why he don't say nothing? I forgets."

"Now Patty Cake, remember what me and your mama told you. Your daddy is being quiet till Jesus tells him it's time to talk. He can see you though. He sees how pretty you are."

"He can? Oh, yes ma'am. I remember. Can I show him the picture now?"

"You sure can, sweetie."

"Look daddy, I drawed a picture of you and me. I'm wearing my new dress. And see here, that there's your guitar. And these is clouds and that's a sun and those trees. I didn't draw a house since we don't got one no more. I hope you like it. You can tell me when Jesus let you. I don't mind you can't tell me right now. I'm a good drawer, daddy. See. Mama and Miss Helen say so. Ain't that right, Miss Helen? Ain't I a good drawer?"

"Yes child. You an excellent drawer. Now, give your daddy some sugar and say goodbye. You can go on and draw Miss Helen another pretty picture unless your mama says it's time for you to go to bed. It's my turn to talk to your daddy now, ya hear."

"Yes ma'am. Daddy, I'm gon put your picture right on this here table for you. Hope Jesus lets you talk tomorrow," Patty Cake said before giving him a kiss and skipping out in her dress, a flurry of joy.

First Lady was happy to finally have a moment alone with Augustus. She had never been a fan of his by any means but there was definitely one thing she believed she had in common with him. She knew firsthand what it felt like to be an outsider. Many years ago, she had arrived in Chinaberry, sweet-faced and honeymoon-fresh, not knowing a single soul but her doting new husband, Reverend Vernon T. Willis, Pastor of No Ways Tired Baptist Church. He ushered her in and sat her right there on the far left corner of the first pew on the right side of the aisle, a sacred place that had long been reserved for the former First Lady in all of her elegance and elo-quence, Mrs. Wisteria Wilhelmina Wilkinson, who had passed two weeks to the day after the former pastor, Cecil B. Wilkinson, had passed. The late great Pastor Wilkinson had built the new sanctuary from the ground up and led the congregation for a better part of twenty-five years, his two crowning moments being, preaching a sermon so anointed that Jesse Mae Cooper started speaking in tongues and ran to the altar seeking salvation (*from that thing she had done in her past that everyone whispered about but would no more in polite company after that day*) and the moment he pulled that crisp white sheet down in one clean powerful swoop like a magician to reveal the brilliant stained glass window depicting the crucifixion in colors of deep crimson, royal blue, garden green, and shimmering gold. There it was to spectators' delight and awe, taking center stage behind the choir benches just beyond the pulpit. It was both a glorious testament and work of art that served the dual purpose of welcoming the proud members of the church and guests, alike, into the otherwise humble sanctuary for praise and worship and in later years, giving their glazed-over eyes some-thing to feast upon to remain awake once Pastor's sermons were reduced to essentially the same four messages over and over again. In his dementia and demise, the deacons took turns at getting the Holy Ghost to support his dedicated efforts and Sister Arlene could always be counted on, with-out fail, to shout every service on cue three fourths into the sermon and for added drama, to nearly faint on First Sundays when she wore one of the fancy hats sent to her by her eldest daughter, Patricia, a successful stage actress, singer, and dancer, headlining in Paris—Paris, Texas, that is.

Well, there Helen was wearing a perfectly tailored red, pink, and white tweed suit. Her freshly hot combed hair was pulled back in a tight bun save thick bangs and topped with a matching pin box hat tipped to the side just so. She sat with perfect posture, head held high, holding her white patent leather pocketbook securely planted on her lap with her stocking-covered legs crossed at her delicate ankles. She was smiling on the outside but crumbling on the inside at the weight of the scornful eyes, some real, some imagined, piercing her fragile body, now held together by a dignity that was her birthright and the love of her husband. She looked straight above into the eyes of her beloved as he stood in the raised pulpit, massaging the sides of the wooden podium waiting for the last note of the hymn to be sung. Her spine steeled by internalizing the authority in which he stood. She resisted the urge to go to him and wipe away the beads of sweat she could see forming at the temple of his forehead even from across the room.

Then the Rev announced with pride that he had taken a beautiful, God-fearing wife and declared they would grow to love her as much as he and then in grand formality, he introduced Mrs. Helen Willis as the new First Lady of No Ways Tired Baptist Church and invited her to stand so she could embrace her new position and greet her subjects. Helen stood, smiled widely, and waved to her left and right before sitting back down quickly yet gracefully. The flock reacted with deafening applause loud enough to quiet the competing sound of gnashing teeth. Sista Debbie Brown politely put one finger up and hurried out of the sanctuary with her head down.

Sista Susan Caldwell started to weep openly and frantically searched for a handkerchief. Sista Crystal Mulligan shifted in her seat and took a deep breath to regain her composure. And Sista Faith Bailey shot the Rev a cutting look that made him grab his neck to check if it was covered with blood. He exchanged an awkward smile with his new bride. Then he opened his Bible, cleared his throat, and called the congregation in with the Word and they responded in the spiritual dance, forgetting momentarily the strange woman in their midst occupying a seat, in their opinion, she had not yet earned. Later at the services' conclusion, it was Pearl who came up to the new First Lady to welcome her and that warm gesture formed the basis of their enduring friendship.

And this very friendship is why she, along with her husband, was happy to take in the Rivers family, and why she now had built up enough courage to speak to Augustus on behalf of Pearl and the children.

"I really hope you can see and hear us Augustus, because your beautiful baby girl is growing up day by day and you don't wanna miss her blossoming. You been in this bed four months and you can fit a whole lot of life in four months. Did you see that picture she did? Ain't nobody help her with that. She did it all by herself. She is a real artist, very talented. We just got to encourage her. She's gon find her way. It ain't been easy for her with Charles gon but yes, she still gon find her way. And Augustus, it may not be my place to say so but frankly, your whole family has had to find they way, especially Pearl. Bless her heart. Let me tell you this. You was blessed when God seen fit to make her your wife. Never hear her complain about nothing. Ain't missed a day's work since she been here. Still help out at church and my kitchen don't know what hit it, the way she be cooking up a storm in there. Yes sah, she been nothing but a blessing to me and my husband. But I say all this to say what you don't see when she brings your food and sits with you most days till she falls asleep right here in this chair is she's tired, Augustus, and not only that, she is reaching for joy the best way she knows how but her heart is heavy. Don't think she know but late at night I hear crying through the walls. A few times, I went to her door and asked if she was alright and she would always say she was but I know different. One night I ask if I can come in and she let me in and I walk over to her real slow. I won't soon forget. She was wearing a bright blue gown and Lawd forgive me if this is wrong to say, but she looked to me to have a halo about her though I reckon it was most likely the moonlight streaming in from the window. Augustus, your wife was the most beautiful I'd ever seen her but I tell you the truth, all that beauty and sadness wrapped up in all that blue just broke my heart to pieces. I sat on the edge of her bed and bent down and hugged her tight and that's when a tear welled up in me that was so determined to get out despite me trying my best to hold it in. Lawd knows I tried. Wanted to be strong for Pearl, you see. About the only way for me to describe it is, it felt like this one little old tear had freed itself from a mighty river and no sooner than I felt its coolness against my face, it had gone back to get another little old tear, then another one and another one until there was an army of tears that was joined up with Pearl's flowing out real heavy now, even whilst she seemed to be smiling but that didn't seem strange to me at all for some reason at the time. Then she sat up on the bed and put her feet on the floor and I sat on the bed beside her and gently laid her down on my lap and then I covered the top of her head like a blanket with my chest. And then the floodgates opened wide and we both cried out everything we ever wanted to say or do or feel and believe me when I tell you, this went on for about an hour, maybe longer, till all of a sudden we heard Patty Cake stirring up a squeak in the bed. Then Pearl sat up real fast and wiped her tears and so I jumped up real fast and wiped my tears and then I tucked her back into bed and the whole time, we hadn't spoken nary a word. Reckon there just wasn't nothing to say that we couldn't say with all that crying we did. I just walked back into my room and climbed back into my bed with my husband and I don't know about Pearl but I slept real good the rest of the night and Glory be to God, I woke up the next day and gave thanks for the morning sun."

First Lady looked over to Augustus to see if she could see a reaction but his eyes were closed and his head was lowered. She sat in silence with him for a spell in case he needed to catch his thoughts up. She also said a quick prayer of thanks, believing in her heart that God was about to move mountains with Augustus.

"Well, I said all that to say, she is just making a way out of no way each and every day. We serve a powerful God and I know He is carrying her but if you ask me, she needs her husband back in every way. That woman loves some Augustus if nobody else do." First Lady laughed. "You quite special in case you don't know but I can tell a good man when I see one. I always knew you to be a hard worker that takes care of his family even if you got some funny ways about you. So I'm having faith that there is a reason you not with us right now and having faith you gon return soon so you and Pearl can continue building up your family together. I'm gon leave you now. Reckon I've overstayed my welcome. May the good Lord keep you."

Before First Lady turned to leave the room, she placed her hand on Augustus' hand and he opened his eyes briefly, took his other hand and placed it on top of hers, and squeezed it. He watched her leave and then placed his eyes on the wall. And before him, stretched out to every corner of that wall in the beautiful, bright colors of nature, was Patty Cake's picture on a grand scale and he held a smile on his face as long as he could before he drifted to sleep.

As soon as First Lady stepped into the hallway, she heard the sobs of Patty Cake coming through the bedroom door. She immediately knew what the matter was. Her dear friend must have made her take off that dress. She felt bad. She didn't mean to cause any confusion when she had given her the dress. She had not known how much it would mean to her. She was just doing her best to make everybody in the Rivers family feel better as they each dealt with loss in various ways.

She opened the squeaky door. "Now Patty Cake, hush up that crying, chile." She joined her on the edge of the bed and Patty Cake leapt into her arms. First Lady rubbed and patted her back and said, "There. There. You know you can't keep that dress on forever."

"It's mines. You give it to me!"

"Ain't nobody taking it from you but we have to wash it up. You got to keep it nice. You just can't wear it every day."

"But I want to."

"Why would you wanna do that?"

"Because it make me pretty and smart!"

"Oooh. Is that what you think? That dress ain't no magic dress. It can't do that. You already pretty and smart. The dress just make you smile inside and when you smile inside, you feel how pretty and smart you are. But there's a lot of things that can make you smile inside. Can you be a good girl, wipe those tears, and help me think of some?"

Patty Cake wrinkled her forehead a few seconds in contemplation and then exclaimed, "Oh I know! Like when I use to play patacake with Charlie or run and play tag?

"Yes."

"Like when mama don't fuss at me."

"Yes."

"Like when you read to me."

"Yes."

"Like butterscotch and pep'mint candy."

"Yes. What else?"

"Butterflies. I love catching butterflies!"

"What else?"

"Daddy coming home and hugging me sometimes or when he used to do that."

"Un-hunh."

"When mama let me lick the spoon after she done making a chocolate cake."

"Yes. What about drawing?" First Lady asked, feeling excited that Patty Cake was already feeling better.

Patty Cake looked down and lowered her voice. "That don't count none. My dress help me do that. 'Member I was wearing it when I drawed daddy's picture with all them colors you give me."

"No, no. You can draw without that dress. Just so happens I gave you the colors the exact same time I gave you the dress. You just have more colors to choose from now when you draw. And tomorrow you finna see for yourself because I want you to draw all these people and things that make you smile on the inside and see don't you feel pretty and smart. Will you do that for Miss Helen?"

She perked up. "Yes ma'am. Imma draw a picture of you too, Miss Helen. You gon be in a new dress like me. What color you want your dress to be?"

"Red," First Lady answered without hesitation, both surprising and delighting herself.

"Miss Helen, I never seed you in a red dress before."

"I think you might be right about that but truth be told, red is my favorite color. Red makes Miss Helen smile on the inside and on the outside."

"Good then. You should get yourself a red dress and then we can wear our new dresses together and be smiling real big. That's how you get to be pretty and smart. Ain't that what you said, Miss Helen?"

"Yes, that's right. You're a very smart girl. Now close them pretty eyes of yours and get yourself some good sleep. You gots a lot of smiling to do when you get up in the morning."

"Yes ma'am," Patty Cake said before settling under the covers and entering into her dreams with inside smiles.

22

"**C**harles!"

Charles stopped playing the piano instantly and smiled in the direction of the door. He loved to hear Cousin Gloria call his name. Firstly, she didn't call him Boy. Secondly, she dragged it out in a high-pitched, melodic way, as if she was singing in an opera. It was music to him. Charles started putting everything in one pile called music or another pile called-not music. Thirdly, when she called his name, it never meant that he was in trouble. It just meant she was looking for him. It also meant a nice warm hug was approaching him. He decided not to answer right away in hopes that she would call him again before she entered the parlor, where she knew she'd find him doing his piano lessons.

"Charles!"

He smiled wider. "Yes ma'am, I'm in here," he responded so as not to be disrespectful. "There you go, sweetie. Oh, so you were focusing on your music. That's why you didn't hear me calling you?"

"Yes ma'am."

"Well, how are you? How are you coming along with the Beethoven piece?"

"Perfect."

"Pretty confident, I see. You can show me after dinner so I can judge for myself. Now, guess what I have here in my hand. I have a wonderful surprise for you."

"A surprise? For me?" Charles jumped up off the piano stool and moved toward Cousin Gloria, who was still standing under the rounded doorway.

"Yes. For you," she said as she hugged him. "You received some mail today all the way from Chinaberry, Arkansas. Here you go, Sir Charles."

Charles held the gold envelope in his hand and just stared at it. Inside that envelope was another world. He had settled into his new life and he liked it in Little Rock. A sharp pang of guilt hit his chest that was quickly followed by dread rushing through his skinny body. What if it was his mama telling him it was time for him to come back? Was his daddy all better and talking now? Was it safe? He wasn't ready to go back. As a matter of fact, he never wanted to go back there. He missed his family, especially Patty Cake, but he didn't miss anything else. He felt important here. Things that seemed to come hard before came easy now. With tutoring from both Esquire and Cousin Gloria, he had improved his reading and writing. He didn't feel dumb. Now he believed that even if he wasn't as smart as Eye, he was pretty smart. Plus, Eye didn't know how to play music like he did. He felt smart enough that he could teach some learning tricks to Patty Cake.

But above all else, he found how to release the blues that had been storing up deep inside. They now flowed out of him through his fingertips on the keyboard. The music he was playing wasn't like his daddy's but it made him feel powerful and that is all that mattered to him.

"Charles, aren't you going to open it? My goodness, I am more excited than you. Go ahead. Open it."

"Oh oh, yes ma'am."

Charles opened the envelope and pulled out a white piece of paper, but he wasn't looking at a letter. It was a drawing.

"Look Cousin Gloria, it's a picture. Looks like Patty Cake drew me a picture! Oh WOW.

It's a picture of us sitting on the porch. When did she learn to draw like this? Man oh man."

"Well, let me see it. My, isn't this something. She is really, really good. I think we have a budding artist on our hands. The Rivers family is the most talented I have ever seen. Well, do you feel better now? It looks like Patty Cake is doing alright."

"I do feel better. Wait. There's something else in the envelope. Another piece of paper."

Charles pulled out a sheet of lined paper that had been folded and placed at the bottom of envelope. He took it out. "It's a note."

"So what does it say? That is, if you don't mind sharing." Charles read the note. It was in Eye's handwriting.

"*Dear Charles. How are you? Fine we hope. We are fine. We miss you. Take care.*

Sincerely, your family and it is signed by Mama, Eye, Patty Cake, and even Reverend Willis and Miss Helen signed it." He dropped his voice. "But daddy didn't sign it."

"That is just great that everybody else signed it. Your father must still be sick but I bet he signed it in spirit."

"Cousin Gloria. I wanna tell you something but I don't want you to get mad at me."

"What is it, Charles? I promise not to get mad."

"OK," Charles said as he ran out of the parlor to his bedroom and quickly came back holding an album. He took the record out of the sleeve and put it on the mahogany-based Victrola, which sat in a corner of the parlor, mostly used for decoration.

First Lady listened. "Jazz? I don't understand. Where did you get that record?"

"That's not just jazz. That is the great Thelonious Monk and Jerry Jam gave it to me at the barber shop. He let me borrow it. Did you know he plays in a band? He let me watch them practice. They *real* good."

"No, I didn't know that. I don't even know him but what's this got to do with what you wanted to tell me?"

Charles closed his eyes and moved his head to the music in a dance. "Listen to that," he whispered so as not to interrupt. Almost three minutes of their silence went by as Monk played "'Round Midnight." Then Charles finally opened his eyes again.

"Man, did you hear that? No disrespect. I appreciate everything you taught me but I don't wanna play Beethoven, Chopin or none of those cats no more."

"Cats? Hmmm… But I thought you enjoyed playing the piano. You are an absolute natural. Don't give up now."

"You got me wrong. I love to play but I wanna play like Monk. When I play, I want people to know I came and I want them to remember my name."

"Oh, I *see*," Cousin Gloria said. "I already know your name, so get on that piano right now and practice playing like Monk playing Beethoven.

If and when you can master that, you are well on your way to making your wish come true. Now let me get dinner on the stove and oh yes, after you practice for an hour more, start writing a separate letter back to every member of your family."

Charles gave her a blank stare and sighed in his head. The record skipped in agreement with Gloria and startled him. Then Monk played on.

Dear Patty Cake: How are you? Fine I hope. Do you still like to play patacake? If you want to we can play when I see you. I received your picture. It was nice. How you learn that? Please can you draw me another picture? Be good and don't get mama upset. See you soon. Sincerely, Charlie

Dear Eye: How are you? Fine I hope. They have a lot of books here. They got a room with just books. I think you would like it. Sincerely, Charlie

Dear Mama: How are you? Fine I hope. I am doing well. They are very nice to me. I have new friends. I mind my manners like you teach me. I am doing well in school. And mama I miss your cooking. Sincerely, Charlie

Dear Daddy: How are you? Fine I hope. I hope you feeling better. I am fine. I am learning to play piano and I am good. Cousin Gloria teaches me and sometimes Cousin Esquire let me watch a band practice. They play jazz and that's the kind of music I want to play. I don't talk to the piano like you do with your guitar but I can play music in my head. That's what I do when Cousin Gloria tell me to cut the music off or to stop playing. I hope you feel better.

Sincerely, Charlie

23

Pearl didn't feel like going to church, which was just as rare an occurrence as finding a five-leaf clover. She sent Eye and Patty Cake on with the Rev and First Lady for Sunday school and the main service. She put in her mind that she would attend BTU, Baptist Training Union, later in the evening. Nevertheless, Pearl got up early to cook Sunday dinner for the Willis family and the Rivers family, which had merged into one. Dinner would just have to be warmed up later. The menu of baked chicken, creamed corn, okra, and biscuits was a special request from the Rev and she was more than happy to oblige.

The house was quiet and filled with the aroma of her handiwork. She was dressed up in her favorite dress-the cream one with the intricate pink paisley print. For now, her long, thick, curly hair flowed freely down her back. First Lady promised to braid it in two French braids later on. Pearl was very modest about her hair, even though she was always getting compliments on it. In fact, sometimes she felt ashamed to have it. It seemed to bring out a quiet envy in some of the ladies and a loud lust in some of the men and both made her feel uncomfortable. Augustus didn't mind her wearing it down. He actually preferred it. She chose to tuck it and pin it away. However, today in her lonesomeness with Augustus being there but not really there, Pearl felt pretty and happy to feel the weight of her tresses. Plus, she couldn't deny that she was feeling this way because just before the Rev walked out the kitchen to leave for church, Pearl caught out the corner of her eye that she was on the receiving end of a look that lingered on perhaps a little too long, and something stirred in her that made her smile on the inside and out. Almost made her change her mind and go to church to both follow behind the source and to seek redemption at the same time.

Pearl decided she had better have her own church with Augustus. When she entered the bedroom, she saw him curled up and sleeping under the red, white, and blue quilt she had made for him. She sat down in the rocking chair and commenced to rocking. With each rock, the chair took pride in its strength and embraced its calming purpose. This chair had replaced Pearl's favorite straw chair on her old porch. She missed that chair, but this rocking chair was like a lullaby, she having fallen asleep in it many nights sitting and overlooking Augustus while she and others told stories, read the Bible, and sang. Pearl rocked on. She closed her eyes and started to hum an upbeat gospel tune, "*Jesus is on the mainline. Tell him what you want. Jesus is on the mainline. Tell him what you want. Jesus is on the mainline. Tell him what you want. Call him up and tell him what you want.*"

Before the next verse came to her mind, she abruptly stopped rocking and opened her eyes to see if Augustus was awake, but he was still asleep and now laying on his back. Seeing him lying there like this looked mighty strange. When had he changed to this position? He always slept on his side. Now he looked like he was casket-ready for his Maker to come take him to that great meeting place in the sky.

Who was this man? He had aged. His hair had grayed. Wrinkles had formed. Where was her strong, handsome, tall groom, so chocolate she wanted to make a dish out of him every time she saw him? Those feelings still remained after all the years that had passed since he asked her mama for permission to join hands with her. She never saw a wider smile on him than that day. Looked like he had just won the biggest prize and it was her. Their future was bright and they couldn't wait to make babies and build a home together, especially Augustus. But that was many moons ago.

A strong wave of resentment welled up the full length of Pearl's body. In this moment, she didn't feel sorrow or pity or love for this stranger lying on his back. She felt something unfamiliar. Something quivered on her face beneath the surface of her skin that felt red hot. What was this new emotion that Augustus was bringing out? Was it hate? It made her eyes blink, her nose flare, and her mouth twitch. All of a sudden, Pearl wanted to slap Augustus into next week, run and meet him there and then slap the taste out of his mouth. She rocked faster and sat on her hands to stop herself from actually slapping him. However, it was her mouth that contained the slap and before she knew it, she had blurted out.

"Just who do you think you are, Augustus Lee Rivers, laying up in this bed for four long months? You ain't the only one that's suffered a loss around here. Look at you. Look like you done checked out of life and you just here waiting for your body to catch on."

Augustus' eyes remained closed and he didn't shift his body. Pearl released her hands and folded her arms. She squinted and twisted her lips. She shook her head in disbelief and disgust.

"Just how you think I feel? My life done burst up in flames just like yours. There ain't no more sitting on my porch in my chair with my children waiting for my husband to come up the road. I ain't got my kitchen no more. I can't move about like I want. Anybody that knows me knows that my kitchen was my heart. You might not be talking but I suspect your brain still working. Lie to yourself if you want to, but you can't tell me that coming home to my cooking wasn't the best part of your day. The good smells in my kitchen might as well been perfume. No, you ain't no hugging and kissing man, but I got sense enough to know how to measure your love just like my seasonings and I believe in my heart you know how to measure mine. You and I both know I gives you what all I gots to give, and don't think that just because you ain't honey this and baby that like many of these no-account puffed up menfolk that spend up most of their money on liquor before they even get home on payday, that I don't appreciate you. Augustus, you're a good man. Me and these children never wanted for nothing. Had everything I needed. So Augustus, like I say, you ain't the only one that's suffered a loss. I'm trying to make due and keep this family going whiles you over here laying on your back. You mean to tell me you ain't got no fight left in ya? You done allowed these here white folks to suck you dry? You done allowed them to turn you into a no-account nigger?"

With that, Pearl jumped up and ran out the room. Soon as she left, Augustus opened his eyes. A lone tear he had been holding back streamed down his face, which he wiped away quickly. He felt the blues rushing to his fingertips. He whispered to himself, "I ain't nobody's nigger. I am Augustus." Then he spoke just above a whisper, "I am Augustus." Then louder, he spoke. "I. Am. Augustus." And then he yelled out at the top of his lungs, "Pearl!"

Pearl ran back into the room and stood at the door, stunned.

"What you done cooked up in there smelling so good? I ain't trying to wait till these other folks eat before I gets a plate?"

Pearl laughed with joy. She clapped her hands and shook them in the air and shouted, "Glory be! Hallelujah! Thank you Jesus!"

Augustus smiled. "And as soon as the good Rev hit the door, make sure you send him my way. We got things to discuss. For starters, I don't like how he been looking at my woman. He can cut all that out right now."

Pearl blushed and just shook her head. Her husband was speaking and she could hardly believe it. She stood frozen at the door.

Augustus got up out the bed. He was thinking that Pearl had already come more than halfway to meet him too many times to count. He knew it was past time for him to travel to meet her. He walked over to her and for a minute, he just stood and looked at her, arms stretched out between them. He was looking down at her with his head tilted and his eyes squinted in a way that felt to him like he was actually looking up at her with a sense of reverence and awe at both her beauty and grace, if such a feeling could be described in words. He ran his long fingers through her thick hair and then he pulled her close and hugged her tight and long and complete. Although it was Pearl who was nestled into his chest, to Augustus it felt as if he was buried into her bosom, like she was taking him inside a peaceful place that he had never known. Then the risings of his spirit and body nudged him to give Pearl a kiss and he did and then another and another at various places on her face, from forehead to cheeks to nose to chin. And then like beats that had never been missed, they parted their lips and kissed each other as Augustus inched backward, pulling Pearl with him toward the bed.

They kissed until their knees gave way, causing them to fall into the embrace of the bed, where Augustus undressed Pearl and then himself, finally breaking free of the chains that had locked and cut into his heart. Their bodies rolled into one another with the urgency of life and death, his hardness wrapped in velvet pressed against her natural softness. Then he placed his strength on top of her and her legs spread wide open as if she was preparing to take in the whole of the universe. At that moment, all he wanted was to run inside of her yet he paused to look into her eyes. In those eyes, he saw past her skin and hue and past her flesh and bones and saw her, Pearlie Mae Rivers, his wife and the words "My God" rolled off his lips. Then he entered her and found the two of them swimming in perfect harmony with a rushing current, two souls in one body.

Pearl, the room, and everything in the room seemed to then call out his name— AUGUSTUS, endowed with greatness and purpose. The name reverberated and echoed as if emanating from the highest mountain peak. The name danced and sang. The name rejoiced and wept. The name pressed against Pearl's ear before it followed the path of her spine down and over the arch of her back and back up again to find them both shivering, and then the name set flight through all the openings of the room because it could no longer be contained. And in this sacred place between lovers, a mighty river broke past all barriers and flowed into an ocean that finally found a shore for its lonely horizon.

24

Augustus asked Pearl not to tell anyone just yet that he was speaking. So when everyone returned home from church that afternoon, Pearl kept the news and didn't say a word about it. They just had to wonder what all her smiling was about. That night after everyone was asleep, she crept into Augustus' room which felt like entering a field of lilies since Augustus had come back to life. She climbed into the welcoming bed with him and laid on his broad chest while he wrapped his arms around her. It was the safest she had ever felt. It felt every bit like home.

Meanwhile, Augustus tried to find the right moment to bring up everything he needed to tell her and none of it was to be easy conversation, so instead he gave her a look which caused her to climb on top of him and lift his plaid night shirt as she lifted her white nightgown decorated with tiny red roses and rode him until they both were lifted high off the bed. They floated up to the ceiling and then tumbled down toward the bed in a million pieces and landed, breathless and whole again. It was too hot to lay in each other's arms but too cold to lie apart. So they laid there fully spent in the pleasure and lull of waves and heat.

A few minutes passed and Augustus heard what sounded like a muffled whistle and saw that Pearl had slipped away into sleep. He needed to wake her up. He didn't want to put off talking to her. After making love, he felt an even stronger urge to bare his transgressions to her. He wanted to close all the spaces between them that he had created over time. He wanted her to know his love as sure as he knew hers to be.

He gently pulled her out of her slumber by calling her name. "Pearl."

"Yes baby," she answered before her eyes opened all the way.

He jumped right in. "Pearl, you know that land you always remind me that belongs to you?"

They both sat up in the bed and Pearl responded, "You know I do. I likes to tease you but everything I own is yours and the other way round, which ain't much at this juncture but I pray we least able to rebuild our house one day."

"That same land I have tilled many a season?"

"Yes. Augustus, *that* land. Tell me. What's on your mind? I know it's something."

"I gots to tell you something that you need to know."

"What you talking about, old man," she insisted as she planted a kiss on his cheek.

Augustus smiled but quickly brought his face back to his purpose. "You already know the ending but I needs to go all the way back to the beginning of the story."

Pearl decided right away that no matter what Augustus was about to say, she would listen with love and understanding, not with judgment. She felt it was real important for him to speak on whatever he wanted to speak on. She figured that a man that was silent for such a long span of time might have plenty to say here on out.

Then Augustus confessed the whole story, including the land deal, how he had received money and buried it, the plan to go up north without the family to become a big city bluesman, how he figured that something of value was on the land beside timber and how this factored in him getting shot. Of course, he didn't mention anything about white women being part of his motivations. Fool wasn't carved so deep on his forehead that he couldn't smooth it out. Then after all the releasing, he apologized for everything and waited for Pearl's response.

A third way into the confession, Pearl had abruptly shifted her body out of the curve of his arm. She had not expected any of what he said. She looked away from Augustus straight ahead to the wall he used to watch all day long expressionless, and she let all that he just shared sink into the silence between them for several long minutes. Let him get a taste of what he had been dishing out for months was her thinking. It was a small act of punishment while she tried hard to walk the path to forgiveness in her mind and heart. Did he just follow all that good loving with "I was gon leave you and the children?" Was this the same man? Could he have really changed so drastically? Did she really know him? She had a flash of him lying lifeless on the bed. She remembered back to Old Lady Miss Corinthia saying he would speak when he recognized it and called it by name. Could the "it" be love? Could the "it" be her? She took a deep breath and settled her questions with a question to him, "So, what's the plan now, Mr. Rivers?"

Augustus leapt off the bed and went around to her side and kneeled on the floor beside her. Then he took her hands and the stage. "First, we gon go up to Little Rock to your kinfolks' house to see how they treating my boy. If everything checks out, I don't see nothing wrong with letting him stay on for the time being. Seems like to me he's on a good path. I just gots to see it with my own eyes. Then whiles we there, Imma get Esquire's take on the land matters. I'll take Eye with me when I do that. He is smart as a whip and can go toe to toe with him and the rest of them other N. Double A.C.P. lawyers with big words. Matter fact, I think he'll make a fine lawyer one day. Whiles we doing that, Esquire's wife can ride you around to look at houses. Make shore you look carefully and put in mind how you want yours to look because as shore as my name is Augustus Lee Rivers, I'm gon build you a house exactly to your liking. Let Patty Cake draw it for you. She knows how."

"Well my, my, my. You shore been doing some serious figuring and I like every bit of it except just one little thing."

"And what's that, pretty lady?"

"If it's all the same to you, I wanna be at that lawyer meeting."

"Woman, anything you say."

Pearl smiled songs and sunshine and hugged Augustus.

"God willing, I believe everything you set out to do is gon come to pass. I really do," she proclaimed.

"Thank you, baby but first thangs first. I'm gon need some outside help with this plan. Now that's where the good Rev comes in."

Then Augustus and Pearl talked some more until there was more to do than there was to talk about doing. They had arrived at that place where actions had to speak louder than words.

25

"Augustus," the Rev called as he went in the room.

The bed was empty because this time it was Augustus that was rocking in the chair.

"Evening, Rev. Why don't you have a seat over there on the bed? It's right comfortable."

The Rev whipped his head around in shock but quickly regained his composure. "I reckon you ought to know. That's been your spot for months now."

"Well you right about that. Couldn't dispute that even if I tried. Got to admit I lost my way. Something grabbed a hold of me and wouldn't let go till it was ready, till I was ready. I've seen some things right there on that wall and some people in this room that I guess was meant for me to see because now I see things more clearly in my mind than I ever did before. So really, I don't regret none of it. What I regrets is how I ended up in that bed. I recall you sat right here in this chair and you likened me to Job, a man that lost everything. I can't say I had as much as Job did but I lost plenty. That's for shore. Lost my house and livelihood. My youngest son was run out of this town. Lost friends or I should say folks I thought was friends. Lost my music. Lost my pride. Damn near lost my mind. About the only thing I didn't lose was my woman. But everything I did, I aim to get back. And let me make this perfectly clear in case there's any doubt. Every last Duncan I know and don't know can kiss my ass—all of them. Now, I appreciate what you done when you took my family in. Not many that would have done that for a man they ain't never had no exchange with. All I needs to know now is if I can count on you and the menfolk in this town under your influence to have my back. Now, I know you ain't never seen me sitting on one of them pews come Sunday morning, not even Easter or Christmas, but let my wife and children stand for me. Plus, I can't rightly say I've been the best neighbor Chinaberry has ever seen but all that's finna change. You gon just have to trust me on that. What you say, can I count on you?"

"Hold on. I let you talk because I understand words are something you gots to get reacquainted with. But before I join up with you in your plan, I want you to see things from my direction. Yes, you're awake now, but you was sleep when I left here early this morning to go put in a day's work. You was sleep when Pearl got up this morning and drove herself to work. I wanna repeat that...drove herself to work since I taught her how to drive and got that truck of yours running better than it did when you was driving it. And as for your livelihood, I arranged for the menfolk you speak on to take turns working your land and bringing in your harvest and I'm satisfied that all monies are accounted for. Pearl give them a small share for their trouble— some of them won't even accept nothing from her at all. And the womenfolk have been bending over backward to befriend her. Of course, they know not to bring any food over here since Pearl is only partial to her own cooking, but that ain't stopped them from bringing over the things needed to mix in the pot. Even old man Reynolds done sent Jeremiah over here a couple times with bags of groceries. What I'm trying to say is whiles you been sleeping, it's a whole lot of folks around here that's been wide awake and I hope that you don't forget that between you stretching your arms and yawning."

"You done?"

"I reckon I am."

"You shore now?"

"Said I was."

"Good. I can't say it's easy for me to sit here and take in all you said but I did take it in and every bit of it was fair. I don't expect I'll be down at the juke joint humming a tune of celebration with everybody tonight. That's not my aim. I wanna state again for the record and man to man that I appreciates everything you done and everything anybody has done for me and my family during this time. But once again, I'm awake now and I am about taking care of my family and taking care of business. I'm humbly asking for your help—excuse me for what I'm about to say—but I swear on my mama's grave, come hell or high water, it's gon get done. The what, the who, and the how can be filled in as I go. So are you gon be a part of it or just hear about it after the fact? Trust me. Your reward will be right here on this earth and doubled up in heaven. What you say? I know the cat ain't got your tongue soon as I got mine back."

The Rev bowed and shook his head no but Augustus looked into his eyes before that and caught a yes. He could work with that.

26

The melancholy midday sun shone down on a lazy Sunday and blanketed David into an unplanned nap. He lay curled up on his porch using his bended arm as a makeshift pillow, deep in slumber with his mouth slightly open to the elements of late summer. Planted in a dream, David was laying on the ground under a canopy of lush, thick leaves and Augustus was sitting against a tree playing his guitar and singing the blues, when suddenly he called out his name, "David," which startled him, and then suddenly he jumped up out of his dream into the reality of Augustus looking down on him at the edge of the porch holding the guitar he had given him.

"Gusty! Well I'll be damn. You nearly scared me half to death. You up walking about! How the hell are you? I was starting to believe that I was never gon see you come out of that room!"

"Howdy, David. It was time for me to get up. Too much work to be done for me to sleep."

"That's right, Gusty. This is how I like to hear you talk. A lot has happened but you can go on. You can start again. Of course I'll help you the best I can. I see you brought your nice guitar, there. What do you say you play it like you know you can? I been missing you and your music. Gusty, you really are the best damn bluesman I ever did hear. Can't nobody work those strings like you do and that's the truth."

"I do thank you for the compliment but I didn't come here to put on no show. No sir, that's the last thing I aim to do."

"You don't have to play just yet if you ain't ready. I can understand that. You got to ease back into things."

"That's the thing. I ain't never gon be ready to play this here guitar again."

"Why you saying that? Come on, don't talk like that. I know you still got it. Just start strumming and humming and I bet ya it'll all come rushing back."

"I don't think you comprehending so Imma have to walk a straight line to the point. Time will tell if I play the guitar again but what I know for shore is—I won't be playing THIS here guitar. I ain't got no more use for it now. I come to return it to you." Gusty extended the guitar into David's hand.

"Now Gusty, this don't make no sense. You love that guitar."

"I can't play no more on something that is covered in blood, my blood, my family's blood."

"So that's what this is about. I told you when I come to see you that I didn't have nothing to do with what happened. I swear to God. I need you to believe me."

"What you don't seem to get, I was meant for dead if your family had its way. My son almost seen his daddy shot dead on the ground. And if it hadn't been for him, that's exactly what would've happened."

"I know this, Gusty, but we're friends. Don't you know I'm torn up about this? My family is my family. We don't think or do alike."

"That may well be the case but I went as far as to trust you. Thought I was like family."

"You were. You are."

"Family don't kill family over no land. I got to put some distance between us. And that starts with returning this here guitar."

"Just keep it, Gusty. You don't have to play it now but maybe you'll get the notion and you could have it right there at your reach."

"Nah, I just don't want it no more. I can't trust nothing it say. Right now, only thing on my mind is taking care of some family business, my family."

"OK, Gusty, I don't have no choice but to accept this. I'll keep it handy for you in case you need to come back for it."

"No. Ain't no use in keeping it for me. Why don't you take up playing? I heard you tell me whiles I was in the bed that you had the blues. This might be just what you need. Speaking of the blues, I saw Cora Lee with little Levi this morning and she shore was singing the blues herself."

"Cora Lee?"

"Yes, Cora Lee Thomas. I'd expect you to remember who that is. Well, she says she been making due these last few months but her patience 'bout run dry now. Said she shoooore could use some help and wondered if she should just go up to the diner with little Levi and go ahead and eat free since he's a growing boy and all and needs to eat as good as Richie and baby Judy eats. I told her she would have to take that up with you directly, you being the pappy and all. So I reckon you'll be handling that real soon. Now I gots to be on my way."

David didn't know quite what to say so he just said, "Wishing you well, Gusty," as he clung onto the handle of the guitar real tight.

"Appreciates that and you just put in my mind something else. My name is Augustus and that's what I go by here on out."

And with a tip of his imaginary hat, Augustus went on away from there. Next stop: Reynolds' General Store.

27

Augustus walked into the store as if months had not passed since his last visit. His slow and quiet open of the door and quick and forceful shut of the door was intentional to jar Callie. She looked up from the counter just as she was handing a male customer his change. For a split second, her eyes widened as if she had just seen a ghost and then she called out, "Gusty!" with excitement.

The customer looked at her with shock and winced. She drew back and hardened her look as best she could.

Augustus spoke, saying "Miss Callie," rather matter-of-factly and then went about gathering up some the ingredients Pearl would need to make some apple fritters.

In the far aisle, his back was to Callie. He heard the door close and he knew that meant that it was just the two of them in the store. He felt Callie tap his shoulder, while calling his name again in a hushed tone.

"Gusty."

He turned around and met the blue eyes he most times had tried to avoid and replied, looking directly into them, Augustus, you mean."

"Oh Gusty, how can you joke around at a time like this? You're back. You're up and all better. You gave us such a scare. I declare, I never thought I would hear your voice again, let alone see you up and about. Are you really fine?"

"Yes, ma'am. Never been better," he responded as he moved toward the counter, leaving Callie no choice but to follow behind awkwardly.

He saw several glass jars lined up on the counter filled with candy. He grabbed a handful of butterscotch candies out of one of the jars. It was everyone's favorite in his family, especially Patty Cake. He then asked Callie to get him a bag of tobacco from the shelf behind her.

Callie said in awe, "I've never known you to chew tobacco."

"I don't but my wife does when she gets the notion."

Callie offered a small, twitchy smile and rung up all the items and asked if she should put them on his bill.

Augustus said, "Yes but I will be paying that off real soon."

"Of course you will. Do you remember me visiting you?"

"Why shore I do. I appreciate you coming."

"Do you remember what I said to you?"

"Yes ma'am. I remember everything."

"About that, I may have said some things...I mean I didn't think you was ever gon talk gain."

"Well, looks like you was wrong about that but so was lots of folks. Anyhow, that's all water under the bridge. Some things meant to stay buried. I suspect you know what I mean."

Callie nodded and looked down.

"Now, I must be on my way. You take care, Miss Callie."

"Alright Gusty, but I can't wait until you bring me some of your best tomatoes soon. My soup just ain't been the same without those magic tomatoes from your garden."

"Miss Callie, no disrespect, but you might wanna get yourself another recipe."

And with that, Augustus left with a bag full of treats.

28

There were only two churches in Chinaberry, one for the whites and one for the coloreds. The one for the whites was made of brick and swayed with song come Sunday morning and the one for the coloreds was made of siding and rocked with song come Sunday morning. No Ways Tired Baptist Church, with Reverend Vernon T. Willis at the helm, his lovely First Lady Helen at his side, and Pearl the choir lead, had something going on just about every day of the week from Sunday school, afternoon service, and Baptist Training Union to Monday Deacon Board meeting to Tuesday usher board practice to Wednesday Bible study meeting to Thursday choir rehearsal to Friday Fish Fry but nothing on

Saturdays, except this Saturday. This Saturday the doors of the church were open. The Rev had called a special meeting.

Not all the menfolk of the church or town were invited, just the five the Rev had determined could handle the task and what it required if they so agreed. One by one, they came in, some looking belly full with supper and some looking like they couldn't wait to get home to a warm plate and their favorite chair. They assembled in the first two pews and after an exchange of howdy dos and a question or two, they figured out that nobody knew what the meeting was about. All they knew was Pastor asked them to be there and that had been enough. They continued to chatter amongst themselves trying to surmise what the occasion was. Was it good news or bad news and why wasn't so and so there?

Then the front door of the church opened quietly and in walked Augustus. Lester Wilson saw him a split second before everyone else because he was good at sensing things since being struck by lightning. Then every pair of eyes followed the direction of his eyes, that big left one and that beady right one. Augustus felt a sea of eyes on him but looked straight ahead as he made firm, dignified steps, almost marching, on the worn beet-red carpet down the center aisle. He pushed his broad shoulders back and held his head high, which added inches to his already tall height. In time, he joined the side of the Rev, who had entered from the back of the sanctuary and was now standing in between the pews and the pulpit in front of the men. Augustus looked over the heads of those gathered while they, on the other hand, fixated directly on his eyes, hoping to meet up with them and read his thoughts, all the while willing their gaping mouths to close.

The first shock was seeing that Augustus had got up out that bed. The word about his rebirth hadn't made it around town yet. But in addition to being shocked to see Augustus up and about, it was an even bigger shock to see him in the house of the Lord. Not a one could remember a time that they had seen him anywhere near a congregation of Negroes since he quit performing at the Tail Feather.

As Augustus stood up there right next to the Rev like he claimed to be his equal, their gaping mouths turned into twisted lips. Sam Hawkins' look said it all and soon everyone in the room had the same look—the look that didn't ask a question but made a statement-*I know this Negro ain't got the nerve to set foot up in this church to tell us or ask us for nothing.* Sure, some of them had helped mind his land while he was bedridden, but any good Christian neighbor would do that for Pearl and the children. Sitting up front in their minds was something none could deny. Augustus hadn't had time for them before so they hadn't had time for him either, and they didn't expect that to change now on either side.

Augustus tipped his hat. Paul Jefferson was the only one still wearing a hat, having forgotten to take it off when he came inside, but he didn't tip back. Augustus finally took his off and then Paul slyly did the same, embarrassed to be forced to follow his example.

The Rev broke the heavy silence. The ears of flies on the wall perked up.

"Good evening, everybody. Shore appreciate y'all coming out. I ain't gon hold you too long because I reckon most of you wanna get home to eat, rest up, or both. As you see, I have Augustus here. I know the last word you heard was that he had taken to the bed after he suffered some losses at the hand of the white folks in this here town, who can smile in your face one day and burn your house down the next day and then on the third day, smile again. And still worse, for good or bad, it ain't no secret that Augustus counted them as friends. Well, he knows better now but he can tell you better than I can so Imma let him speak for himself. All I ask is for y'all to simply consider what he say. That's it. Augustus, the floor is yours."

"Good evening, everybody. First, I wanna thank y'all for coming out here on the Rev's call. Mighty shore if I would've called you, the turnout would not have been the same. Second, to anybody that's helped my wife and my youngins along the way, I for shore wanna thank you from the bottom of my heart. Nobody appreciates it more than me the kindness you've shown. And even though I already thanked the Rev for all he done, him and his wife, I wanna do so again before others so there's no mistaking on where I stand with that. I know y'all wondering why y'all been summoned here so I aim to get right to the point. Ain't no other way around it but to say it. I need your help. Now before you shut me down, please give me a listen. The man that stands before you here today ain't the same one as before. I reckon to start off, you'll just have to take my word on that."

Sam Hawkins, who never met a negative thought he didn't like, spoke up because it was his nature to do so. "Hummin' Gusty, Gusty, Augustus, not sure what name you go by these days, I'm glad to see you back up because I don't wish no man down, so I don't mean no harm, but you said you was gon get straight to the point and it still looks to me like you taking the long way around. I, for one, wish you would go on ahead and let us know just what you need us for because I ain't got all day. I gots things to tend to."

"OK, Sam, I can respect that so I'll get right to it. The land my old house sat on before it was burned down has something of value on it, something that made the Duncans wanna shoot me dead for. I made a terrible mistake and signed it over to Peter Duncan. The deal we made allowed for me to stay on that land as long as I was alive and then after I passed, he could claim it. Let me tell you, I ain't gon lie, it sounded like a steal of a deal at the time. I guess I was thinking too fast and too short and if I'm gon tell it, I might as well tell it all. I had it in my mind to take the money I got and go up north to Chicago to try my luck playing my guitar. I was just about ready to leave my family behind to get a taste of a life I've heard tell of but didn't think I could ever have a chance to have for myself. This ain't nothing I'm proud of, but I've had plenty time to think on it beginning when the life of my right arm just ran out of me leaving nothing behind but pain. Then I lost my house and my youngest son, who saved my life, had to be sent away. Can't even imagine if I had lost my wife but I did lose my way. I couldn't find no words to describe what I was going through and my guitar couldn't talk for me neither. I don't expect for y'all to rightly understand all I'm saying or trying to say, but it's the honest truth. But know this, right now, there ain't a part of my body that wanna run away from here now, least not before I set some things straight. If and when I leave Chinaberry, I won't be running."

This time Bill Canton, a man of good reason and generally good cheer, spoke up. "I think we can all agree, it took a mighty big man to say what you just did, so I don't mind saying go ahead and tell us exactly what is it that you need. I can say my ears are wide open."

"Thanks Bill. Appreciate that. I aim to find out exactly what's on that land that them Duncans want and think they got. Once I figure that out, I got to do what I can to reclaim it."

Sam jumped in, "What? I was right there with you for a second but now I gots to ask. Man, is *you* crazy?"

"Sam, respect where you at," the Rev demanded.

"Sorry, Rev." Then he started again. "You might as well kiss that land good-bye. Them white folks ain't giving nothing back. You see they willing to kill for whatsoever's on the land. And what you know now about the land that you didn't know before, when you was so quick to sell it and kiss your family good-bye for some stardust and to chase some white gal, no doubt? Was you gon run away from here with Callie Reynolds? We ain't blind and we shore ain't stupid. Everybody see you sniffing around over there at the store all the time. It's a wonder you ain't been shot dead already while you gots one of the most beautiful ladies, inside and out, in this whole blasted town. That's right. I said it. Why shore, I can't blame a man for having some dreams of going up north. Heck, I got dreams of my own but never once did I have leaving my family behind in my dreaming. And another thing, I ain't never had no problem with who you picked to be your friends, just who you come to for help when you down and out. I suspect you agree, as you stand here before us today, you need to get better at picking."

Some of the other men shook their heads in support of Sam. He had said what they were thinking but hadn't planned to bring up until later amongst themselves with Augustus long gone.

"I opened myself up so I reckon I have to be prepared for what walks in. I'm glad you said your peace but if I may sum things up for you, I'd be much obliged."

"Waiting," Sam added.

"Bottom line. My plans done changed and I have it on good authority that the land is worth far more than I sold it for. Then too, I ain't spent not one penny of the money I was given neither."

Sam wasn't done. "As far as what I know, that land wasn't even yours to sell in the first place. Tell the truth, that land belongs to Sista Pearl, don't it? Is your name anywhere on that deed?"

"Deed? What belongs to my wife belongs to me. No disrespect, but I think you stepping out of your boundaries now."

Tim Collins, a peacemaker and deep-thinking kind of man, chimed in to head off what was on the tip of Sam's tongue. "Well that might be generally so, but not when it comes to the law. Seems to me, that deal wasn't no good at the gate and it just went on down from there. You need to find yourself one of them lawyers who can tell you all about this stuff much better than me."

"Tim, I thank you kindly. You got my wheels to spinning. This ain't over. But back to why I need you. I'm asking y'all to meet me over there at midnight with your shovels and flashlights. Before dawn, if it's something to be found on that land, I believe we can find it if we work together."

"No disrespect, Augustus," Sam said, "I'm glad you a changed man and all, but what's in this for us? It's gots to be something in it, because I really don't need no trouble with them white folks. And another thing, we're meeting in this church and I see Sista Pearl every Sunday and then some, but frankly I ain't never seen you sitting in any of these pews."

"Can't dispute you on that and your question is fair. I give my word, for whatever it's worth, to y'all that's willing to help me that y'all and this church will be taken care of in good measure depending on what's found and even if ain't nothing found."

The Rev chimed in, "I can vouch for him. I've prayed on this situation and I aim to help him but every man here is free to make up they own mind."

"Well your word, Pastor Willis, carries a whole lot more favor. If he's passed muster with you, count me in," Bill Canton announced with surety in his voice.

"Show of hands?" The Rev made inquiry and looked around the pews of the sanctuary.

All five men, one by one, raised their hands, Bill being the first and Sam being the last.

Augustus smiled widely, said a quick thank-you, not wanting to press his luck by saying anything further or staying any time longer. Then he proceeded to go around and shake everybody's hand.

The Rev said, "Alright, this meeting has come to a close and now I got to do my duty. Let's close out in prayer and I look forward to seeing all y'all at midnight AND in church in the morning." All eyes shifted towards

Augustus, Lester's big left one and his beady right one leading the pack. Augustus shook his head in the affirmative and the Rev said a prayer. At its conclusion, Augustus Lee Rivers put his hat back on, bid farewell, and walked out the church building the same way he walked in, broad shoulders pushed back, head held high. They all watched him until they couldn't see him anymore and then another conversation sprang out in No Ways Tired Baptist Church. The flies did a jig. This would hold them until Sunday morning.

29

The men knew they could not leave their homes in the midnight hour on this mission without telling their wives what Augustus had asked of them. They were not those kinds of husbands with those kinds of wives. Not all of the wives were in agreement with the plan, but all were in agreement with helping the Rivers family in any way they could. They reasoned the family had suffered enough and for some odd reason they couldn't explain or foresee, this night felt like a peek of sun coming through and they wanted to be a part of it.

The women decided on their own that they would go and gather with First Lady and Pearl while the menfolk carried out their plan. Then they went into their cupboards and iceboxes to see what they could find to take with them; never good to come empty-handed where you know there is a need, was their way of thinking and doing. Those that had babies, scooped them out of bed in the middle of their dreams.

So even though there was no set plan for the women, they came with the men and the babies to the Willis' house like it was No Ways Tired Baptist Church for Watch Night service. No one seemed surprised at the nature of the showing up so they greeted each other with hugs and smiles and went about fellowshipping.

The living room quickly filled up. All in all, they squeezed in. Even in the smallest of places, there was always room for one more. The eldest women sat on the couch. A few, less well-positioned, sat in chairs made for sitting and one sat in a chair that normally sat in a corner for the comfort of passing ghosts. First Lady and Pearl made pallets with quilts to soften the wood floor for sleepy and sleeping children. The men stood at the edge of the room closest to the front door in a semicircle facing the women. Some were talking and some looked to be in deep contemplation.

A pushy heat took advantage of the hospitality meant for others and showed itself in without invitation. It made conversation one-by-one and left a strong, yet negative, impression with each encounter. Cool, fragrant breezes had to be conjured in the minds of the gatherers to withstand his rude company. It got so bad that skin cried rivers of sweat and even ambitious mosquitoes drowned, defeated and bloodless. First Lady dipped into a box of church fans she found and passed them all around; there was beauty in their design and power in their sway.

The room grew silent for a whisper when the Rev asked through exaggerated gestures and a clearing of the throat that all eyes be placed on him. Then he wiped his forehead and said a simple five-word prayer with all authority in his stance and the strength of his voice, "May God be with us."

Then he looked over to Augustus and Augustus, in turn, gave him a nod that said, "I'm ready. Let's go." Nothing more said, the men kissed or hugged or waved to their wives, depending on their nature, and departed into the night with Augustus and the Rev at the lead and Sam Hawkins dragging from the back, weighed down by fear and doubt in his pockets and a block of jealousy in his heart.

Some of the heat left with the men and some of the heaviness of the living room was lifted. Then it was just the women and the sounds of the night in the dimly lit room, cast with intermittent flickers. Dissatisfied with the brevity of her husband's prayer, First Lady left the room and returned with a jug filled with water and an empty wooden bowl she had received as a gift from Old Lady Miss Corinthia. She placed the bowl on the coffee table in the center of the room in the circle of the women and handed the jug to Sista Odetta to have the honor of performing a libation prayer. As the eldest there, she accepted the great honor, and rose with a smile.

She took a moment to gather her thoughts within every strand of her silvery gray hair, the deep wrinkles of her flawless bronze skin, and the strength of her defiant bones and then she spoke, "Ladies, first and foremost, all praise to God Almighty who is already in our midst and who is already working miracles our eyes can't even begin to see. Blessed be His Holy Name. Amen. Amen?"

The ladies nodded, "Amen. Amen."

"And now we wanna call on those that come before us for they many blessings given to us, their strength, and wisdom."

"Yes. Yes."

"May they add another layer of love and protection for our brethren as they go about their way like soldiers off to battle."

"Yes Lawd."

"To our ancestors, our roots, I say, may them that's searching hear your voice and may your spirit guide them and place them where they need to be on that land."

"Ashe! Ashe!"

"Now my sistas, call your loved ones by name. Wake them up, sistas, wake them up and give thanks to God Almighty for all they done for us!"

"Harriet!"

"Robert!"

"Martha!"

"Sojourner!"

"Nannie!"

"James!"

"Lydia!"

And they called many more as Sista Odetta poured the water into the bowl, which represented the ground, the earth, and they all responded in unison, "Ashe! Ashe! And so it shall be and so it shall be." Then the spirit of the women that had raised the spirit of the dead with a reverent shake, slowly began to subside. They inhaled and exhaled over and over again until they finally slowed down the quickening of their hearts into a calm, rhythmic beat. Then they bowed their heads, closed their eyes, and kept praying to themselves for the situation at hand and for any situations that might soon be at hand.

For a while, they sat quietly like they were waiting for a storm to pass, but then Pearl couldn't keep the song to herself that she had been humming all along inside her head so she started to sing, low and slow at first, "Ohhh, I got a feeling that everythang's gonna be alright. Ohhh I got a feeling that everythang's gonna be alright. It's gonna be alright, be alright, be alright."

And then the others joined in louder and faster and with more spirit one-by-one and two by-two in perfect pitch and harmony. "Ohhh, I got a feeling that everythang's gonna be alright. It's gonna be alright, be alright, be alright."

Pearl led, "My mama told me that everythang's gonna be alright." The women responded, "My mama told me everythang's gonna be alright. Gonna be alright! Be alright! Be alright!"

First Lady led, "Jesus already told me everythang's gonna be alright. Gonna be alright!

"Be alright! Be alright!"

Sista Odessa led, "The Holy Ghost has confirmed it, that everythang's gonna be alright." The women responded, "Holy Ghost has confirmed it, everythang's gonna be alright. Gonna be alright! Be alright! Be alright! No matter what you're going through. It's gonna be alright, be alright, be alright. Ohhh I got a feeling that everythang's gonna be alright. Oh my, my, my. It's gonna be alright, be alright, be alright."

And they went back and forth and around the circle, each getting a turn to lead, and together in unity, they clapped and the babies woke up and they kept right on singing deeper into the night that was now on the brink of day, "I believe it. Do you believe it? Alright! Alright! God said it. Gon be alright! Gon be alright. Ohhh I got a feeling, it's gonna be alright. Be alright. Be alright! Hallelujah! Hallelujah! Yes! Yes!"

And everybody in that room knew in their heart that everything indeed was gonna be alright by personal testimony because they believed that in one way or another, God had picked them up and turned them around and placed their feet on solid ground. Pearl knew because she had lost just about everything she had but He still had seen her through. Sista Odetta knew because she had come that far by faith leaning on the Lord, trusting in His Holy word and He never failed her yet. Another elder knew because she come too far from where she started from and nobody told her the road would be easy and she didn't believe He brought her this far to leave her. Another knew because too many times to count, He had made a way out of no way. Another knew because she could have been dead sleeping in her grave but He woke her up that morning clothed in her right mind and started her on her way. Still another knew because while she was trying to figure it out, He already worked it out. Yes, everything was gonna be alright leapt from the depth of their souls, rocked the room, and bounced off the walls. It was the singsong of saints. It was blessed assurance. It was a call for a miracle and an expectation that one was on the way.

And right outside, nature was having church too. Frogs croaked real low, crickets chirped real high, and a lady cat in the distance could not hold back her shrilling cry even if she tried. The night stood on full alert and in everything and everywhere, there was a big stir and a collective *Lawd Have Mercy on Me.*

Yet after a good while, a hush returned to the room. The women became still once more and graciously breathed from their core. There was complete silence, all but the waves of heat. The meditations of their hearts now rested on the menfolk, their safe return, jubilation, and faith.

30

The men piled into three vehicles. The Rev ended up riding with Augustus after everyone else had quickly paired up. Augustus was still trying to adjust his truck back to his liking. Pearl had made it her own since she learned to drive. It had a woman's scent that used to be fleeting but now was embedded in the fabric. He did not like it. He also did not like the fact that Pearl had learned how to drive but most of all, he didn't like the fact that the man sitting to his right had taught her and in his own truck. Exactly how close had he sat when he was doing all that teaching? Did he make her laugh like he did? Had he touched her? Had she responded? Sure, he appreciated the Rev's help but he still didn't trust him as far as he could throw him when it came to his wife. Just as he was reminded of how much he really didn't care for the Rev or his loud cologne meeting up with Pearl's scent, another location in the mind told him he needed to put that aside and concentrate on the task at hand.

The two men didn't speak the entire way. As they approached the little road that led to the Rivers' land, the only thing that could be heard was gravel crunching underneath the wheels.

Then they finally arrived. The other two trucks in the caravan filed into the left and right of them side by side. Augustus stepped out and slowly walked around to the front of his truck. Now he was seeing with his very own eyes what he had only heard about. Where their house once stood was a stark nothingness over debris and seared grass. His eyes and mouth widened then closed as he hung his head. Tim Collins squeezed his shoulder to comfort him. Augustus lifted his head and looked dead-on at the nothingness again. They all stood there in a perfect line in varying heights and sizes, with straight necks and strong backs facing the absent house in a respectful silence. Moments circled the moon and Augustus inhaled a deep, heavy breath. He moved his thoughts to the blessed fact that it was a house. Houses aren't lynched and hung on trees. People are. A house can be rebuilt. You can't bring back the dead. He breathed out. He was ready to move forward. Some lessons must be learned quickly.

Sam was the first to speak. "So here we are. What we gon do first?"

"We gon dig till we find something looking to be found," declared Augustus.

"Sounds like a plan to me," the Rev added with a snappy clap.

"Men, grab your shovels and pair up. Tim, you can come with me," Augustus said. He wanted to make sure that he didn't wind up with the Rev by his side again.

This time Sam was the odd man out of the seven. "Good, I work best alone," he proclaimed as he cut the ground with the force of his shovel.

Augustus knew the land like the back of his hand, or so he thought. He directed each team to the four corners of the property. He and Tim took the furthermost northern area, near the line that separated the garden from the dense woods, and not far from the sycamore tree where he had buried the money he received in the land deal. He already knew that he would have to somehow return that money to Peter Duncan and get out of that deal, but he hadn't quite figured on just how he would do that. That's where Pearl's cousin Esquire and his N. Double A.C.P. friends in Little Rock would come in handy, according to what the Rev had told him. All his attention now was focused on finding something bigger than what could fit in that sorghum syrup can he had used to hold the money and his soul.

Nature conspired on the side of the men and held back flying, crawling, and four-legged creatures while keeping an eye out for bad-natured two-legged creatures. The full moon with its bright eyes could see far beyond the parameters of the Rivers' piece of land. She had every angle covered no matter which way you looked. So nature took hold of Chinaberry and in the shadow of the night, each team started searching and digging. Before long, the men began singing impressions of songs that had been sung back home, in the middle passage and then in chains and under the threat of the whip and then in the guarantee of no to low pay and at the risk of imprisonment, and always at the grip of terror. They were all freedom songs. Each group could hear the singing of the other men in the distance as if they were part of different tribes in different villages yet in perfect knowing.

For hours, they dug and searched and sang. They took turns resting and playfully calling each other fools to be out there in the middle of the night looking for who knew what or possibly nothing at all, but kept digging and searching and singing. Something of value had to be on that land and Augustus was determined that they would find it by dawn.

Tim Collins took advantage of being alone with Augustus. He decided it was his duty to ask him questions to satisfy his curiosity and other folks' too.

"I don't mean no harm in asking, but what you reckon caused you to not talk like that? Don't get me wrong, I know you been through a lot but was it a nervous breakdown what you had? Some folks say you was fine until Old Lady Miss Corinthia came up in there and put some roots on you. I ain't gon lie. Folks was taking bets on whether you'd ever step foot out that house again in your right mind and shame to say I was one of them. And look here, man to man, folks started talking about Pastor Willis, like how he might be a smidgen too neighborly with that sweet, purdy wife of yours. No disrespect to the Rev or Pearl. Everybody knows he's a changed man and she's a saintly woman. Of course, I wasn't in *that* talk. Just what I heard."

Augustus stopped digging long enough to give Tim some special attention. Then he said in all seriousness, "Keep my wife's name out your mouth. As for the rest, glad I don't pay none of y'all to think about my business or I'd be broke for life. I don't owe no explanation but I can put some things to rest right now. I ain't had no nervous breakdown and Old Lady Miss Corinthia ain't done nothing to me. If anything, she done something for me. No sah. I just needed some time to think things through. Can't say it was more or less than that. What matters now is I'm walking and talking in the here and now and done on speaking on the past. You got that?"

"Well, I can't deny you..."

"Tim, stop your yapping and help me dig, I think I see something."

"You ain't the only one! I see something too!"

The two men dug some more and then Augustus said, "Step aside." He reached down deep and pulled an object out of the dirt, looked at it, jumped back and threw it back to the ground.

"Well I'll be doggone, Great Jehovah! Is that what I think it is?" Tim asked but he already knew.

"Bones. We done found a skeleton, my God." Just then Bill and Lester came running over.

"Y'all ain't gon never guess what we found!"

"Bones," Augustus and Tim responded together.

"People bones, NOT animal bones." Bill wanted to make sure they were talking about the same thing.

Then the Rev and Paul called out as they ran toward the expanding group. "Y'all, it's skeletons under this ground. Counted least four."

"Was this some kind of cemetery at one time?" Tim asked

"No such thing. If I were to take a guess, these are our missing peoples, the folks that left out and never came back," Paul responded.

"Glory be! Could these be the people that's gone missing all these years? We've all heard the stories. May God rest their restless souls in peace," the Rev said solemnly.

Then in the distance, folks heard Sam yelling. They had forgot all about him.

"Augustus!"

"He must've found some bones too. He probably scared to death. Old Sam is scared of the boogeyman," Paul joked.

No one else saw the humor in what Paul said because there was a time and place for everything and this wasn't the time or the place. Everybody started walking in the direction of Sam's yelling and then they spotted him running toward them.

"Augustus!"

As they came upon him, they noticed his hands were covered with something. They all thought it looked like blood and then he yelled out, "Oil!"

"What?" They all asked eagerly with their mouths, eyes, or both."

"Oil! There's oil on this here land!" Sam shouted.

The men looked at each other and jumped and clapped and hit backs and hooted and hollered. All but Augustus who stood quiet and still.

Sam got right up in Augustus' chiseled face and rubbed oil into his skin, mixing it with a layer of sweat and then he repeated. "Oil, Augustus. You rich. Do you hear me? Oil!"

That's when the other men noticed that Augustus had not been a part of the celebration, so they took their hoot down to a hush to match Augustus' quickly as they could.

Sam stood his ground, with no more than two inches between them. "Are you deaf *and* mute?" He pushed his words to the limit to shake a re-action out of Augustus but Augustus didn't budge.

Instead, Augustus shut out everything but the moment before him and grabbed both of Sam's hands still dripping with grainy black crude, looked him square in his eyes, and said in a deliberate and serious tone, "What you don't know is there's bones on this land, too. Oil *and* bones." He dragged out the words to say loudly what he was saying lowly. "Oil and bones and blood. And as far as I can see, they all worth something and they all worth fighting for." He dropped Sam's hands, and no sooner than he had done so, he felt a great bolt of lightning rush through his body that sent shock waves to his fingertips. His hands shook uncontrollably. Then Augustus was knocked off his feet and fell to his knees. The moon pulled his eyes upward and he stretched out his arms to her and then he cried out blues for the blood, blues for the bones, and blues for the oil.

31

The sun had dashed inside out of the rain and its warmth could be felt by those being happily entertained in the Carters' fancy parlor; the perfect backdrop for such occasions as this. Charles, in a new white shirt with a dapper polka dot, burgundy bow tie and gray, dress pants with a sharp crease, played the last note of the jazz piece on the freshly tuned ebony piano. He looked up to wide smiles and hand clapping from everyone that had gathered around him that festive Sunday afternoon after church. All dressed in their finest, his family's obvious pride encircled him, a family which included the Carters and Patty Cake, Eye, Pearl, and Augustus who had the biggest smile of all. That is, if you didn't count Miss Patty Cake in her pretty golden yellow ruffled dress with matching bows, the same color as the butterscotch candy Charles had given her upon their reunion. She was so excited to be back with her Charlie, who now knew how to make music just like she now knew how to make pictures. Beaming and blooming, she plopped right down on the paisley emerald, peach, and gold velvet, cushioned bench, forcing Charles to scoot over by her body's say so. She hugged him wildly but tight and started pecking on the keys real hard and fast until she determined that she liked the sound of the black keys better and decided to just play and sway to her own little tune on those keys, up and down, down and up the piano scales.

She stopped abruptly to everyone's relief and faced Charlie. "That was nice, how you play, Charlie. You gon teach me to play like you? And I don't like to play patacake no more. Plus, I want everybody to call me Ruby now but sometimes they forgets," she said, lowering her head.

Charles smiled as he lifted her chin back up. "Good, Ruby," he said dragging out the "ooo" sound in her name and looking directly into her bright eyes. He remembered back to when he would play patacake with his baby sister over ten times in a row. He never really minded though. Seeing her now made him realize just how much he had missed her and he hoped they would never be separated again. He also had to admit that he was happy to be back with Isaiah, who had discovered the Carters' library and was off to himself in pure heaven between the pages of a book.

Charles continued, "I can teach you a song if you teach me how to draw one of those nice pictures you draw."

Ruby nodded yes and asked, "Charlie, does playing the piano make you smile on the inside and outside?"

"I reckon so," Charles answered with a puzzled face.

"Good," Patty Cake whispered.

Then she returned to her own style of piano playing until she could get that lesson Charles just promised. This time, she took her pecking up to full-fledged banging.

Pearl, who was chatting with Cousin Gloria, whipped her head around and waved her hand in the air at Ruby and admonished, "Not so loud, Patty...I mean Ruby. Not so loud," as everyone laughed and dispersed from the piano or parlor altogether.

After a few minutes more with Ruby on the piano, Charles found his chance to break away. As soon as he stood up, Pearl noticed his movement out of the corner of her eye, and beckoned him over to her as Cousin Gloria exited to the kitchen.

"Yes ma'am, mama?"

"Mama don't want nothing. Just wanna tell you how much you done made me proud. Cousin Gloria say you been minding your manners and we all see how you done took to that piano. You get music from both me and your daddy, you know."

"Yes ma'am, but just wait till you hear me play jazz, mama."

"Now I don't know about that jazz, son. I'm shore Sista Caldwell can teach you how to play the organ at church. They all miss you back home. I hear tell you been getting your lesson too. Eye might not be the only lawyer in the family just yet. Ain't that right?"

"Yes ma'am, mama." Charles was shaking his head no in his head to the notion of playing in church and to being a lawyer. He was going to be a famous jazz musician and nothing was going to get in the way of that.

Then Pearl drew him into her bosom and hugged him real tight. By the time she released him from her hug and he had started breathing again, she had planted three butterscotch candies into his pants pocket.

"Thanks mama," he said through a smile.

Pearl winked at Charles and simultaneously brought her pointing finger vertically to her lips and uttered "Shhh" and left to find Cousin Gloria to discuss the bake sale. It was an idea Cousin Gloria had and Pearl was excited about it. She was thinking she might even open up a bakery. Cousin Gloria told her it was high time she got paid for her gift and she agreed that sure would be nice.

Charles, with fat pockets and a lightness in his steps, walked over to Augustus, who had returned from another visit to the assortment of desserts displayed in the dining room on the French buffet table with the scalloped carved apron and the signature, delicate curved feet, design details that the lady of the house certainly appreciated and hoped her guests did as well. A very content Augustus was sitting quite comfortably in the corner in a vibrant peach, tufted velvet, wingback chair. He had thought to himself as he settled into the chair that it felt like a hug. With no concern to proper etiquette that the delicacies of the room politely whispered, he devoured with his eager hands a big chunk of Pearl's sinfully delicious, three-layer chocolate cake that made it all the way from Chinaberry.

"Daddy," Charles called, taking Augustus out of his sweet-induced trance.

"What's on your mind, Baby Monk?" Augustus asked as he licked some butter cream frosting off his fingers and gingerly placed the delicate floral, porcelain dessert plate on the three-legged golden gilt end table to his right.

Charles chuckled. "You like how I play, daddy?"

"Listen here, son. You real good and gon get even better if you keep at it. You got what it takes to go real far with this. Just keep at it. You gon be alright. Yes. You gon be alright. My son, a big-time jazz musician. I like the sound of that."

"I wanna go up north one day and play, daddy. Think I can make it there?"

"Why shore you can. Can't see why not. You're a Rivers, ain't ya?"

"But what about you, daddy? Who you talk to since you ain't got your guitar no more? You don't miss it none? You still got the blues?"

"Son, the blues got me. Don't reckon that's gon ever change. Don't forget though. I still got Windy City, thanks to you and your mama. But let me tell you a little secret. Eye been learning me how to read for understanding. Just reading ain't enough. You gots to read to get an understanding. So for now, I reckon books is my new guitar and all them words is my music. You might not understand what I'm saying now, but you will. Remember your mama's song—*We'll understand it better by and by*." He ended, grabbing Charles and rubbing the top of his head playfully. Charles, in the embrace of love, smiled all the while thinking to himself, "*Just when in the world is by and by?*"

32

Augustus too asked himself when was by and by again and again until the answer was crystal clear in his head. He decided that the by and by had caught up with him. Having got his family settled in Little Rock, the very next day Augustus kissed Pearl goodbye, packed two roast beef sandwiches and a big slice of chocolate cake, and headed back to Chinaberry singing the blues the full length of the journey without his guitar.

Hours later, Augustus arrived in his hometown. He didn't want to chance being seen because he wasn't ready to be seen. Augustus went directly to his property and parked as close to the woods as he could. He still felt the absence of his home as a pang in his heart. He walked to the sycamore tree in the color of night. At the base of the tree, he dug deep into the ground until he felt the coolness of red dirt cover his hands. Finally, he felt the roundness of the top of the tin sorghum syrup can filled with what he deemed his future before. He took the can and dusted off the dirt. Then he sat down and leaned against the trunk of the tree. He tuned out the chirping and howls and dancing of nature to hear his own thoughts. He searched the stars one by one for solace but having found none, he turned to staring at the can he held in his hands. He did this a good long time. He marveled at how at one point, its contents represented three great riches to him, wealth, happiness, and a path to freedom. He thought so hard that he heard the gunshot in the woods and the can almost jumped out of his hands.

He reflected on the months he spent in the seeing room. Flashes of the scenes that he saw on the walls flashed before his eyes. He also saw the faces of the people who visited him to help break his silence. In all, there had been nine—Old Lady Miss Corinthia, Pearl, The Rev, First Lady, Eye, Patty Cake, Callie, David, and Peter. All of their words echoed in his head.

He also couldn't help but to see himself on his old porch playing his guitar and humming and singing the blues. That's when he thought about Blind Eye Joe from the Tail Feather. He learned that he had passed away from cancer while he was bedridden and unable to speak. He figured that he not only died from cancer but the blues too. Augustus was filled with so much regret, never having the chance to say he was sorry, to thank him for what he taught him and the kindness he showed him despite his peculiar ways. He sunk his head real low and one lone tear flowed down from his eye and rested on his cheek before he wiped it away with the back of his hand and raised his head back up. Everything he thought about seemed like a long time past.

He emptied the can and counted the bills one by one and concluded he had grossly miscalculated the costs of freedom. He had sold himself short. It had been a bad deal, a really bad deal to say the least. But he realized that his true fortune was still beyond the horizon and he needed to do what needed to be done to bring it in closer, not just for him but for his family, the definition of which had expanded along with his newfound sense of responsibility. He stood up, took the money and put it in his billfold and left the empty can there. He headed over to the Willis' house to see if they would take in an old friend once again for the night. Early in the morning, he would head back to Little Rock to get a plan together.

He, along with Esquire, Pearl, and Eye, met with a team of lawyers at the N. Double A.C.P. and found out that the color of the white man's law was on their side. At marriage, Pearl had done a quitclaim deed that gave Augustus one-half rights of survivorship of the acres. In turn, when he made the deal with Peter Duncan, he made him a beneficiary of only his half. Augustus was to retain full surface and mineral rights to his half of the land until the event of his death. Therefore, the lawyers told the Rivers that they had rights to the oil discovered on the land. It was all written in black and white. Even so, since he was dealing with folks who had their own laws, he could not stand on that alone. He needed to talk to Peter Duncan man to man and let him know the deal face-to-face.

It was also learned that the land that the Rivers owned was once owned by the Duncans. Pearl's father acquired it from his old chum who had acquired it from Walt Duncan, David and Peter's father. Walt Duncan lost the land when he became delinquent on a debt to the old chum. This all happened when Peter was a little boy and before David was even born. Anyone that carried the history of Chinaberry knew Walt Duncan to be an unfair and unjust man to most whites and an evil and vicious man to all Negroes.

And with the discovery of human remains on the land, the colored folks had put two and two together and figured that Walt Duncan must have had something to do with the disappearances of colored folk in those days. But what could they do now but honor their dead, seek simple justice, and leave room for God's wrath. Whether Walt acted alone, they could not say but Peter, for one, did know the truth. On his deathbed, his father had entrusted the knowledge of the whereabouts of his secret burial grounds to his favorite son Peter and directed him to put the land back in the hands of the Duncans. The greatest irony of all was that Peter had no idea that oil was on the land. He had simply wanted to reclaim the land to pay homage to his father and his perceived trophies that were buried there.

Even before Augustus went to Little Rock, he and his comrades had gathered the bones they found, gave them their proper respects, and put them to final rest near the sycamore tree in an enclosed space never to be disturbed.

33

So at the changing of the leaves from a sea of greens to bright oranges, yellows, and reds, in broad daylight, Augustus looking and smelling like new money, rode back into Chinaberry with a posse of sorts, not in his usual plaid shirt and dingy denim overalls but in a sharp, black, pinstriped three-piece suit, starched white dress shirt, and a slender, silky gold tie that said money or sent a message above that he was ready when *He* was. The posse included Esquire and his other lawyer friends from the N. Double A.C.P., and a white Oil & Gas Real Estate lawyer from Texarkana, who was also a friend to Esquire. After heavy negotiations were made with the Leasing Agent from the Oil and Gas Company, the drilling was set to begin.

All of Chinaberry was buzzing at the news. Some of the same colored folks who looked at Augustus with such scorn before now looked at him with a mix of envy and admiration and respect. Some folks looked with dollar signs trying to recall if they had ever done a good deed for any member of the Rivers family, living or dead, so they could potentially cash in on their windfall. And the majority of the white folks had another look altogether. It wasn't one easy to describe. Perhaps it was what hatred, envy, fear, and helplessness looked like when mixed together.

Feeling overwhelmed about everything happening so fast, Augustus, for the first time in his adult life, began to pray for guidance and strength. He also humbly sought the counsel of the Rev, who was more than willing to provide it. So it made sense that on the day he planned to pay a visit to Peter Duncan, he asked the Rev to accompany him. They met up at the church and went to Duncan's Diner together, in their own separate vehicles.

Augustus knocked on the front door of the diner. Elizabeth Duncan, Peter's wife, was just finishing tidying up so she could close the diner and get home. When she saw Augustus, a sense of fear came over her face. Augustus saw it and felt it and his heart sank a few inches. Her face used to greet him brightly and eagerly.

"How you doing there, Miss Lizzie. Mighty good to see you. Been a good while," he yelled through the window.

She walked over to the window and spoke through it. "Yes, yes, good to see you too, all up and about. Good evening, Vernon."

The Rev returned the greeting with a polite nod.

"Y'all boys come too late. I'm just about to close up. Maybe you can come back tomorrow."

"Well actually Miss Lizzie, we come to see Mista Pete. Thought we could find him in the back room yonder where he mostly be."

"Gusty, he is indeed back there but I don't believe he is looking for visitors. Now why don't y'all just run along and come back tomorrow."

"Miss Lizzie, no disrespect but I aim to see Mista Pete today," he insisted by giving her direct eye contact.

Elizabeth was caught off guard by his directness and she didn't appreciate it. She frowned but then relaxed her face. After all, it was just Gusty and she needed to get home. She threw her arms up and let out a heavy sigh. "Oh fine. Come on around to the back then, but you got to know you're about the last person he wanna see, Gusty. He ain't like you use to know him. I hardly know him myself. Now, I've got to go home and get supper on. Go on back yonder if you must but don't say I didn't warn you and Vernon, you might wanna say a prayer before going in." And then Elizabeth turned the sign around from "OPEN" to "CLOSED" on the front door and left praying her own self.

When they got around to the door of the back room, Augustus stopped in his tracks, turned to the Rev and told him that he must go in alone. The Rev told him that he understood and that he would go wait for him in the truck. He started to walk away but something told him to turn around.

"Before you go in there, something's been weighing on my heart to say."

"What's that good Rev?"

"Let's just be honest here, I ain't never respected you one iota."

"No secret at all."

"But God as my witness, you alright with me now."

"Is that right?"

"Yes sah. That's right. Granted, still waiting on you to walk through them church doors but even a blind man can see you're a changed man. And I mean that in more ways than one. Look at them threads. Sharp. I see I need to make a trip up to Little Rock if that's how y'all doing it up there."

"Serious though, on behalf the church, we thank you for everything you done. You are a man of your word."

"Don't need no thanks."

"Know you don't. Getting all the same."

Augustus smiled. "OK now. I got to go on in that room and set some things straight. But listen here, if anything should ever happen to me…"

"Let me stop ya right there."

"Ain't no use in stopping me. All I need from you is a promise that you'll watch after my family."

"That goes without saying but remember God got your back."

"OK Rev, I see a sermon coming up the road so it's time for me to go but wait, I need you to do me a favor," Augustus said as he reached into his pocket and pulled out a piece of paper folded tight. "Can you make shore my son Charlie gets this?"

"Why you can give it to him your…"

"Promise me," Augustus said with resignation.

"I promise." And then the Rev did the least expected thing. He hugged Augustus and Augustus hugged him back. It was quick but strong.

Then Augustus, not bothering to knock, entered like he had done so many times before. This time felt different to him though. Something told him that this would be his last visit to this room. There was plenty space for Hummin' Gusty in there but he reckoned not much at all for Augustus. He advanced in the room slowly with measured steps. The room smelled like leftover catfish floating in the air from Patsy's kitchen, whiskey, and stale, dusty, and cluttered if that was a scent. He was use to this smell and had grown very comfortable in it, as if it could be bottled up and made into a cologne to be splashed behind his ears and on his neck. It was the scent that swarmed around what previously made him a happy man, performing for the Duncans, who he regarded as friends. He now believed that it was all in his head but then again, he still hadn't let go of David all the way. There was a part of him that still believed in David or at least he wanted to, for his peace of mind. It was too painful to bury their friendship. Unlike the others, they had shared too much. It had to have been real, but there was still an ounce of doubt that plagued him, so he had to keep his distance to move on and focus on a new life for him and his family. He and David would not be able to work it out with or through the guitar in the woods or in this room with his brother Peter, Bubba, and George, looking on and that was just fine at this point. Everything had changed, some for the worse, but mostly for the better.

Augustus was halfway in the room before Peter realized he was no longer alone. He was hunched over a table, drinking from a half bottle of Ancient Age one-hundred-proof Kentucky straight bourbon whiskey but when he spotted Augustus, he gulped the rest of his drink down and put the empty bottle beside three other empty ones. He was dressed in a plaid red shirt that was unbuttoned disrespectfully low. His sleeves were pushed all the way up. His hair was disheveled and greasy, unusually long, and his chin was covered with prickly stubble. Augustus was shocked to see him looking this way. Peter had always prided himself in the way he dressed and carried himself, and he looked to have never done a hard day's work in his life, but not today. And now that Augustus was closer to him, the scent he was accustomed to morphed into a monstrous funk of booze, body odor, and bitterness. Augustus covered his whole face to adjust.

"What the hell you doing on my property, boy," Peter snapped with fire in his already puffy, bloodshot eyes, as he picked up one of the bottles and slammed it on the table for no other reason than to add emphasis to his words and disgust at the sight of Augustus.

"Well, can't say I'm here to hum no blues," Augustus responded as he looked over at the corner, his former stage, where his chair sat empty. He

249

also spotted in the opposite corner, stacked to the maximum with canned goods, the shelves that Joe Baby had built without receiving his proper pay. Augustus knew now—and knew back then—that the craftsmanship of those shelves was impeccable and would stand the test of time and Joe Baby deserved to have been paid what Peter promised and then some. A wave of regret came over him and his heart felt heavy at the thought of speaking ill on Joe Baby's reputation as a carpenter to defend Peter's lies as an unjust man.

Peter broke Augustus' thoughts in half. "I see you been around them uppity niggers and don't know yourrr place no morrre," Peter said, slurring his speech soaked in whiskey.

Augustus straightened and hardened his posture to regain his sense of confidence and purpose, reminding himself why he even returned to this room. "Look, Pete, I didn't come here for this line of talk."

"That's *Misterrr* Pete. You must have come in here with a death wish. Is that what you want? To end up strung up on a tree. I will light the damn match myself, the way you eyeballing me with that damn smirk on your face like you better than me. Damn good-for-nothing niggerrr," he stammered while yawning and scratching the back of his neck. He was exhausted, drunk, and sleepy. He had not had a good night's sleep since he had heard about the discovery of oil on the land that he believed should have belonged to him and the Duncan family. He felt like folks, white and colored, were laughing at him behind his back for letting a colored out-smart him. He felt his wife no longer wanted him and his kids no longer respected him. He felt like his brother hated him and no longer looked up to him in any way. But most of all, he felt like he was a loser who had dis-appointed his father long dead, whom he revered more than anyone. And now to top it off, here Augustus was right in his face when he should have been dead and buried in a shallow grave or better yet, thrown into a bloody river. Self-pity and hate blended into one and was spreading through his body like a brush fire destroying all sense of reason in its path. He wanted to choke Augustus to death but then again, he just wanted to disappear into a slumber and forget everything that had gone wrong. Forget everything he thought he was but now knew unequivocally that he was not. He was naked and his skin could not stretch enough to cover the ugly truth.

Augustus took a long, deep breath and reached into his pocket and pulled out a thick leather billfold. He pulled out the very same bills that Peter had given him for the land that he had been storing in the sorghum syrup can buried in the ground. "I came here to return this here money to you," he said, holding the cash.

Peter laughed. "A deal's a deal."

"Well, I can't disagree with you none on that. Smart businessman like you must've known my land was sitting on top of all that oil."

"I ain't worried about that none. Soon as you dead-Pow- that land will be back in its rightful hands, pointing an imaginary gun at Augustus and pulling an imaginary trigger. "Well, by the time that happens, I reckon all the oil be about dried up." "Not if I can help it," Peter spit his words out.

"Way you talk, you aim to finish what you sent your cousin out to do. Speaking of which, I shore hope he's doing better than I heard." Augustus' chest was thrust out and his fear was too far out his reach now to grab. Todd Duncan was stricken with a sudden paralysis in his legs and was bedridden. The colored folks wondered if Todd's double helping of Miss Patsy's flavorful soup, a special recipe she got from her Auntie Bernadette that lived down in New Orleans, had something to do with his inexplicable illness. They seemed to recall that Miss Patsy's no-good husband suffered a similar affliction a few days after he had the audacity to show up at the diner for supper with his new woman and slurped down a double helping of that same flavorful soup. The Duncans even got so desperate they called for Old Lady Miss Corinthia to see if she could cure him. She took her fee and stayed in the room a good thirty minutes. Then she came out and told them that Todd could one day walk again. All he had to do was to recognize it and call it by name. Then she shouted something in a language they didn't understand and left them dumbfounded. She departed by cane as she had entered, but now with ten more bills than before tucked in her brassiere.

"That's right. Unlike him, I ain't gon let no youngin get in the way of making shore you buried six feet under like my daddy, God rest his soul, did to the rest of them uppity niggers like you done got."

Augustus felt his face twitch and burn and the muscles in his temple expand. He wanted to punch Peter dead in his face, knock him to the ground and beat his evil, hateful ways out of him. He closed his eyes briefly with this in mind but when he opened them and looked over at Peter, all he saw was a pathetic man and he couldn't help but to pity him. It was in this instance that he determined that the man, if he could call him that, was sick and unworthy of battle. The land and its riches belonged to the Rivers family and wasn't anything he or any of the Duncans could do about it. Augustus believed that he had done what he came to do. So he stood up, placed the bills on the table where Peter was sitting with his head buried deep in his folded arms and started to leave.

Peter, who had zoned out in his drunken stupor and despondency, was startled back awake by Augustus' close presence. He jumped up in time to see him headed to the door and yelled, "What, you turning your back to me while I'm talking to you, boy."

Augustus kept walking and then he heard a click when he was two steps from the door. He swung his neck and looked back and there stood a wobbly Peter inches away from him with a pistol. Before things could fully register with him, Peter was forcing him across the room with the barrel of the gun pointing to his head. Once they reached the empty chair in the corner, he commanded Augustus to sit down.

"Now, boy, it's show time. Getta humming," he directed, still pointing the gun at Augustus.

Augustus responded in a steady voice, "My name is Augustus."

"Peter! What the hell you doing," David yelled upon rushing into the room.

"I'm about to finish this here ornery boy off. That's what I'm doing," Peter barked.

David, with anguish and panic in his eyes, looked over at Augustus. He brushed his hair back with his fingers over and over again. He was sweating profusely. He looked at Peter and then at Augustus and then back to Peter. His heart was beating so fast but he needed to appear calm and think. Peter was pointing the gun and singing. David needed to stop thinking and act if he was going to get Peter to let go of that gun. He slowly approached his brother and demanded as gently as he could in a very controlled and stern voice, "Petey, I need you to hand me the gun."

Peter turned the gun at David and then back to Augustus. He rubbed his eyes with his free hand and stumbled back. He let out a loud laugh and exclaimed, "Petey? You ain't called me that since we was boys."

David continued, "Peter, I said give me the gun. You don't wanna do this."

"Don't tell me you're taking up for this here coon. You always were a nigger lover. That's why Pa couldn't trust you to take care of family business. You think this here will be the first time I shot and killed one of these. Hell, naw. Pa even took me to see one hung up in a tree when I was little. You know he loved me way more than you. Damn weak mama's boy is what he always called you."

"Peter, don't talk like that. That's all in the past."

"Goddam, you started it when you called me Petey!"

"Just give me the gun and you can get home to Lizzie and get yourself some nice hot supper. Gusty's about to leave out of Chinaberry right now anyways. I'll see to it myself," David pleaded with both arms stretched out to his brother.

Peter ignored David and turned back to Augustus. "Hummin' Gusty, I don't hear you humming."

David locked his eyes to Augustus' eyes but within a fraction of a millisecond, Augustus broke free from David's redemption-seeking gaze. He jumped up and lunged at Peter and knocked the gun out of his hand. There was a great commotion. Then a shot rang out and then another. It all happened so fast. There was a thundering, collective gasp heard throughout Chinaberry. The moon blocked the sun's view and the sky became pitch black.

The Duncan brothers lay side by side in a pool of blood that flowed wildly like a spillage of runaway wine. The gun lay in between them covered only with their fingerprints and their blood. At his demise, David's eyes were closed shut instantly like the slamming of a heavy door but Peter's had been flung wide open and left frozen.

Augustus' knees buckled as he looked around the room that seemed to be spinning and tried to make sense of what just happened. He thought of the numerous times spent in that room. He heard his gut-wrenching howl and the intense resonance of his hum. He heard laughter and clapping, and coins dropping in the cup. He heard the sweet melody of his mother's heartsongs, the beating of his father's drums, the soul-stirring spirituals of his beloved Pearl, and the cry and ecstasy of jazz emanating not just from Charles but from Isaiah and Ruby Lee. It was all the color of blue from sky to cobalt to midnight and every shade in between.

He braced himself against the shelf and looked over at David and Peter. He inched toward them and knelt down beside Peter and closed his eyelids. Then Augustus took a deep breath and rose to his feet. He walked over to the far wall and tore down the dusty Confederate flag, ripping it where nails had secured it for years and other measurements of time. He covered the Duncan brothers with the tattered, lifeless flag. Then the legendary Augustus, with deep brown skin bathed in ancient, dusky rivers and loved by a luminous sun and moon, took the stance of a mighty oak and walked out the front door.

Epilogue

The sun was unusually warm and kind and carried a soft breeze that whispered in the trees, which had been a great comfort to all who had gathered earlier that day under the wide open autumn sky. Now only Reverend Willis and Charles remained behind. Charles requested a moment with his father in private and the Rev agreed to wait for him in his Chevy.

As he approached Augustus, Charles held a piece of wrinkled paper tight in his hand. Once before him, he placed weight into his slender body, pushing his chest outward, and took a deep breath before he spoke.

"Daddy, I want you to know that I got the paper right here. Reverend Willis give it to me just like you asked him. And everything on it, I'm gon make shore it gets done. Can you hear me, daddy? Riverstown gon be built. Imma make you proud, daddy. I promise you that."

Not knowing what else to say but not yet ready to leave, Charles stood silent looking downward at his father until there was a bristling at his feet that broke the stillness of his thoughts. He then folded the paper and returned it deep into his trousers pocket. He lowered himself to his knees and rested them on the browning grass covered with crisp wind-tossed leaves. His boyish face held the intensity of a wise old man. He looked up at the sycamore tree and then over to the smooth grey headstone. He, Pearl, and Eye had chosen the words together and Ruby Lee had given her blessing. Joe Baby, Chinaberry's finest carpenter, even built the casket a size to accommodate Augustus' old guitar, Windy City.

He read the engraving out loud with a steady voice that boomed with confidence and pride—*In Loving Memory of Augustus Lee Rivers, A Great Man, Blues Musician, and Citizen, 1920 to 1957*

And then Charles Lee Rivers laid across the fresh damp grave and rested his head against a pillow of red dirt, which he imagined to be the chest of Augustus and closed his eyes. After a good while, a spirit patted him gently on the shoulder and moved him to sing, "*By and by, when the morning comes, when the saints of God are gathered home, we'll tell the story how we've overcome, for we'll understand it better by and by.*" Soon he was singing through a stream of tears and for a brief, shimmering moment, set against an orange-streaked, indigo sky, the sun and moon embraced each other and the great Augustus Lee Rivers smiled as he stepped off the train with his guitar in tow.

Gratitude

I express my deepest gratitude to the following for being a part of my journey to fulfill my dream of seeing my work in the hands of readers and in the embrace of bookshelves.

To my precious daughter: Sasha Ariel

To my parents, my biggest fans: Farrell & Verdene Chiles

To my grandparents: Robert & Lydia Johnson (*both passed on*) and
James (*passed on*) & Louise Chiles

To my Johnson and Chiles families: my loving uncles, aunts, and cousins

To the ancestral literary spirits: Dr. Maya Angelou, James Baldwin,
J. California Cooper &
"Mama" Zora Neale Hurston

To the master teacher mentor: Marita Golden

To the brother mentor: Kwame Alexander

To the great ones: Nikki Giovanni & Toni Morrison

To the prayer warrior muse: Valarie Jean Bailey

To the cultural remembrance muse: Beth McGruder

To the super encouragers: Lydia Watts Bell,
Jacquelyn Briggs,
Juanita Britton,
Gwendolyn Burrell,
Olu Burrell
Samantha Kirby Caruth,
Devona Cole,
Olivia A. Cole,
Meri Culp,
Catherine Davis & Family,
Tinesha Davis,
Althea Dixon,
L. Michael Gipson,
Rosalind Stewart-Johnson,
Patricia Spears Jones,
Aarum Lindo & Constance Moore,
Tashia Mallette,
David Miller,
Michelle Morales,
Benita Robinson Osbey (*passed on*),
Bola Oyedijo,
Goldie Patrick,
Tajamika Paxton,
Tiffany Pertillar,
Courtney Peterson,
Jay Sambasivan
Wendy Sherman,
Donna Maria Smith,
Annie Watson,
Carolyn Woodson

To those who helped me reach
a major milestone: Khadijah Z. Ali-Coleman,

        Valarie Jean Bailey,

        Lydia Watts Bell,

        Gwendolyn Burrell,

        Olivia A. Cole,

        Meri Culp,

        Catherine Davis,

        Lucy Anne Hurston,

        Alonzo & Jessica Knox,

        Daryle McGhee,

        Kimmoly Rice-Ogletree,

        Tracy Squatrito,

        Uncle Wesley & Auntie Elvie Stewart,

        Michelle Talbert,

        Keisha Walton, &

        Lindsay A. Young

To circles of support: GCS,

        Wrap-around Porch,

        The "O" Family,

        #TheSociety,

        Literacy Empowerment Action Project (LEAP),

        DC Public Library,

        Coffy Cafe,

        Busboys & Poets,

        Watha T. Daniel Library Workshop &

        Shaw Writers' Group,

        my SFUHS crew,

        my GU Crew,

        Soul Hoyas,

        Women Writers of Color Brunch Group,

A Course in Gratitude Circle,
the Mastermind,
Liberated Muse,
family, friends,
& Social Media loves

To those who provided invaluable editorial support: Cherise Fisher &
Nira A. Hyman

To my elementary school spelling teacher who cultivated in me a love of
words: Ms. Jessie Caldwell

To my GU Professor for calling me into his office that day to discuss my
writing: Professor George O'Brien

CPSIA information can be obtained
at www.ICGtesting.com
Printed in the USA
FFOW02n1654230216
21765FF

9 780997 135442